THE WRONG BLOOD

Manuel de Lope was born in Burgos, Spain in 1949, and is the prizewinning author of over a dozen novels. He has lived in Switzerland and England, and is now based in Madrid. *La sangre ajena* (*The Wrong Blood*) is the first of his books to be translated into English.

John Cullen is the translator of many books from the Spanish, French, German and Italian, including Enrique de Hériz's *Lies*, Yasmina Khadra's Middle East Trilogy, and Margaret Mazzantini's *Don't Move*. His translation of Philippe Claudel's novel *Brodeck's Report* won the *Independent* Foreign Fiction Prize in 2010. He lives in upstate New York.

pbk

MANUEL DE LOPE

The Wrong Blood

TRANSLATED FROM THE SPANISH BY
John Cullen

VINTAGE BOOKS
London

Published by Vintage 2011

2 4 6 8 10 9 7 5 3 1

Copyright © Manuel de Lope 2000
Translation copyright © John Cullen 2010

Manuel de Lope has asserted his right under the Copyright, Designs
and Patents Act 1988 to be identified as the author of this work

Originally published as *La sangre ajena* in 2000 by Arete

First published in Great Britain by Chatto & Windus in 2010

Vintage
Random House, 20 Vauxhall Bridge Road,
London SW1V 2SA

www.vintage-books.co.uk

Addresses for companies within The Random House Group Limited
can be found at: www.randomhouse.co.uk/offices.htm

The Random House Group Limited Reg. No. 954009

A CIP catalogue record for this book
is available from the British Library

ISBN 9780099551850

The Random House Group Limited supports The Forest
Stewardship Council® (FSC®), the leading international forest
certification organisation. All our titles that are printed on
Greenpeace approved FSC® certified paper carry the FSC®
logo. Our paper procurement policy can be found at
www.randomhouse.co.uk/environment

Printed and bound in Great Britain by
CPI Bookmarque, Croydon, CR0 4TD

Will He . . . Fill the void veins of Life
again with youth?

WILFRED OWEN
War Poems

Verano era aquél, verano hazía. . . .

Fray Luis de León

CONTENTS

One

THE WEDDING

IT WAS THE MONTH OF MAY, or the month of June, in any case summer was near, and within only a few weeks the war would break out, although nobody knew this at the time, and those who had premonitions couldn't go so far as to believe them, because fear rejects what the intuition accepts, and they wouldn't have been able to convince anybody anyway. And so it was the month of May, or the month of June, in wedding season. The midday sunlight exaggerated the radiance of the meadows on the banks of the Bidasoa River. The mountains retained their thick semi-darkness, and the waters of the river were subsiding to their lowest level. On one of the sharpest curves in the road from Irún to Elizondo, a curve of most unhappy memory, the huge roses climbing up the façade of Etxarri's Bar proudly displayed themselves to the sun. People who know about roses maintain that rosebushes with large flowers were fashionable for many years, and that roses as plump as a wet nurse's breasts bloomed in the gardens; and such a plant had sprouted up on the façade of the big, rambling inn, which stood with its back to a riverside meadow. The building had been a roadside inn for mule drivers and carters until 1924, and then a cheap stopping place for truckers and automobilists when the road was partly cobbled and partly blacktopped around 1933. By then, rosebushes bearing large roses had gone out of style, and visitors to the Etxarri inn were always surprised by the size of the roses on its front wall, because diminutive tea roses were the current fashion in every garden.

Three men dressed as if they were on their way to a wedding arrived in a black Citroën 11, which had been washed that same day or at the latest the day before, for its chrome parts shone like mirrors, its waxed metal surfaces gleamed, and its windscreen and windows dazzled. Its whitewall tyres, quite rare on this model, looked as though they had been scrubbed with a toothbrush. The dust of the road had deposited only a thin, velvety veil that extended no higher than the vehicle's fenders. Its occupants, who had been riding with the windows down so that air would circulate, alighted at the door of the bar. One of the passengers was a rich man from the town of Vera de Bidasoa. Of his two companions, there was little to say, but the proprietor of Etxarri's Bar knew the rich man from Vera. He owned a hardware store as well as a half interest in a paper factory.

As the three men, sheathed in their wedding finery, entered the café, they wiped their faces with their handkerchiefs. The rich man from Vera, a tall, fat person, continued without stopping across the half-lit room, heading for the dark door of the latrine, where he intended to urinate. 'Let me have a glass of water,' he said as he walked. The other two men stepped up to the bar and shooed away flies. The bartender, the owner of Etxarri's, always kept a loaded double-barrelled shotgun within reach under the bar. As he fetched three glasses from the cupboard, he thought that those men could be going to

THE WRONG BLOOD 5

a wedding in Lesaka, and he also thought that they could be going to a wedding in Irún, and in any case, he thought, no one would have washed and polished his car like that if he didn't intend to go to a wedding. For the same reason, no one on his way to a wedding seems like a dangerous man, and experience taught that dangerous men can come *from* a wedding, after the dancing and the drinking and the horseplay, but that men are not dangerous before going *to* a wedding, and so the owner of Etxarri's Bar gave no thought to his loaded shotgun. He let the water run for a few seconds until it flowed cool from the tank. When this modern cistern was built, the inn's water had begun to take on a ferruginous taste, because of the pipes or because of the tank itself, which had been manufactured out of anodized sheet metal, but many people liked the rusty taste, and some thought the rust might be beneficial to bones and teeth. Without waiting for the rich man from Vera to return, one of the other two took a drink from his glass and smacked his lips in delight.

Two or three minutes passed, and the rich man from Vera who had gone to the latrine did not reappear. The owner of Etxarri's Bar figured that it must have been two or three minutes, enough time for the flies to start landing again here and there. The bar was submerged in semi-darkness, like a sacristy. The only window had a southern exposure and let in a great rectangle of sunlight half filtered by the rosebush that spread over the façade. Those who knew Etxarri's in those days say that the stuffed head of an African buffalo hung on the wall right next to the window. Even some years later, the African buffalo's head was still there, surmounted by its great helmet of horns, with long, almost feminine eyelashes above big brown glass eyes, parted lips revealing four yellow teeth, and a thrusting snout, black and shiny, as if the animal had plunged it into honey or marmalade. New visitors to the bar would raise their nostrils and admire the gigantic head, which almost touched the ceiling, and ask how the head of an African buffalo could have wound up in the valley of the Bidasoa. Regular customers, on the other hand, would contemplate the African buffalo's head with consummate naturalness, as if it were the head of a fighting bull, and make rude jokes about its horns. What's certain is that the innkeeper either didn't know where the head had come from or never cared to give an explanation of its provenance. He would talk about an uncle of his who had been a sailor, and on other occasions he would talk about another, much less probable uncle who had been a hunter. The bar top was made of coloured artificial stone. Near the window, there were two wooden tables, placed end to end and furnished with benches, where the truckers used to eat and where the mule drivers had eaten before them, and where the Romans may have eaten long before the mule drivers; but after the war, the wooden tables and benches were replaced by normal tables with four places and tablecloths. In the rear part of the house, next to the cow barn, facing the meadow, and under a kind of porch that had once been a hayloft, one of those long tables could still be seen, transformed into the back wall of a henhouse or rabbit hutch, with boards forming the side walls and roof and a metal screen covering the front. An arch behind the bar framed a mirror and the glass shelves where the liquor was kept. The rarest bottles, containing spirits no longer to be found, stood on the top shelves, out of reach. On the right-hand side of the bar, nickel-plated and gleaming like a Rolls-Royce, was the coffee machine.

The second visitor did not appear to like the ferruginous water from the sheet-metal tank, the same water that others praised as the most unusual of mineral waters, and it was evident from this that he was an outsider. 'This water tastes terrible,' he muttered in a low voice. Many people, including some of the locals, thought the same thing the stranger did, and the owner of Etxarri's Bar didn't bat an eye.

'We're on our way to a wedding,' said the first visitor, crossing the room and admiring the rosebush from inside the window. 'May I pick a couple of roses when we leave?'

'Of course,' the innkeeper said.

The third glass of water remained untouched. The rich man from Vera who had gone to the restroom seemed to be in no hurry to come out. In those days, the man who ran the Etxarri inn was in his early forties, and there were some who knew he was not an Etxarri, that is, he wasn't a member of the Etxarri family, although he was known by that name because he presided over the inn, and the name of the inn could not be changed. Whether or not this man's uncle had sailed the seas or hunted buffalo was a question of little importance. The master of Etxarri's Bar was distrustful by nature, as keepers of inns often are, and when the old-style roadside inns and taverns went out of existence, the innkeepers' distrust passed, by the same right and the law of communicating vessels, to the proprietors of the small, cheap hotels known as *hostales*. He was an ugly man, with an apron perpetually tied round his waist so that he could dry his hands, and he cared little about the roses on the façade, because they were his wife's department. His wife was not in the bar on that day. She herself was indeed an Etxarri, a member of the family that had established the inn in the days of the mule drivers, or in the days of the Romans, and the man she called her husband, even though he wasn't, had formed the habit of acting as though the inn belonged to him. But that wasn't what was important, nor would he cite it some years later, when it was a matter of taking legal possession of the property without any more right to it than what might have accrued to him from sharing a bed, that is, without any right supported by documents or implied in his name; but the war had caused so many difficulties that few people raised questions about any property rights to the ruins of the inn. No one knew for sure whether there might be titles or documents somewhere, or whether the inn and its meadow and the half-dozen oaks that constituted its share of the forest could belong to anyone who didn't bear that name, nor could any civil-law notary testify to any of this, and the upshot was that the innkeeper was called Etxarri, too, although he wasn't a member of the family. He had a stepdaughter, that is, the daughter of the woman who shared his bed and a previous man, but that day the stepdaughter wasn't in the inn, either. The girl had recently reached her sixteenth birthday, and from time to time her stepfather opined that she needed some discipline, which took the form of blows, administered either with his hands or with his belt. Of course, no one imagined that the war would break out in a few weeks or that the girl, María

Antonia, would suffer what she suffered, which will be related in due course. On that day, the owner of Etxarri's Bar was alone. He drew back slightly from the counter. At this point, he felt more curiosity than distrust in regard to the three men, who he was convinced were on their way to a wedding, even though he had only two of them in his sight, because the rich man from Vera de Bidasoa, whose name, the innkeeper knew, was either Leonardo or Leopoldo, was still in the restroom. Five minutes passed, and the innkeeper shooed away the flies again with a corner of his apron. One of the men, the one who looked the youngest and who had asked about the roses, turned towards his friend. 'What's your uncle doing?'

But the innkeeper knew that mature men have bladder problems or worse. He didn't know whether the men were going to pay for their three glasses of water, even though one of them was untouched and the other two only half empty, nor did he consider asking them to pay if they didn't; it was free, his medicinal water. Behind the house and the meadow, the mountainside rose in a steep slope to the spring whose water was carried from there to the cistern, and laying the requisite pipes and building the tank by means of which running water passed from the spring to a tap in the inn had entailed an investment, which it was only just that the innkeeper would attempt to recuperate, at least in part, by charging for a glass of water. He would see about that later, or he wouldn't see about it at all. The shooed flies had taken over the rectangle of sunlight that came in through the window. The man who looked like a boy stepped through the curtain of light and flies and stood by the window again. For a moment, he contemplated the automobile. Then he looked around the bar. He raised his eyes to the buffalo's head and examined it with indifference, as if he were a frequent visitor to the inn, or as if his young life had been replete with buffaloes. After that, he returned to the right side of the bar. And then he lost patience. 'Don't you think something's happened to him?'

Ordinarily, no one requires more than a couple of minutes to urinate, although it's said that women take longer than men and that obese men take longer than women, and there are probably scientific reasons that justify this point of view. When the young man asked his question, the three of them – that is, the two customers and the innkeeper – simultaneously turned their heads towards the rear of the bar and started moving towards the toilets. Light entered this area through glass panes on a door that faced the luminous green meadow and opened under the porch, where a rabbit hutch was kept. There were no ladies' and gentlemen's rooms, there was only one latrine, and generally anyone could urinate for as long as he or she wished. Although the drinking water from the spring was connected to a tank and the tank to a tap, the toilet facilities had not been connected to a septic tank, so that waste water was carried directly into the river after passing through a proper toilet, a white porcelain bowl stamped with the calligraphy of the Manufactures Villeroy Frères, of Bayonne. One may suppose that in those places and those times, even toilets were smuggled. The nephew stepped up to the latrine door and rapped on it discreetly with his knuckles. At the other end of the bar, the buffalo thrust his snout forward.

'Is everything all right, Uncle?'

The door was neither open nor locked, and they had great difficulty pushing their way in. Inside, the rich man from Vera de Bidasoa was lying on the floor, wedged between the door and the toilet bowl, with his fly open and his eyes rolled up, dead or almost dead from a stroke. They had great difficulty opening the door because the rich man's body was obstructing it, but in the end they managed to haul him out of the latrine and drag him a few feet into the dining room. It was unthinkable that a rich and ample man should die in such a confined space as that privy. But to say that he was a rich man back then is not the same as to say that someone is a rich man now, when much more capital runs through the veins of the valley, although that's no reason why anyone, even in those days, should have had to die in a latrine. His travelling companions loosened the starched collar of his wedding shirt, while the innkeeper opened the back door, the one that faced the meadow, and then hurried to open the front door as well, so that air could circulate. Nobody thought about closing the rich man from Vera's fly. He was still breathing. They put damp towels on his forehead and concluded at once that they urgently needed to get him out of there and take him to where he could be helped.

There was a wooden bench that had been used as a butcher's table for quartering pigs and as just a bench ever since pig-slaughtering days had come to an end, and in any case there were no pigs at the inn, because rabbits and chickens were considered more profitable and required less work. The man's head was resting on that bench when he emerged from his throes. His eyes, which had rolled up in his head, finally began to focus and to seek something they could understand. But he could understand nothing, nor could he grasp where he was. So it happens with the dead to whom fate has granted the right to open their eyes again. The man from Vera rubbed his nose. No one on the point of death who is thinking about his soul ever rubs his nose. His arm rose clumsily, and he dragged the back of his hand across his nostrils, indifferent to his nephew, indifferent to his companion, indifferent to the other witness, Etxarri, the master of the inn, but the rich man's gesture, which relieved his nose of mucus and facilitated his breathing, at least manifested his will to live.

They put him in the black Citroën 11 that was waiting in the sun to take its passengers to the wedding. It was an elegant, spacious automobile, designed like a gondola, with an engine as reliable as a ship's. In those days, there was a metal plaque nailed to an electric pole outside the inn, and on this plaque a skull was crossed by a streak bearing the words DANGER OF DEATH. Another sign with the face of Christ was nailed to the door of the inn, and the words under the face were ERREGIEN ERREGIA, which means 'King of Kings' in Basque, but which could also mean 'I shall reign'. These signs were nothing but relics, or they later became relics, and even as rust was devouring their metal and causing their enamel to flake off, time was causing other damage. New embankments were excavated and built, some curves were flattened, and the arches of a new concrete bridge straddling the river were raised above the very roof of Etxarri's Bar. As has already been mentioned, these days there's much more money circulating through the veins of the valley.

It's well-known that rose plants are named according to their variety and grafts, or according to fashion and current events and colour. Back then, there were roses called Lady Macbeth, or Marquesa de Urquijo, or Presidency of the Republic. There was an old variety of rosebush called Titanic. A pearly white rose that didn't look like much but had a most fragrant scent was named Essence of Love. Any catalogue of rosebushes offered a summary of the visible and invisible world of those years, arranged in parcels of flowers that were capricious or enigmatic, but identical in their perfection. Nobody doubted that there would exist in years to come a variety of rose, probably blood-red in colour, that would be called July Eighteenth, because that was the day the war began, and after the war, or even during the conflict in some gardens, somebody would think of giving that name to a rosebush in order to commemorate the victory or celebrate the satisfactory turn of events; the names of rose varieties establish a terminology of passions and enthusiasms so evocative that they live on in the eyes of those who still remember the name of a given plant. However, let no one dare to imagine that anyone on the other side, the losing side, either during those three accursed years or later, might feel the sweet and sinister urge to cultivate rose plants in the courtyard of a prison or against the wall of a cemetery and call them Euzkadi, October, or Revolution, as if the roses they produced would also take a side in the conflict, would deny themselves to one group and bestow themselves on the other, as arbitrary as victory or disaster, and like them indifferent to future returns of spring, the fervour of anthems, the pangs of grief, and every sort of flag. And so it was that María Antonia Etxarri, the inn family's daughter, did not remember the name of the enormous roses that grew up the façade of the building. On the other hand, whenever she saw the ice delivery van, María Antonia couldn't help remembering the night when she was raped. At the time, she was a girl of sixteen. Many years had passed since then, and she still didn't know whether what happened that night was what people called a rape. Before that night, she had known two men. The first of them had gone down to Oyarzun at the beginning of the war and was her first lover, although he had never been her boyfriend. The second man had also gone down to Oyarzun, but she didn't know whether he'd done so to kill the first man or to sign up to fight in the war. Now this second man had indeed been her boyfriend, but somehow she had never heard from either of the two again; they had faded away, like travellers disappearing into a fog. The third man in her life, the one who would rape her, had not yet appeared, but she had a feeling that he was getting closer.

Because of the first two men, her mother and stepfather had slapped her and called her *txona* and whore, *txerria* in the language of the house, and then, when María Antonia and her stepfather were alone, he had touched her breasts. But some time afterwards, when the men arrived from Pamplona, having come by who knows what roads, her mother and stepfather had fallen silent, and then they had run off to Oyarzun,

and María Antonia was left alone with all those soldiers. Some
of them wore espadrilles, some had uniforms and wore boots,
and others dressed in a wide variety of clothing, but all wore
the red beret of a company of right-wing militia, the Carlist
requetés.

The troops did not number more than twenty, and they
were accompanied by three mules, which were loaded with
the men's equipment and several cases of ammunition. An ice
delivery truck, requisitioned along the way, had been armed
with a light machine gun, which was set up on the roof above
the driver's cabin. On one side of this vehicle, one could read
the words *Fábrica de Hielo*, 'Ice Factory', written in blue-and-
white letters, with snow on the F and the H. The same words
were written on the other side of the truck, but someone with
white paint and a brush had added another, longer phrase
above the snowy letters of the Ice Factory: 'Long live God,
who never dies, and if He dies, He rises again.' This short
prayer was the unit's slogan. The conscripts installed on the
ground floor of the inn would shout that slogan fervently,
along with songs and cries of 'Long live' and 'Death to'. Many
of the militiamen were boys not more than twenty years old,
and some of them looked as young as María Antonia, but
probably none of them, experienced though they were at getting drunk, had ever got close to a woman. Thirty metres from
the house, the armed ice truck guarded the brow of the hill.
The three beasts of burden needed fodder. They had been put
in the stable, next to the rabbit hutches, where the cows had
been housed until the girl's mother and stepfather dispersed
them on the mountainside before running away.

So it was that María Antonia found herself in charge of the whole place. It had been her stepfather's idea to convert the inn to a bar, thus making the most of its excellent location on the road, near the bridge and the river. In addition to being in a strategically good spot for turning a roadside inn into a bar, Etxarri's also had the advantage of dominating the crossroads, a fact that had not escaped the lieutenant in command of the unit, a swarthy, unshaven young man, his belt unbuckled and the top three buttons of his army jacket undone after a three-day march. The lieutenant and a sergeant took up quarters on the second floor. That was where the mule drivers had slept in the past, and twenty years later, when Etxarri's Bar had become a prosperous business, that was where the fishermen would have their rooms, that is, the sportsmen who would come from Madrid or Bilbao in big black cars with enormous boots for the opening of the salmon season. Two men had been posted to the attic, where previously there had been only doves. The soldiers' rifles protruded from the small windows. It is likely that they were asleep at their post, because nothing could be seen from up there, except for the forest of fir and oak trees on the other side of the river and a few pale columns of blue smoke rising from the bottom of the valley.

The unit formed part of Colonel Beorlegui's forces. After an operation around Vera de Bidasoa, where his men had pushed past the village but failed to get across the Endarlatza bridge, Beorlegui had decided to execute an indirect manoeuvre, dividing his troops into small support units and a main advance force and moving out over difficult terrain and along forest trails in order to fall upon Oyarzun. These matters were all very far from María Antonia's thoughts. They seemed equally far from the thoughts of the young militiamen, who shouted curses at Judas and praise to the Risen Lord and beat on the wooden tables in the dining room with clenched fists before passing out, exhausted, on those same tables, their rifles leaning against the benches and their faces placid in sleep, several of them with two or three deaths on their shoulders, accumulated like two or three eternities through service in some firing squad, and others, or the same ones, with death waiting ahead of them, so close, so soon that they could almost dream of it. On the morning of their arrival, they had sat down outside the front door of the house, under the climbing rosebush, to take off their espadrilles and treat their blisters and relieve their swollen feet, and they had hardly noticed whether they were in enemy territory or not, because after the surprise at Vera de Bidasoa, it wasn't clear which redoubt in the valley or which hillock had remained under their side's control. María Antonia had a feeling that one of those soldiers, if not more than one, was going to rape her. Barefoot, lounging in the field or on the stone bench, they looked like lads on a day trip, and later that afternoon, when a sudden rainstorm drove them into the kitchen, they cursed like drunken day trippers, too. The men stationed on top of the ice truck covered their machine gun with canvas and took refuge inside the vehicle. The men in the attic retreated from the embrasures and waited for the cloudburst to pass. Rain lashed the glass panels of the balcony on the second floor, where the only officer in the troop was in a discussion with his sergeant. The lieutenant had asked for some lunch to be brought to the room. It was past five in the afternoon, but neither he nor the sergeant had eaten anything yet. María Antonia climbed the stairs with a tray in her hands. There was some of the week's bread, wine, and chorizo, along with some chestnut purée from the previous winter. The soldiers had dispatched two large cheeses and then cooked some potatoes, which each of them had eaten with his individual field rations. María Antonia pushed open the door and entered the room. The dark, abrupt lieutenant, who could not have been more than twenty-five, was drying his hands on a towel. He pivoted round, turning his back to the balcony. María Antonia stood still in the doorway. Her mother and stepfather's bed was inside this same room, in the space partitioned off as a bedroom. The spread was on the floor. The wardrobe stood open, and its mirrored door reflected the unmade bed, a pair of calf-length leather boots, and a military bandolier and belt, complete with holster and standard-issue pistol, which hung from one of the brass balls on the bedposts. The girl noticed that the lieutenant was barefoot and must have been sleeping with his army jacket on since he arrived.

'Who's this kid?'

'She was in the house,' the sergeant said. 'Her parents ran away yesterday.'

'What's your name, *muchacha*?' the lieutenant asked.

'Etxarri,' the girl said.

'Leave our lunch on that table. And stay away from the soldiers,' the lieutenant said.

María Antonia crossed the room and put the tray where she had been told to put it. Behind the rain, the valley was suddenly torn by glittering sunlight, and although the down-pour continued to beat against the windows, a strange, sunny luminousness flooded the parquet floor. Reflections of the wine danced on the table. Neither of the men paid any attention to the girl when she turned to go. After she left the room and began to walk down the stairs, the sergeant closed the door behind her with his foot.

When it stopped raining, the soldiers went outside again, some stretching, others rubbing their eyes, all of them young country boys, much like the boys in the surrounding villages, and all day long María Antonia had felt that one of them was going to rape her. But she wasn't afraid. She assumed that that was, in some way, what had happened on the two previous occasions, even though it wasn't, and she also assumed that her mother and stepfather had beaten her and called her a tramp and a slut precisely because it wasn't, and because she had let herself be taken in. The young soldiers were wearing trousers that were too big for them and outfits that were generally the wrong size, and one or two of them were in their underwear; when they stepped out of the dark kitchen, all were dazzled by the brightness of the late afternoon sun. They took down the stuffed buffalo head, brought it outside, and set it on a rock some fifty or sixty metres away. Some of the troops took target practice, and a bullet split the buffalo's left horn. Then they stopped, because just as they had orders not to loot, they surely had orders not to waste ammunition, either. One of the men who had been posted to the attic shouted something to his comrades on the ground, and several of them laughed, and others shaded their eyes with their hands and squinted up at the eaves, where they could see a big smiling head and a rifle barrel sticking out of the opening in the dovecote. A rumble of artillery fire came from the direction of Erlaiz, and no one could tell if the steam rising from the valley was coming from the rain or if the rain was putting out a fire somewhere down there. The fields looked as though they had been polished. The mountainsides took on the fir trees' sharp shadows. The blaze of twilight gave the leaden clouds blood-red outlines, but the most intense brightness, beyond the mountain crests, shone from the sea.

A while later, the lieutenant came down from his room and the two men stationed in the attic were relieved, as were the two serving on the armed ice truck. Those who had gone down to the river to wash their socks returned, sending rocks rolling down the embankment as they came. The sergeant gave a few orders as well, while the officer headed for the bridge, from which point one could see the succession of hills and the river winding among the firs, and from there he examined the valley, aided by a pair of black binoculars whose brass fittings were shiny with use. Darkness was falling. After a few minutes, the lieutenant returned. 'Mess and turn in,' he told his men. 'Tomorrow's a fiesta.'

'A holy day of obligation, Lieutenant?' said one of the soldiers, who was wearing an undershirt and drawers and shaking out a blanket into the cool twilight air.

'Shut your trap,' said the lieutenant, without hesitation.

'Does anyone have any aspirin?' the sergeant asked.

Someone had two aspirin tablets, well wrapped in a piece of newspaper, and he gave one to the sergeant, who put it in his mouth and threw back his head and started chewing. Then he took a long pull on a canteen. Then he clicked his tongue and belched.

Night was coming on quickly, and only shadows could be seen, moving from one side to the other, unpacking equipment and carrying bundles. The men gathered in groups of three or four to prepare their mess. The kitchen cupboards and various corners of the inn had been searched, not violently, because the soldiers had quickly confiscated sufficient bread and provisions for the following day, and with the exception of sugar, which was not to be found inside the house or anywhere else, they needed nothing. They turned on no lights and lit no fire. Some of them laid blankets on the floor of the kitchen and the dining room and settled down to sleep. Two or three went out to the stone bench beside the entrance to smoke cigarettes, whose dim embers intermittently lit up their faces with a serene glow. Others bedded down in the stable with the mules, because it was a warm and welcoming stable. After exchanging a few words, however, the men decided to take the mules out into the field so that they could graze. María Antonia Etxarri, unafraid, went out and sat near the three smokers, and then, when they withdrew, she took a seat on the same bench, near the entrance, and remained there with her arms folded across her belly and a blanket over her shoulders, listening to the strident breathing of the soldiers sleeping inside the house and the concert of the owls that had been born the previous spring and the dull thud of the hobbled mules' hooves as the beasts grazed in the darkness.

The lieutenant went to spend the first part of the night with the men whom he had relieved, the ones who had been on duty atop the ice truck. There were two or three of them. He sent for the girl, and María Antonia, pressing her arms against her belly, thought that the moment had come, and that they were going to rape her when she joined them. There were no men who wouldn't do the same. Thirty metres separated the house from the brow of the little hill where the ice truck was parked. The top cover of the machine gun mounted on the ice truck was silhouetted against the night sky. As María Antonia walked up those thirty metres, the frozen letters of the Ice Factory gradually appeared and grew clearer, blue and white on a blue background paler than the thick darkness surrounding the ice truck, as if it were a circus truck painted with some kind of glossy or glittering paint, and as if those fantastic letters, snow-crested like mountaintops, were announcing the imminent opening of a circus show with ice, seals, and penguins. The lieutenant was sitting inside the truck, on the driver's side. His window was down, one elbow was sticking out, and he was smoking like the others. He turned his head as the girl approached the truck. The two men beside him craned forward and looked at her, too. 'What do you think of this girl?' the lieutenant asked.

'She looks human, Lieutenant,' one of the other men said.

'Go up to the room. The sergeant wants to ask you to perform a service.'

The girl crossed her arms, pulled the blanket over her shoulders, and turned round. Neither the lieutenant nor his two

men were the ones who were going to rape her. She was afraid
to retrace the thirty metres, because her heart was pounding
in her chest and she couldn't see where she was putting her
feet. In church, the priests taught the children such behav-
iour, telling them that they had to be obedient, even in time
of war, even though they could escape and disappear on the
mountain with the cows after setting fire to the hayloft, and
then, for decades to come, the house that had sheltered Etxarri's Bar would be nothing but a burnt patch, a few charred
beams on ash-covered ground, and nobody except a very few
people would know that María Antonia Etxarri had set the
house on fire to save herself from being raped, but instead of
doing that, remembering other reasons and other rains, María
Antonia obediently mounted the stairs to the room, doing as
she had been told, fearing only the barrage of blows she would
get from her stepfather should peace ever come.

The door was open and the sergeant was waiting for her,
wearing a rustic undershirt and long drawers. When she
arrived, he looked at her and said, 'I'll have to thank the
lieutenant.'

A lighted oil lamp stood on a console table, filling the
room with shadows and shimmers worthy of a sacristy. The
sergeant invited her inside and closed the door behind her.
His face was illuminated and sad, or at least that's the way
she remembered it, giving it the features of a boy who had
perhaps been promoted to corporal on the very day when he
enlisted, and then promoted to sergeant because of the need
for non-commissioned officers or because of some warlike

deed accomplished on one of the many occasions a war of
that sort would have offered, and after the passage of so many
years, that closed face, which contemplated her with neither
malevolence nor kindness, without even any desire except to
assuage desire, had taken on in her memory the expression,
between bad-tempered and foolish, of bridegrooms married
against their will. He didn't smile, nor did he bare his teeth.
The lieutenant had turned the room over to him for just this
situation, which promised to be awful from the moment the
sergeant closed the door behind the girl, and she, who had
often heard her mother and stepfather fighting in that room –
and years later, the best customers would take up quarters there
during the salmon-fishing season – she dropped the blanket
that she was still wearing over her head like a shawl, and since
she knew what she was going to be obliged to do, she hoped
only that the man would not force himself upon her violently,
and that the young soldiers downstairs would never find out
about what was on the verge of happening in that room. She
had heard men compared to dogs, and she had watched the
packs when they were released during hunts. The indecisive
sergeant made no move for several seconds. His profile was
silhouetted against the moonlight on the balcony. He told her
to lie on the bed and pulled his woollen undershirt over his
head as if he were peeling off his skin. Then he sat on a chair
and removed his long underpants, tugging first on one leg and
then on the other, as though stripping off a long, two-fingered
glove. She had never lain on her mother and stepfather's bed
nor, except when doing the cleaning, did she ever enter their
bedroom. But she lay on the bed as the man had told her to

do, and the man lay down beside her. He had big, cold hands. They seemed rather nervous, perhaps from shyness, perhaps from excitement. The brass balls at the foot of the bed gleamed while the bedsprings groaned, and her only hope was that the other soldiers wouldn't hear what was going on and wouldn't wake up in a state of lecherous agitation that nothing would be able to restrain. He threw her skirts over her face as if he were opening a trunk full of fancy clothes and undid the long drawers she used to wear in those days. Then he threw himself on top of her, and without her moving a muscle or shedding a tear or feeling either pleasure or pain, except for the alien warmth in her insides, the ungainly, naked man, covered with the sweat of war, as defenceless as a dog in the bed, raped her.

The sergeant turned over onto the mattress, lit a cigarette, and caught his breath. 'Today's my first wedding anniversary,' he said. 'My wife's in Pamplona, and the lieutenant understood that I needed a woman tonight.'

The cigarette left some shreds of tobacco on his lips, and he spat on the floor.

'Your name's Etxarri?'

'Etxarri.'

'There are some people named Etxarri in Pamplona.'

The man didn't speak again, and when he began to snore, she was able to leave the room. She picked up her blanket and spent the rest of the night in the kitchen, where the other soldiers were sleeping. She heard the changing of the guard and the lieutenant returning to his room. Then she fell asleep, too.

Colonel Beorlegui's forces ran into difficulties in their advance upon Oyarzun. In the to-and-fro of the war during those days, the Etxarri house changed hands three times, and it seemed as though each force had carried off a piece of the building. A mortar shell ripped off one corner, bringing to light a wallpapered bedroom and the sad bed with the brass balls. When the bridge over the river was blown up, stones and pieces of rubble struck the roof, and an eave was detached when fire destroyed a beam. But then the war gradually moved away. No one knows when the ice truck came back, stripped of its machine gun and transformed into an ambulance, and later, during the years of shortages, stripped of everything that could serve any purpose and finally stranded in a field, where it became a refuge for a clutter of cats, with its snowy letters eaten by rust, its broken headlights like the hollow eye sockets of an animal carcass, its tyres and seats gone, and its remains delivered up to the advancing nettles. No one knows with whom the sergeant spent the first anniversary of the war or the second anniversary of his marriage. María Antonia, indulgent as she was, still didn't know whether she had been the victim of a rape or whether, in the springtime of her sixteen years, she had been a second wife for that man. 'Long live God, who never dies,' the young troops of his company would fervently shout. Death surprised some like an early visitor, leaving behind as a sign of their time on earth the satiny sheen of some campaign photographs of them, young soldiers followed by their patient, immemorial mules, which seemed to carry all their exploits and all their sins, until they could carry them no more. María Antonia Etxarri's mother did not return, and it turned out that she was in a cemetery on the other side of the border, but her stepfather came back, and Etxarri's Bar eventually started doing a good business. María Antonia went into service, first in Vera, in the house of the rich man who had suffered a stroke in Etxarri's while on his way to a wedding. His name was Leopoldo, Don Leopoldo, like Leopold, King of the Belgians, and he behaved like a patriarch towards her. Some time later, she went to Hondarribia to serve in the house on the country estate called Las Cruces, and she preferred Hondarribia, because although she had been born in the valley and raised in the valley, she had always (even more now that she was old) liked being near the sea.

Some more particulars about Etxarri's inn:

Work on the new bridge began with the excavation of foundations on both sides of the stream and the pouring of gigantic concrete bases, placed diagonally across from one another with respect to the line of the current. Anchored in those concrete blocks, the bridge's iron framework, with beams as thick as a man's arm, grew upwards, anticipating the construction of the only arch. This new bridge vaulted the river in a single span, altering dimensions, modifying perspectives, and soaring above the old bridge, which had been poorly reconstructed – its ancient, hewn stones were reused – shortly after the war. The highest point of the elegant curve upon which the new bridge's concrete deck rested rose some ten or fifteen metres above the chimney and the ridge pole on the roof of the inn. Around this time, after the expropriation proceedings, the place was abandoned. What the war had been unable to do was accomplished in the peace: The roof developed holes, and moss and ferns began to grow on the tiles and in the recesses of the attic windows. Soon the sign that read *HOSTAL* fell off, and the big, rambling house once again became a ruin as in the days of the muleteers. The rosebush on the façade, the one with roses as fleshy as a wet nurse's breasts, grew wild and started throwing shoots into the meadow in a kind of disorderly procreation, and these offspring produced roses that were smaller but perhaps more robust. It was as though the rosebush were emigrating from the premises and demonstrating its ability to cope with the dark rivalry of the brambles in order to reach the woods and traverse the crests of the mountains and perhaps even – who could tell? – cross over into France. The new route of the highway, a comfortable, gently winding road, opened onto an embankment cut into the mountainside about halfway up and then ran along the opposite slope like an asphalt ribbon among the thick mountain foliage, and all this so that trucks with five axles and loads above thirty tons might have a smoother ride to Pamplona. By then, María Antonia's stepfather was dead, and it was she who received the money for the expropriation.

She was, by that time, an old woman with clever hands and a strong stomach, the housekeeper or servant or custodian or caretaker of the house where the wedding reception had been held (and later we shall have to speak of that wedding), a conceited but shrewd woman, weaker and more rheumatic than she herself might have wished, but still capable of lifting a bucket of water with only one hand, and capable as well of shouting insults over the villa's delicate rosebushes and garden wall at anyone making a racket with a motorcycle or at the baker who hadn't stopped to drop off her bread. The proprietress of Las

Cruces had died a few years previously, and the house was kept up by sorcery or by the servant's presence and certainly not by the distant solicitude of the late owner's family, who lived in Madrid and couldn't even spend their summers in the country house, because it didn't belong to them any more. One could recapitulate the landscape of bygone days by standing on the promontory of Hondarribia and gazing around in a circle. The young girl who had arrived there as a servant had been transformed into a wild animal, as if time had stripped her of her flowers in order to cover her with a skin like woven esparto and a cap stiffened with tar and turn her into something between a fox and a porgy, because there was as much innocence in her as there was shrewdness, and everything depended on who spoke to her and who came to see her. Her body was essential. She hated horses, an attitude that was somewhat surprising in a woman who had known three men, or perhaps was based precisely on that fact. The maintenance of the Las Cruces house was her responsibility, since an unusual last will in her favour had made the place hers. The property overlooked a magnificent landscape surrounding the broadest and most open stretch of the estuary, and from Las Cruces one could descry a watercolour horizon in the tender blue and green of the other shore, the buoys off Hendaye, the heights of Urruña, the masts and wind-whipped flags in the seaside resort of Saint-Jean-de-Luz, the radio transmitter, the casino in Biarritz, and the big department stores in Bayonne, all in a single, compact picture, just as María Antonia's misty imagination could have desired. She could see the Customs Service's grey motor launches. On the French side, the glass-enclosed miradors sparkled in the

twilight sun. One could always, while admiring the view, conjure up the landscape of a former battle. During the fall of the
fort of San Marcial and the burning of Irún, there were people
on that other shore who rented miradors and well-situated
farmhouses so that they could follow the spectacle of the war
from the safety of their side of the frontier. At the other end,
one could discern a point of light that came from the Amuitz
lighthouse. Also visible from the villa, among the trees of a
park on the Spanish side, was a country estate that the former owner never forgot to point out to her visitors, and which
had belonged to the late Eulalia de Borbón. But to return to
the Etxarri inn, to the construction of the new bridge that
cancelled out the bend in the road where the inn stood, and
to the old bridge, upon which the Etxarri inn had founded
all its hopes since the time of the Romans and their succes-
sors the mule drivers – in these matters, even María Antonia's
elementary imagination found food for thought. It was the
combat of gold and blood, which was resolved with the victory of gold. Not even she, with all her ambition – a woman
of the woods, thrice possessed by men with equine members
– could have conceived of the millions stipulated in the work
contract for that bridge, or of the amounts that were thrown
around in the government ministries and in the administrative offices of the Public Works, or of the modern require-
ments of traffic, but she knew all about the blood that had
been spilled on that bridge during the war, and she moreover
felt, however obscurely, that she carried in her veins the blood
of the innumerable generations of Etxarris who had run the
inn until it was taken over by the last Etxarri, her stepfather,

who was not a true Etxarri but a false Etxarri, but who, for the results he'd obtained and on a posthumous accounting, could be considered one of the family. None of that could have any effect against the gold represented by the bridge-building contracts and the exigencies of transportation, but a portion of the budget wound up in María Antonia's pockets anyway, and on terms she could never even have dreamed of. Her property was expropriated, and the expropriation filled those pockets of hers with gold. She was old and rich in the way peasants are, suspicious, and less than friendly to strangers. Nobody cared about the consequences of this chain of events, except for the gardener, a distant relative, or some cousin, who would never get rich. In regard to her function on the little estate in Hondarribia, to which she had come as a servant when she was a young girl and her late mistress practically a newlywed bride, nobody and nothing, not even a bulging bank account, could have persuaded her to leave service and go into retirement. The cheque from the Ministry, duly deposited in a bank, had amounted to something like eighteen million pesetas, and in the three or four years that had passed since, interest had accrued upon that principal, and neither María Antonia herself nor the gardener nor anyone in the vicinity who was aware of the existence of her fortune could guess what María Antonia would do with such a mass of money.

This was the state of affairs on the day when a grandson of the late owner – after asking permission from the present proprietress, his grandmother's former servant – was coming to stay at the house in Hondarribia for a few months. One of his first acts would be to identify the deceased in a photograph taken on the afternoon of his grandmother's wedding, a pallid sepia memento corroded by acid and set in a silver frame, barely more important than the two little porcelain dogs that were kept in the same glass cabinet, petrified like two small companion animals that might have belonged to the Señora and might in some way have been buried with her. The bride smiled in a lost paradise of tulle and lace and orange blossoms. The photograph showed neither how much weeping she was to do nor how little she had wept until then, nor was there any visible sign of the two tears of emotion she had shed during the ceremony or of the sighs she would utter that same night, but these are things that very few portraits of women allow the viewer to discern. María Antonia Etxarri heaved her own sigh. She felt veneration for the woman who had been her Señora. The bride in the photograph was a young lady of twenty-five at the time, while she, María Antonia, thrice possessed by three stallions, was a tender girl of . . . how old had she been? She herself could no longer be certain. The calendar of sentiments knows no certainties, but she had kept everything in her memory. There could be no greater misfortune, no greater solitude, than memory.

Miguel Goitia's plane had landed in Hondarribia at seven o'clock. He'd loaded the bulk of his baggage into a cab, and he himself had taken another cab, which preceded the one carrying his things and brought him to Las Cruces. Standing at the large window that overlooked the estuary and part of the broad mouth of the river and the open ocean, he could indeed see the sparkling miradors and the tuna-fishing boats painted red, green, and blue in the incredible softness of the evening. The old breakwater, planted with tamarind trees, was crowded with the last summer visitors. There on the other shore, amid the gleaming windows and the delicate mist that descended from the crests of the mountains, the lighthouse on the French coast was emitting signals, and the buoys had begun to send out synchronized flashes. The sea extended out towards the setting sun, caught in a sieve that came down upon the horizon at the moment when dusk fell. Soon the first star would rise. Unless the simultaneous weariness and exaltation of travel were obstructing his understanding, the great panoramas seemed to contain a message, and he considered the possibility that the sea before him, into which the gigantic beast of the Pyrenees would someday sink, was going to make all things more meaningful than ever before. Miguel Goitia turned from the window, stepped over to the glass cabinet, and picked up the framed photograph. 'Is this my grandmother?' he asked.

The robust servant, wearing a black cap set at an angle on her head like a beret – she said it was a mourning cap – replied in the affirmative. The deceased, the Señora, the bride, Grandmother Isabel – the person pictured in that photograph was all of them. For her grandson, who had seen little of her when she was alive, she was only a distant and uncertain childhood memory. He replaced the photograph between its permanent sentinels, the two little porcelain dogs, and moved away from the glass cabinet. The servant moved away in her turn, dragging one leg. White slipcovers shrouded the furniture in the drawing room, except for the table, whose covering was an old, patched tablecloth. The portraits and paintings on the walls, visible in the half-light of the room, were condemned to a mysterious opaqueness. The adjacent room was the dining room, and the one communicating with it had been the living room, after having been the smoking room, or the sewing room; in any case, the distribution and use of the rooms on the ground floor were not determined by their appearance or by the furniture they contained, for each space seemed to have been used capriciously for any function. At some point, Grandmother Isabel must have eaten in the sewing room, in winter or in summer – forgetting that gentlemen had smoked there in other lifetimes – or asked to be served in the real dining room, or even in the drawing room, in front of the big window. A door with a brass handle led to the kitchen. From there, a flight of stairs descended into the cellar. As for the other rooms and the attics, it would be better to leave consideration of them for another time. Hostess and guest mounted to the second floor. María Antonia went about opening doors and ventilating strongholds that had resisted the entrance of fresh air for quite some time. There was a leak in one of the bedrooms. The water filtered through the centre of a magnificent halo, which on stormy days let fall an intermittent drop, like an astronomical signal, into a chamber pot placed exactly perpendicular to the circle. The ultimate cause of this drip was a cracked tile on the roof. On the ceiling, concentric, delicately veined patterns were forming, patterns such as those one can observe in certain agate stones, paler or more intense according to the severity of the rainy season in the

year when they had taken shape. In all probability, the white
china chamber pot that caught the water from the leak was an
object saved from the Etxarri inn, and although the servant
wouldn't say so, it could be considered a survivor. At the turning of a corridor, Miguel Goitia confronted the stuffed head
of an African buffalo with a split horn, and María Antonia
neglected to explain that the rather shabby trophy came from
the inn and had survived the war and all the post-war years
with less damage and loss than many men. However, anyone
familiar with the two locales – that is, the Etxarri inn at the
crossroads and the Las Cruces villa in Hondarribia – could
have told that one of the two had pervaded the other through
the subtle introduction of symbols and emblems that assur-
edly were not limited to the buffalo head and the china chamber pot. Knowing eyes would have detected María Antonia's
influence in the house after the Señora's death and the expropriation and destruction of the inn. Thus her universe now
extended beyond the kitchen, where she spent so much of
her time, and her room, which had always been the servant's
quarters. She had gradually taken over the rest of the territory,
just as a certain species of phagocytic amoeba takes over the
space previously occupied by a rival species. They went on
to the room that the grandson was going to occupy for the
anticipated duration of his stay on the estate. It was a room
with a view of the sea, located on the north-eastern façade of
the house, just above the drawing room, where a few minutes
previously he had contemplated his grandmother Isabel's picture. A door led to a bathroom with blue, bevelled tiles, white
baseboards with a golden fillet, and a frieze in the same style,

with garlands of flowers. The bathtub stood on four lions' feet, like a Roman sarcophagus. The bedroom that the servant had chosen for him communicated with another bedroom, which contained a double bed. Another door, half closed, led to the room with the chamber pot. The chosen room was well-maintained and in good shape, except for the damp stain he detected near the window. Perhaps María Antonia had left in that room, too, some object from the inn, some fetish or device charged with magnetic power, but knowing eyes would have been unable to detect it at first glance. Then they would have guessed that the bed itself, with its brass balls, could have been stored for many years in the attic of Etxarri's after the stepfather had turned the roadside bar into a cheap hotel. This was quite possibly the case, and also quite possibly not. A factory in Elizondo had produced beds of this type, and there were many in the region. Whether it was the case or not – and it probably wasn't – every room in the house had preserved a certain nobility, which remained unaffected by the ceiling leak that dripped into the chamber pot or by the melancholy aspect of this bed. Miguel Goitia put down the small case he was carrying. He had heard the taxi with the rest of his baggage driving up, and he went down to wait for it at the entrance. The servant followed him, closing doors as she went. A loose shutter was banging against a window somewhere. The sparrows of late afternoon had settled on the telephone wires, and at the moment when the cab driver opened the enormous mouth of the vehicle's boot, the birds took flight.

With eighteen million and more in her bank account, María Antonia did not feel obliged to unload anybody's luggage, and she confined herself to observing the operation from the porch with her hand on one leaf of the double door. Goitia was travelling with two suitcases and a trunk. The trunk appeared to be filled with lead. In fact, it was full of books, but they weighed as much as General Zumalacárregui's bronze bust. The taxi driver and the gardener got the trunk out of the automobile. Then, using a rag he kept in the glove compartment, the driver wiped his hands, like Pontius Pilate abdicating his responsibilities. Goitia and the gardener carried the trunk to the house. Then they came back for the suitcases, and Goitia paid his fare. Although it looked as though he'd be sleeping in the bedroom next to the room with the chamber pot, Goitia preferred to instal his books on the ground floor, and he and the gardener lugged the trunk inside. In the meanwhile, María Antonia had removed the white slipcovers from the furniture in the drawing room and draped them over a chair like an armful of limp, useless ghosts. The dying afternoon light cast a dull pall over the drawing room. María Antonia switched on a couple of lamps and withdrew. In very few words, the gardener had made it known that the kitchen floor tiles were soiled with mud tracked in from the garden, and this information had put her in a bad mood. Goitia shrugged. The servant re-emerged from the kitchen with a mop and an enormous bucket of water as Goitia was dismissing the gardener. She had changed her outfit; under the black skirt she'd had on before, she was now wearing a pair of blue trousers. She began to scrub away the traces of mud with obstinate, pendular movements. Then she looked up at Goitia with a spark of mingled reproach and affection in her eyes.

'Where's the telephone?' the intruder asked.

María Antonia gestured towards the sewing room.

There was indeed a telephone, and it was to be hoped that the line had not been cut. Next to the sewing room was what probably had been the gun room, containing a desk and two empty glass cabinets. In point of fact – although Goitia could not know this – that small chamber had been the original smoking room. In any case, he decided to put his books in there, for although the servant thought he was a medical doctor, he was actually a doctor of law, a lawyer, and he intended to spend the next four months studying for the competitive examinations to become a civil-law notary. He had no intention of dedicating himself to anatomical dissections, as he did in the servant's turbid imagination, and therefore he needed a small chamber, a desk, and some bookshelves, not the kitchen or the cellar for dismembering cadavers, no matter what she might have fancied. But all that was to become clear in the following days, after the servant and the intruder had made mutual efforts to communicate.

Goitia turned to her with a tyrannical gesture. 'Is there a clean armoire on the second floor?'

'They're all clean,' the servant said proudly, without taking into account the invisible proliferation of microscopic fungi that imparted an odour of penicillin to those enclosed spaces.

'I'll carry up the suitcases,' Goitia said.

María Antonia once again recalled the eighteen million and more that she had in the bank and made no offer to help. One after the other, Goitia hauled the two suitcases upstairs. They were lighter than the trunk filled with books and heavier than what he had really needed to bring with him, but then he wondered whether he shouldn't have added a whip or some kind of weapon in case the old woman, despite having authorized his presence, should decide to attack him.

When he went back downstairs, the servant had disappeared, but as happens with certain animals, a trace of her smell had remained in the drawing room. Goitia stepped into the little sewing room, where he planned to make a couple of telephone calls. Before his eyes, framed under glass, was an embroidered cloth that figured cats playing with a basket full of yarn balls, and next to it was another framed cloth embroidered with an exceedingly elaborate upper-case letter, covered with garlands of flowers. The letter was an I, the initial of his grandmother Isabel. Outside the window, an aeroplane rose into the sky, between the line of country houses and the trees and half-inundated fields that hid the airport runway. The airliner was a silent artefact. The roar of its engines could be heard only several seconds later. It was gaining altitude, high enough for the sun to cast a glittering reflection onto its fuselage. It veered smoothly north-east, tilting its wings, and then traced a broad curve to the west, as if it hoped to escape in triumph with the gold of twilight and flee to the advancing night. Then it changed direction and hurtled southwards. It was the plane Goitia had arrived on, flying back to Madrid.

It's not impossible to imagine what that drawing room was like in darkness, separated from the sewing room by a door that stood ajar and allowed a square of light to fall on the chessboard of the tiled floor. A gloomy lamp with a green glass shade had been turned on in the gun room. In the sewing room, Goitia took refuge under the circle of light shed by a lamp with a parchment shade, crouching beside the nearby telephone table with the Bakelite receiver in his hand. There was something grotesque about this lawyer, this young, modern doctor of law, squatting in a sewing room adorned with kittens and embroidered letters and turning his back on the virile associations of the room with the green light. But one can imagine the drawing room in darkness, and without the shrouds that usually covered the furniture: bathed in the glow of the refulgent moon, which varnished the room's old mahogany, awakening silver reflections, and so desolate in appearance that it seemed to live only for the beyond, represented in this case by the deceptive, watery lamplight shining through the window onto the dark garden. There was an enormous ashtray, batrachian in form, with an inscription, IX FROG-FISHING COMPETITION − GASTRONOMICAL SOCIETY OF MENDIETA, but no date. This object came from some celebration that had taken place in the Etxarri inn. The guests at this gathering had sung

> *Go Mendieta,*
> *You're the greatest. . . .*

or something of the sort. Or maybe

> *The Gorri-Gorri's wife,*
> *the one who does the Charleston.**

Gorri means red in Basque.

Or there was also

> *The woman soft and white*
> *has legs that thrill the sight,*
> *and an ass beyond all praise. . . .*

María Antonia wouldn't have been able to remember those songs, because the men who sang them were her stepfather's old pals, but she did have a hazy memory of a competition where the size and healthy appearance of the frogs the contestants caught counted for as much as their quantity. While the frogs were still alive, their rear legs were cut off with sheep-shearing scissors and then breaded and fried, or cooked in *pil-pil* sauce, or prepared in whatever innovative way a member of the Society might imagine. Back then, men were cruel with frogs and cruel to one another. This kind of fishing had little to do with salmon fishing, or rather their relation was the same as the one between that large brass ashtray and the silver ashtrays to be found here and there, small ashtrays, engraved or repoussé, taking in the moonlight as though receiving the consecrated host. The unoccupied, nocturnal drawing room existed in a certain timeless flux. The collection of small ashtrays had been one of Grandmother Isabel's wedding presents, but old María Antonia was unable to put a date on it, just as there was no date in the inscription for the IX Frog-Fishing Competition on the bronze ashtray.

But the wedding itself, represented in the drawing room by the silver ashtrays, had taken place in May, or in June, on a day excessively hot even for the recently begun season. Because of the heat, the wedding banquet was held in the garden, where the guests could scatter among the trees, although the men, who habitually flee the sun, took refuge in the house. The couple had been married in the church in Hondarribia. A chorus of villagers, beggars, and busybodies watched the bride enter that beautiful edifice, riddled by the centuries and the salt sea air. Isabel was dressed as in the photograph; her fiancé wore the uniform of a captain of artillery. Someone in the crowd said, 'Captain, you don't look like the groom.'

The groom must not have heard this comment or simply didn't reply. Some of those present held the view that weddings where the groom is a military man and wears his dress uniform are fine and striking spectacles; others, however, thought that the anonymous remark contained something more than a mere reflection. In any case, few people choose to be married at their summer holiday home, and the decision may have been dictated by circumstances, or it may have been due to Isabel's desire to be married within sight of the sea. One of the bride's witnesses was missing. At first, no one noticed his absence, and no one could know at the time that the absent witness had suffered a stroke in the latrine of Etxarri's Bar, an ignominious place for a witness in such an elegant wedding. The big black automobiles surrounded the church, and then they drove out in a caravan to the estate. Some of those vehicles would later become authentic museum pieces, and others, beginning shortly after the war broke out, would provide transport for a general staff or other group of officers, or would serve to carry Falangists to the front with the Falangist proprietor of the car behind the steering wheel, or would get taken on a joyride by a bunch of euphoric militiamen after they had requisitioned the vehicle or shot its owner. In any case, on the day of the wedding, anyone who admired those stupendous velvet-black cars, gleaming as wedding automobiles always do, anyone who admired them there would have thought about the coming summer, about excursions to the casino in Biarritz or to eat crabs in Lesaka, and no one would have given the least thought to a war, because wars never announce their imminence in the way that posterity will imagine they did. The groom brought along four witnesses: two members of his family and two regimental comrades. The bride had more than enough witnesses, even though the man who was her father's associate in the paper-manufacturing business had not shown up. There are people who admire superior vehicles as treasures of mechanical science, and who consider the internal combustion engine the most attractive invention since the steam engine. The wedding caravan included a Bentley, two Panhards, and a Peugeot 601, as well as other models that may be tricks of the memory, because it's possible that they were models from after the war or from after the world war. In any case, nothing seemed more impressive than a gathering of fine automobiles, and it was a pleasure to stand close to them, knowing that you'd never be able to get your hands on any such steering wheel, and knowing, too, that those machines were a scarce luxury, only to be seen in groups at certain funerals and certain weddings, just as canons, bishops, and cardinals gather in cathedrals for certain solemn celebrations.

A canopy was stretched between two lime trees, in a spot

where those two lime trees stand no more, because the fashion for shady parks was succeeded by the fashion for expanses of lawn in the American style, which is also called the English style. The guests assembled in that spot. Food and drink were also available on three other tables – two parallel boards adjoining opposite ends of the main table – which formed a horseshoe round the cedar tree. After the ceremony, when the bride, accompanied by the sound of automobile horns and a flight of seagulls overhead, arrived from the church, she entered the garden as a young married woman, but her veil, her emotional state, and the somewhat shy attention with which she extended her hand all showed that she was still a bride, because at that age, so tender and so febrile – barely twenty-five – a woman of her class was a shy virgin, even though she might have attended many a witches' Sabbath in her secret heart. She went into the house to take off her shoes for a few minutes and throw her veil across a bed. She briefly shut herself up in her boudoir to fix her hair and check her make-up in a dressing-table mirror. Then she went outside again to receive the guests' congratulations.

The ladies' hats of those years, the so-called picture hats, were just as remarkable as the automobiles, and one might have talked about the hats as well, but they were much less interesting than mechanical science. A lady who lived in Vitoria, an emotional person, came up to pay her respects to the bride. This lady was on the arm of a gentleman, the bride's uncle by marriage, who smiled under his moustache, exhibiting both his teeth and his good appetite.

'I wept in church, Isabel, to see you looking so pretty.'

'Thank you, Aunt.'

This was the moment to present the groom, for the aunt and uncle had only seen his name on the wedding invitation and had been unable to greet him before the ceremony. 'Let me introduce Julen.'

'Pleased to meet you.'

'Pleased to meet you.'

'You've chosen well,' the older gentleman said. 'You've chosen a chicken thigh,' he added, observing the captain's rosy complexion above the collar of his military jacket, or perhaps thinking about going over to the refreshment tables.

'Thank you, Uncle.'

The courtesies were brief. Other picture hats and moustaches pressed forward. The groom was Julio Herraz, or Julen Herraz, according to the degree of intimacy and familiarity his name evoked, or Captain Herraz to those who met him somewhat later, when he attached himself, with his rank and function, to the Defence Junta of Azpeitia, a few days after the war began. But that decision would have nothing to do with his loyalty or his courage, or with what others would afterwards call his wrongheadedness. Be that as it may, the thirty-year-old captain, five years older than his bride, had come to get married and not to give explanations of what his future conduct would be, even if a clairvoyant capable of seeing imminent events would have dared to ask him to justify himself. He was wearing white gloves and a sabre. He had uncovered his head and was carrying his uniform cap under his arm. A civilian can hardly imagine how difficult it must be to get married while wearing a sabre and to refrain from dragging it on the ground, from tangling its tassels, from using it to strike chairs and benches. The captain removed his right glove to shake hands with the wedding guests. After half an hour, when the guests had taken their seats, he and his two regimental comrades went into the house, precisely so that they could leave their sabres in some convenient place. For reasons having to do both with economics and with some obscure prestige, the wedding banquet had been contracted out to the officers' mess in the Loyola barracks. The cooks arrived with giant field kettles for boiling lobsters, the quarter-master corps sent vans filled with wines and liqueurs, and the waiters were young men performing their military service to the Republic, offering a series of trays laden with canapés and fried snacks. All these unexpectedly glamorous items issued from the kitchen of the villa itself, but it was the groom who had requested them. Some guests remarked to their companions that army recruits and orderlies made the best waiters, but at bottom many of the attendees thought that the wedding was irregular, and that neither of the parties had wished to open their wallets. An orchestra consisting of five musicians and a vocalist, likewise quartered in the barracks, enlivened the end of the meal with elegant music, followed by the Gorri-Gorri Charleston, as if they wanted to complicate their function and vulgarize the party. Later, as night fell, there was dancing on the veranda. Everyone looked on while the bride's father opened the dancing with his daughter, acknowledging the fact that he had finally married her off, as if, right up to that moment, he could have avoided the unavoidable, and also acknowledging the fact that from that moment on, it would be the captain's job to satisfy his daughter's caprices, given that he, the father, had already sacrificed his opinion to her supreme caprice, namely, the idea of marrying the captain. Then, as was the custom, the father of the groom, a widower and tax inspector, invited the bride to dance, while the bride's mother allowed the groom to lead her out for a few turns. Then the groom and bride danced together. Someone remarked, 'Look here, the dove is dancing with the chicken thigh.'

Captain Herraz danced with his shoulders stiff and his neck stretched, as if his body were attached to a hanger. He held his wife round the waist with a gesture learned at officers' balls. Although her eyes were tired, she did her best to keep smiling as she threw her head back. She had lost an earring, but she didn't know it. Someone had picked it up and clutched it in his fist, wondering whether earrings found in such circumstances should be restored to their rightful owner, or if they had some greater significance.

'Gold digger,' somebody said, watching the couple dance.

'Do you think the captain has married the young woman for her inheritance?'

'Not just for that,' someone else added, observing the breathless bride's heaving bosom as the dance ended, noting her smile and her half-open lips, and envying the place Chicken Thigh would occupy that very night.

When this group passed near the newlywed couple, conversation ceased, and the guests raised their glasses and murmured something. On the other side of the wrought-iron gate was a gathering of people from Hondarribia, who had come out to see the wedding at the country estate of Las Cruces. Back then, Hondarribia was still a village where a wedding at the vacation home of some summer residents could be considered a social event. A man on horseback came down the road, and his torso, hieratic against the half-lit landscape, glided past above the line of broken glass crowning the garden wall. But nobody appeared to be paying any attention to this enigmatic vision, and with the passage of the years, when recalling a wedding celebrated so long ago, it may all seem grotesque, strange, or simply unreal – a memory of playing with figures decked out in wedding finery amid flowers and balustrades, or of wandering in a labyrinth of bushes, or of seeing the torso of a horseman above a garden wall as he rode by during the magic moments when twilight was falling – for real life had offered one of those sequences that would never be repeated except in the theatres where what were then still called talkies were shown. In the end, memory adopts images that originated in films. Garden walls were no longer crested with broken bottles, no longer bared their teeth to intruders or glinted like jewels in the capricious moonlight, and this was not because men were less cruel or had chosen to eschew the most primitive manifestations of cruelty, but because tastes had changed, or because those were more violent times, when garden walls were defended with guns; and therefore a horseman's upper body, remembered as riding past at twilight on the other side of a garden wall topped with broken glass, could be seen again only on a cinema screen.

Candelabra had been brought out from the house to

illuminate the garden. A garland of coloured lightbulbs hung from both sides of the canopy spread out between the trees. The girls had shared out the flowers that decorated the tables. The younger children were asleep in wicker chairs, and the faces of the ladies, who had drunk anisette and coffee, were faded and sad. One overturned chair lay on the grass. Some gentlemen strolled through the park. Others withdrew to smoke. Many further details of the wedding could be recounted, but so many years have not passed in vain, and therefore probably no one, with the best will in Spain, could obtain more data than what might spring from the most suggestive sequences of some old-fashioned films, or from the scenes in Rubens's painting *The Garden of Love*, but even in the garden of love there is room for conspiracies and slander, spoken by the rascals who appear between the balustrades of palaces in certain canvases by the Old Masters. The green lamp suffused the gun room with an aquatic glow. The shadows were projected all together, arising from a single body, like the different heads of a mythical animal.

'Cavalry has become meaningless,' Captain Arderius remarked. He was one of the groom's regimental comrades, and he was addressing the group of men who, like him, had retired to the smoking room to enjoy a Havana cigar. 'Infantry is the army's spinal column, but only mobile artillery can decide the outcome of a battle.'

'You're talking about tanks?'

'I am,' said Arderius with a smile, flattered to see that his laconic allusion had been understood.

The young and glossy captain sniffed the bouquet of his

cognac before bringing the glass to his lips. He was a tall, gangling fellow, and a thick, unmilitary lock of dark hair hung down above his eyes. His regimental comrade, also in attendance as a witness for the groom, nodded in wordless assent. The men around them fell silent. Only a very few of them were interested in military matters, and then only as they might have been interested in a new hunting technique. At the time, the gun room was decorated with two illustrations depicting deer harried by dogs. When her mistress was dead and she herself had become undisputed mistress of Las Cruces, María Antonia Etxarri, who didn't like packs of hounds, removed those pictures from the wall. Afterwards, one could distinguish the pale, dirty rectangle left behind by each of the frames, and inside the rectangles, lines of a more intense green than the faded colour in the rest of the wallpaper. In the glass cabinet, against a background of red felt, were a hunting rifle, two Sarasqueta shotguns, made in Spain, and one Purdey, of English manufacture.

A man with drooping eyelids, either bored or depressed by the conversation, raised his glass of cognac at the same time as the captain. Two rock crystal ashtrays lay on the desk. The Havana cigars were producing thick stumps of ash. The newly-weds had departed a moment earlier, having bidden farewell only to the guests who were closest to them. They would stop in Saint-Jean-de-Luz before going on to Biarritz, where they would spend their honeymoon, and then, who could tell? Someone declared that the couple's astounding intention was to abandon Biarritz for Paris and enjoy an authentic honeymoon in the capital of France, but that was someone who had dreamed this project after falling asleep while reading a novel. As for the rest of them, it wasn't that they considered Parisian honeymoons the stuff of novels; it was that they could not conceive of a honeymoon spent north of Biarritz. However, the newlyweds had not really left. They had mounted to the second floor and changed their clothes, but not in the same room. The bride took off her wedding dress, separated by a partition wall from Captain Herraz, who hung his uniform on a hanger. An orderly carried the suitcases out of the back door, and then the couple stepped out. Several automobiles had already left. The deliberate revolutions of their engines, as slow and powerful as ships' engines, could still be heard. Another automobile's horn began to honk merrily.

'There go the lovebirds,' said a man standing next to the window, cigar in hand. Then he turned to his companions. 'Come on, Captain. Let's hear some more about the coffee-pots on tracks.'

'The tanks?'

'That's it, the tanks.'

'Say what you want,' said the man with the drooping eye-lids, 'but the real shock force is and will always be the Spanish Legion.'

There were a few moments of silence. The Havana tobacco made tongues drowsy and thoughts slow. It's possible that some belated memories slipped back, with deferred nostalgia, to their own honeymoons. Then conversation began again.

'Where do the lovebirds plan to nest?'

'In the Loyola barracks,' Arderius said. 'Although Chicken Thigh has put in for a transfer to Madrid.'

The man with the drooping eyelids closed them. He saw himself travelling on the road to Saint-Jean-de-Luz, where he would spend his wedding night, and used the liveliest colours to paint his image of what a wedding night could be. Only once in his life had he possessed a virgin, and she, unfortunately, was now his wife. The placid, sturdy cognac had ignited a vague spark of lechery in him. The desire to be in the groom's place opened a twisting road in his imagination. He finally recovered and peered darkly through one half-closed eye. 'It's not a superstition. The best way to ensure that your wife will eventually make a cuckold of you is to take her on a honeymoon trip to Paris.'

The others burst into laughter. In the smoke-filled gun room, tobacco and cognac were increasingly dulling everyone's wits. The guests were saying their goodbyes, and there was a perceptible bustle of waiters clearing away dishes. The members of the orchestra were storing their instruments in their cases, while a couple of women called through the bushes for a lost child. The Havana cigars were consumed, and those solid gentlemen, as slow and ungainly as sacks of cement, began to set themselves in motion. The gun room would never again be so densely populated as it was during those moments, nor the house, either, nor the garden. The groups of automobiles and curiosity-seekers gradually dispersed. Before long, the last person left the garden. Captain Arderius and his comrade in arms, after giving the matter some thought, went to a whorehouse in Irún. Later, as was the custom in their regiment, they exchanged whores, so that each of them might try the one whom the other had chosen. It's not rare for a wedding to end in a brothel. Could Miguel Goitia have heard the comments made about his grandmother on her wedding day, about how beautiful she looked – which was just as she did in the photograph with the silver frame – he would perhaps have been flattered, but he would have been less pleased to hear the derogatory remarks made about his grandfather, Captain Herraz. Or Herráiz, because no one in Hondarribia could remember exactly, and the name wasn't even spelled correctly on the rolls of the unit the captain joined in Azpeitia a few weeks after his return from his honeymoon and a few days after the military rising was proclaimed in his barracks. War transforms not only people's lives, but even their names and surnames. No one who wasn't curious or crazy would have bothered to verify the spelling of the captain's name after so many years. Similarly, had no one told him about it, Goitia would never have found out the significance of the empty gun room, so someone would have to tell him about it. The pictures of the hunted deer were gone, as were the shotguns in the cabinets, lined with red felt, where he was shelving his books. The smoke from half a dozen Havana cigars had dispersed at the same time as the memories. A collector of cigar bands kept the bands from the cigars the men had smoked at the wedding. On those bands, the initials of the bride and groom were intertwined: *J* and *I*.

The cellar of the Las Cruces house contained more objects salvaged from the Etxarri inn than the total scattered through the rest of the house. The inn's white china crockery was packed away in wooden ham crates. There were thick drinking glasses and various sets of cutlery. There was, in fact, enough tableware to set up a restaurant, but the Las Cruces promontory, even counting the residents in the neighbouring houses and the summer vacationers as potential customers, could not match the advantages of a good crossroads location, and it was for this reason, and not only because of her age, that María Antonia Etxarri had rejected the idea of opening a dining establishment. But sometimes, as the shadows fell and she dwelt upon the schemes and projects that filled her head, she would fantasize about having her own successful business, like the prosperous enterprise that her stepfather had made of Etxarri's in the years following the Civil War, after she had already gone into service. Had that business been hers, she thought, her life would have resolved itself into an entirely different shape. It sometimes happens that well-to-do ladies bequeath their houses to their maids. Now she had the Señora's house and more than eighteen million in the bank, but everything had happened too late, when she was no longer strong and her time was short. These were nocturnal thoughts. Upon the Señora's death, the Las Cruces house belonged to her. There had been documents and a will, and if she was now allowing the Señora's grandson into the house, she was doing so for reasons that were of no concern to anyone, least of all to the grandson, who was there by an unspoken right of usufruct, whether to prepare for examinations or to write a book or to dissect cadavers or to save goods and chattels by means of the law made little difference to her. The grandson had barely known his grandmother. Old María Antonia had no reason to talk about the reasons why. As with many other things in life, it was enough to admit that it had been so.

She went down to the gun room, where Goitia was arranging his books, and gave him a key. Then she asked him if he wanted her to prepare something for dinner.

'I'll dine in the village,' Goitia said, and the old woman, much relieved, withdrew.

She had an apron on over her skirt. She'd taken off the blue trousers she wore under it when she had to wash the floors or clean the house. The mane of her hair was bound at her nape with a black ribbon, and when she turned round to remove the slipcovers, which had been left on one of the chairs, it was possible to admire the thick, wavy locks that hung down the length of her spine, as if she were a girl suddenly grown old, seen from behind. She had a peasant's broad hips. Age had drawn her shoulders together, but they must have once been broad, too. Nonetheless, in the earthy grace of her movements as she bent forward, and in the way she spread her arms to gather up the linen pile from the chair, as she might have gathered up a sheaf of hay, there was something fresh and adolescent, like a figure captured in perspective by the eye of a painter and transformed into a couple of vigorous charcoal lines so that posterity could see in the old woman the graceful girl she had been. It was an instant. Then María Antonia turned round, embracing an armful of slipcovers. Swaying, her head thrown back, she passed in front of Goitia on her way to the wardrobe where they were stored. Goitia stepped aside with a book in his hand. And then she smiled, as if she found this boy less unusual, on the whole, than she had feared. Few could know, however, that María Antonia's smile was equivalent to the face other people make when they detect a bad odour.

Impeded by her load, she passed Goitia and then turned round in the narrow corridor so that she could use her buttocks to push open the door to the service area. When she did so, Goitia could see her hands, fingers interlocked, clutching her white, bulky load. 'Would you like me to help you?' he asked, still holding a volume of the Civil Code.

The old woman's reply was laconic and seemed fierce: 'Stand aside. I can do it by myself.'

Accustomed as she was to living in silence, sometimes stones issued from her mouth when she spoke, and perhaps that was why she spoke little, or spoke earthily, like a quarryman. She mitigated the effect of her words with another indecipherable smile and then disappeared into the linen room, where Goitia would later store his trunk after emptying it of his books. Soon she came out again, her posture upright, her hands free. She hesitated in the hallway, as if she'd forgotten something, unsure whether or not to go back to the drawing room. Then she could be heard in the kitchen. She wouldn't have liked to be obliged to prepare dinner for anyone or to carry anyone's suitcases, and she preferred to dine alone. She had her habits. As she ate, María Antonia thought about that bronze ashtray, the one inscribed for the IX Frog-Fishing Competition. She could remember very well the dinners in Etxarri's on the days of the competition, when she would come up to the inn from Hondarribia to help serve. It was said that the best frogs came from Zugarramurdi Pond, frogs as big as toads. The best snails were the ones that lived in the wall of the cemetery in Vera de Bidasoa. And the best crayfish could be found in the clear streams of Lesaka. Every village had its pennant, which bore the image of a batrachian, a crayfish, or a snail.

Goitia finished shelving his books and hauled his trunk into the living room. Then he went up to the second floor, to the room the old woman had assigned him, with the intention of unpacking his suitcases. When he turned on the landing, he came up against the buffalo head, which guarded the corridor. He thought he had run into a monster and was barely able to suppress a shout. There was a serene, unmoving gleam in the animal's big glass eyes. The split horn gave it the aspect of a dismasted ship. Goitia stepped past it, lowering his head as a precaution, and entered his room. The first lights of night spilled through the open window, drawing a phosphorescent square on the geometrical pattern of the floor. Goitia turned on the light and closed the window. Then he sat on the edge of the bed, unable to make up his mind to unpack. Finally, he decided to go out to dinner and picked up the jacket he'd worn on the plane.

From the outside, he could see that half the façade was covered with climbing plants that had not yet begun to lose their leaves. Under those plants, unknown to Goitia, there was a heraldic shield, probably invented by a great-grandfather who had made his fortune in the paper or wood business, or by canning anchovies, the same ancestor who had built the house and ordered the carving of the coat of arms, which showed an oak, a wolf, and – some said – a can opener, taking for a can opener what was actually a spear transfixing the

wolf's body, but little memory of that shield remained since
the climbing plants had covered it up. Through the black glass
windows of the drawing room, he could make out a lamp
that was throwing a pool of yellow light onto the lawn. One
of the corners on the top floor was built up into a tower, or
a dovecote, and surmounted by the silhouette of a sailboat,
cut out of sheet metal, which served as a weather vane. That
night, the boat was sailing over a placid sea of clouds and
oscillating a little in the west wind. Another light in the depths
of the house disclosed the hidden life of the old woman in her
kitchen, sitting before a plate of fried fish and a bowl of turnip
soup. Just as he didn't see the heraldic shield, Goita was also
unaware of that humble dinner, where the risen Christ himself
could have broken bread with old Antonia and blessed her as
he blessed the disciples at Emmaus. The porch light, a sixty-
watt bulb enclosed in a bronze cage, indicated that the house
was inhabited, and to some neighbours, it signified more than
that. It meant that there was a guest at Las Cruces, because
only on rare occasions had they seen the light still burning
at such an hour. Goitia crossed the garden and opened the
entrance gate. It closed behind him with the melodious whine
of oxidized iron, and when he looked back at the house, it
appeared in the midst of a symphonic perspective: tower,
lights, foliage. He identified his room by its window, which
he had reopened before going out, intending to air out the
space and anticipating the pleasure of sleeping that night with
the smell of the sea in his nostrils.

Retracing the road by which he'd arrived in the taxi, he
descended the slope in the direction of the village. When he

reached a dark crossroads, he grew disoriented, turned back, and took another blacktop road, which ran between rows of streetlights and a series of one-family dwellings and then past taller buildings, apartment houses inhabited by summer vacationers. Some apartments were in darkness, while others had lights and tables on the balconies, under the broad eaves of the roofs. He could hear anonymous voices, fragments of conversations, and the sound of bottles being uncorked. The trees formed a vault above his head. Between their trunks, he could see the estuary, spread out like a black sheet, and the rosary of lights on the other shore. The orange tint of the sky indicated the spot where the road intersected with the motorway. The landscape, at once black and luminous, seemed strangely charged with emotion, and Goitia came to a momentary stop, deeply affected. His surroundings might just as easily have seemed sinister. The inky estuary, made slightly iridescent by the reflections from the low clouds, was receiving the undulations of high tide, slow and powerful, as if a monster were sleeping under the water. Goitia felt the fascination of the early-falling autumn darkness. He stood still for an instant, facing the great void of the sea and of the night. Then he continued on his way down to the beach. The outdoor cafés were deserted. Finally, he reached the village. Comforted by the smell of wine, beer, and sawdust emanating from a tavern – it was as if, after a period of time suspended in the cosmic void, he had come upon humans – he entered and sat down to order his dinner.

It was around eleven o'clock when he started back home. He went up the road with his hands in his pockets and his jacket collar turned up. The night was thicker than before, and the landscape, because of the wine he'd drunk, or because of his digestion, had taken on a velvety texture. The wrought-iron entrance gate again sang its sorrowful, rusty melody. It needed a good oiling. Before going into the house, Goitia took a walk through the garden. He passed under the porch, went round the garage, and returned along the side of the garden wall that adjoined the neighbouring property. He stopped to smoke a cigarette, and then he heard someone greet him.

'Good evening.'

The wall was sufficiently low for him to make out a silhouette of middle height, slightly less dark than the dark garden that surrounded it. The shadowy shape was illuminated, somewhat, by the light from a streetlamp. Goitia threw his match into the wet grass and returned the greeting.

'Good evening.'

'My name is Félix Castro. I'm your neighbour,' the amiable voice said to the nonplussed Goitia. 'Lovely night, isn't it?'

Goitia agreed. The stranger stepped closer to the wall. With unexpected familiarity, he asked, 'You're a doctor, right?'

'A doctor?'

'Old Antonia told me you were a doctor.'

'I'm a doctor of law.'

'Ah! That's not the same thing.'

'No, it's not.'

The anonymous face was hidden again by a half-moon of shadow. Misinformed by the old woman, the doctor had been expecting to meet a young colleague. He'd seen the young man arrive in the late afternoon and watched him and the gardener shift the trunk and the suitcases. He'd thought that introducing himself would be the proper thing to do, but now he wasn't sure that he'd chosen the right moment or employed the degree of diffidence, the hesitant mildness, advisable to a gentleman when presenting himself to someone he didn't know. Goitia remained silent. That way, his neighbour would have to see that his intrusion was inopportune, because the young man wanted to smoke his cigarette and enjoy the night in solitude, just as the other feared. The doctor remained silent in his turn, even though he was burning to ask Goitia at least a few of the things he would not have dared to mention without the protection of the night. And among all those things, the most trivial, the one which, more than any other, awakened in him an almost childish curiosity, was his desire to know Goitia's opinion of the automobile that had been shut up in the garage of the villa for the past fifteen or twenty years, a Morris Oxford, immobilized, mounted on some wooden blocks, a vehicle with a body like the vault in the Church of the Good Shepherd, four cylinders of nearly a litre each, and a chassis like a railway carriage, and he also wanted to ask Goitia what it was like for a youth to find himself in a big, run-down house where the only thing that wasn't missing was wine – the neighbour knew this because old Antonia had told him – and where there was surely no lack of ghosts, either, even though they were the ghosts of the guests who had attended that wedding long ago, the occasion for such a large gathering of automobiles, among which the Morris Oxford had not seemed out of place. Automobiles fascinate people in the same way that horses do, and the honourable, affable man who had appeared on the other side of the garden wall was fascinated by automobiles. He himself owned a fine, relatively recent model – if one could consider 1966, the year of his Renault Frégate, recent – but he was also fond of 'crates', as vintage automobile enthusiasts affectionately called their old relics, and he had managed to salvage from a garage in Vera de Bidasoa a Citroën 11 Légère that had belonged to Don Leopoldo, the rich man from Vera, the King of the Belgians. It was a marvellous automobile, ahead of its time, with front-wheel drive and hydraulic brakes, practically undriven since its owner had suffered a stroke while on his way to the wedding of the new neighbour's grandmother, and Doctor Castro could have talked at length on that subject, too. He would have liked it had old Antonia's young guest been a physician like himself, and not so that they could talk about medicine, a science the doctor practised only by intuition, but so that a generic closeness might have been established between them as members of the same profession. He would also have liked it had young Goitia been interested in vintage automobiles, but that's an interest a boy acquires in childhood, when he can hardly even dream yet of putting his hands on a steering wheel, and then, in his mature years, his fascination brings him a certain comfort, for those same old cars, those Panhards, those Citroëns, those Morrises, end up representing what he so ardently desired and could never possess.

All that involved more than the doctor could have expressed, even in a long and descriptive speech. In the meanwhile, old María Antonia had finished her dinner and was sitting with her knees together and her shoulders hunched in front of the television set that she kept in the kitchen, under the calendar. On several occasions, her neighbour, Doctor Castro, had offered to purchase the Morris Oxford, which she had inherited with the house, but the old woman was still holding out. There was always the possibility that in some less sanctified but more practical future phase of her life in that same house, in Hondarribia, she might acquire a driver's licence. She stretched and yawned in her chair, bored by the all but incomprehensible television programme, and she could have gone out onto the porch, from where she could have seen the young intruder who had arrived that afternoon chatting in the dark with the doctor. And she wouldn't have liked that, because her ancestral distrust made her suspicious of men's conversations. At the moment, the doctor was asking the grandson if he was planning a long stay, and if the old woman was prepared to accept it. The boy replied in the affirmative, or avoided replying by declaring that he didn't know, and then the doctor perceived, in spite of the darkness, that the grandson wasn't exactly a boy but rather a young man, with the face and features of an adult and a slightly severe look, despite his youth, as befitted a doctor of law. Old María Antonia would have been interested in what they were saying about her. Because it is written in the book of Job: *Now shall I sleep in the dust; and thou shalt seek me in the morning, but I shall not be.* If the grandson and the doctor were talking about her, that lesson could be of some use to them, as well as to anyone else who might be seeking witnesses to his sojourn on Earth. But the old woman didn't go out onto the porch, because she had fallen asleep in the kitchen chair, in front of the television, as if she had taken a drug, and she woke up only when she heard Miguel Goitia's footsteps as he went up the stairs to his room.

Two

THE HONEYMOON

D ATES. Naturally, Doctor Castro knew it was going to be necessary to give dates, not only for his young neighbour's information, if it so happened that the newcomer was interested in dates, but also to put his own thoughts in order, because after half a century's worth of calendars have gone by, dates establish terms and margins that are easy to understand. His new neighbour, the youth who was studying for the rigorous, competitive examinations to become a civil-law notary (and not dedicating his time to dissecting cadavers, as the servant had imagined), rarely showed his face. In four days, the doctor had twice seen him going down to the village for dinner, once encountered him in the village itself, where they swapped greetings, and once exchanged a few words with him over the garden wall, on an evening when they had both gone outside to contemplate the fall of dusk. Not much contact, but all the same, it was enough. Sometimes the lad strolled through the garden with a book, which could have been a volume of poetry, or it could just as easily have been one of those compact handbooks that summarize the tricks of the notarial trade. The doctor did not have a great deal to say on these specialized matters. As for poetry, if Miguel Goitia really was walking about with a volume of poems under his arm, Doctor Castro would not have very much to say on that subject, either, except to offer two verses from his beloved Góngora, or to recite a stanza from the *Epístola moral a Fabio*, which brought him back to his high school days: *Ya, dulce amigo, huyo y me retiro* – 'I flee away, sweet friend, I take my leave' – and it was most unlikely that the youth, if he was indeed reading poetry, was reading that kind of poetry. No, it would be modern poetry or it wouldn't be poetry at all, at which point the doctor returned to his first hypothesis, namely that the compact but hefty volume Miguel Goitia carried around under his arm contained notarial prose.

He had seen him studying by the light of the green lamp in the former gun room, where the youngster had set up his office. Once or twice, he stepped out onto the porch, arched his back, stretched, ran a hand through his hair to clear his head, lit a cigarette, and remained for a few minutes in the imposing shadow of the house before walking out into the garden, in his slippers, wearing canvas trousers and a knitted shirt and waistcoat, rather light clothing for an autumn night. In the rear part of the house, the light from the kitchen indicated that the servant was still up and about, preparing the next day's meal or recording the previous day's expenses. The two of them had arrived at a kind of financial agreement, according to which the boy paid for his food a week in advance. This fixed price did not include dinners; for those, Goitia walked down to the village. The old woman, therefore, had only to compare the tally of the grocer's and baker's bills with what she received from her guest each week in order to determine whether she was making any money from him or, figuring in the electricity he used, just breaking even. Old María Antonia had a good head for figures. She'd always been adept and accurate in her accounting. As far as the idea of considering her guest as something other than a guest was concerned, such a notion never crossed her mind, whatever the boy's connection might have been with the Las Cruces estate. And the doctor, who inferred other blood connections, deeper or more enigmatic, couldn't help admiring the old woman's stubbornness, as one admires an iron mask or the remains of an indecipherable writing system that refuses to provide testimony to a previous existence.

The second time he spoke to Goitia across the garden wall, Doctor Castro learned several things. First: The competitive notarial exams were scheduled for December, and so the boy planned to stay in Hondarribia for a couple of months to study without any possibility of distraction. This information had not much bearing upon what the doctor had in mind, but it was worth noting. Second: The boy had hardly known his grandmother Isabel, and this was only the second time that he had ever set foot in Hondarribia. The revelation did not seem to surprise the doctor. He examined Goitia's face, behind which was hidden the blood of other names. By the glow of the youngster's cigarette in the darkness, Doctor Castro could make out the young man's features as they stood near the hedge, where they had stopped to chat. The boy's father didn't count for very much. He'd died in an automobile accident years before (questioned by the doctor, Goitia explained that his father had been driving a powerful blue car but didn't reveal the make or model). In the eyes of the doctor, what counted were the youth's maternal bloodlines, and that was the lineage he was seeking in Goitia's features, and if he'd dared to go a little further, the doctor would have enquired into what had kept the boy's mother away from Hondarribia for so many years and into the reasons why she had never come to visit his grandmother, why she had not shown up after his grandmother's death, and why she had never returned to the country house after marrying that Goitia fellow, who had taken her away to live in Madrid. That was the basic question, the one the doctor was chiefly interested in, with all the rancour, real or imagined, but in any case unassuaged, that could be inferred from it. In the third place, or as the third piece of information, the doctor was able to ascertain that during what appeared to be the young man's breaks, he strolled about with a syllabus of material for the competitive exams under his arm, and not with a book of poetry, as the doctor had conjectured with deliberate naïveté; but that insight was as little relevant as the first, although it did introduce a kind of banal, prosaic, solid accompaniment to the true importance and mystery of the second bit of information.

The doctor didn't dare propose to the youth that each of them should leave his garden by the respective garden gate, meet in the road, and take a walk together to admire the magnificence of the sea at night. Those days, the low tide was beginning shortly after dusk, exposing phosphorescent beaches and sediments of mud and sludge where the garbage and debris swept along by the river shone like precious jewels. An entire, living world of microscopic animals ran between the tiny rivulets and inside the cracks in the rocks that stuck up out of the water. The night smelled of iodine and sea bottoms, like a potent aphrodisiac. A few hours later, high tide would begin, filling the estuary with slow, thick, silver-backed waves, as if the black sea were mercury. Had they taken a nocturnal walk, the doctor would have drawn young Goitia into conversation, and they could have gazed in admiration at the astronomic marvel of the living ocean, punctual as a watch, but the old man dared not make the proposal. The reason was obvious: The doctor hauled his right leg behind him like a piece of wood. Nobody could converse and enjoy the night in the company of a lame person with a leg that seemed to weigh a hundred kilos. The doctor knew that, and he was sufficiently tactful and discreet to refrain from imposing such a situation on anyone. But he intended to invite Goitia to his house one night to have a drink with him under his porch, where the doctor would be able to stretch out his leg comfortably as he warmed the glass of cognac between his palms, and he would offer his guest a cognac, and the two of them could gaze out through the trees from there and contemplate the ocean's exact, nocturnal, pendular movement, and then they could turn their eyes towards the upright shadow of the other house, that is, the villa of Las Cruces, and the youth would thus obtain a point of view both somewhat different and somewhat unusual for anyone who had not lived through years of misfortune, confusion, and injustice.

That night, however, he preferred to keep up the conversation without extending any sort of invitation. Leaning on his cane and shifting his body weight to his bad leg, which served as an axis of rotation, the doctor turned towards his young neighbour by pivoting as though on a pillar. On such autumn days as those, his gimpy leg made itself felt, and he was quick to find cosmological reasons (such as the concert of the moon and the tides) to explain the evident accord between his leg and the change of season. His eyebrows were shiny with dew. He was a tall man, and his rebellious leg had done nothing to diminish his stature; it was as if from earliest youth the bones of that leg had been fastened together with an iron nail and had developed in telescopic form.

'A doctor of law,' the doctor said. 'There have been no visitors to this house since your grandmother died, my boy, and it's normal for an old neighbour like me to be surprised. And it's normal for old lady Etxarri to be surprised, too. Is she treating you well, my boy?'

'I needed a quiet place to study. She wasn't opposed to my coming.'

'Naturally not.'

Goitia remained silent. In the area where they were standing, the wall separating the two gardens was barely four feet high, like the walls that sometimes separate two meadows. Goitia lifted the cigarette to his lips, and the glowing tip gave his eyes a discreet gleam. Once again, the doctor surreptitiously examined his features, insofar as the darkness, mitigated by that very brief illumination, would allow. It was like interrogating time and looking for dates marked in old calendars, not because of what was suggested by the youth's features – the cheekbones illuminated when he drew on his cigarette, the pale forehead reflecting the light from the porch, the profile of the nose, as dark as a ship's keel – not because of that, no, but because of the doctor's own memory, which at that instant was applying itself to the youngster's face, seeking a confirmation that genetics or the heritage implicit in his features might have deposited there. He looked at the boy on the other side of the garden wall and felt attracted by him. Tall, powerful, and manly, with a deep chest where there was room for every sort of feeling, the doctor concealed the secret and refined passion that the youth had awakened in him. And in any case, that wasn't the reason why he was seeking the young man's company. The doctor banished a cluster of thoughts from his mind and returned to his improvised chatter.

'Watch what you eat. Otherwise the old woman will serve you nothing but lentils and protein, and the proteins may turn out to be worms,' the doctor went on. 'To tell the truth, I suspect that she'll treat you like a first-class guest and spy on you through the door to see if you're studying whatever it is you study, even though she doesn't believe it's possible to be a doctor of anything but medicine. Two months is a whole lifetime for an old woman, and she knows she's going to have you for two months. Has she asked you for news of your mother?'

'No.'

'Of course not. I knew your grandmother, and I knew your mother a little, too. I don't find it surprising that the old woman isn't interested in hearing about her. Autumn is the real season of delights in Hondarribia, but one must admit that it can get a little boring,' said the doctor, suddenly changing key. Then he felt obliged to give a little geography lesson, which the notarial candidate surely didn't need. 'What you see over there,' he said, pointing his cane at the darkness, 'is one of the buoys in the waters off Hendaye. Those streaks of light are the trucks crossing the Behobia bridge – trailers and semitrailers with five or six axles. And that beam slicing through the trees above our heads comes from the Amuitz lighthouse. One of these days, I'll ask you to bring out one of the cars I keep in my garage and I'll take you to lunch in Biarritz. I can't drive, so I need a chauffeur,' he added, giving his bad thigh a sonorous thwack and remembering that he'd already talked to Goitia about his modest automobile collection. 'You might ask the old woman to let you take the Morris out, but that motorized whale must have owls nesting in its cylinders by now.'

'I wouldn't dare ask her that.'

'And she'd turn you down if you did.'

'Besides, I think I have too much studying to do.'

'All right. I was just trying to be a good neighbour.'

'Thanks anyway,' Goitia said, trying to cut the conversation short.

'How could it be otherwise? Heaven knows, people would say that Isabel's grandson, a diligent young man, comes to Las Cruces to study hard and turn himself into a notary, and then he meets his grandmother's former neighbour, an old man, almost an invalid, who invites him to go on excursions in automobiles nearly a century old.'

'That's not what I meant,' Goitia said, thinking about how glad he would be to get back to his books.

'I suppose not.'

The doctor was silent for a few minutes. He'd planned to lead the conversation in other directions. He thought about saying to this lad, 'I witnessed your grandmother's wedding. I wasn't the kind of witness who greets the bride at the altar and then signs the marriage certificate, I wasn't even a witness as an invited guest, but from my side of this garden wall, I was a discreet witness, as unknown to the eyes of your grandmother and her family as a callow young doctor could be, recently arrived here, with both legs still intact, someone who might prove useful in the future, or perhaps just a neighbour you say hello to without even asking him what happened to his leg or ever once inviting him over for coffee.' The doctor thought about saying all this, but between the past events those words awakened in his memory and the real, present situation on that September night fell the veil of the war, its fabric composed of other visions, something that young Goitia was possibly indifferent to and in no position to understand anyway.

'It's a beautiful night,' the doctor said, lifting his nostrils to the sea air and the sharp smell of freshly mown grass. 'But you're going to catch cold with no covering but that thin waistcoat. Besides, as you said yourself, you have two or three hundred topics to go over.'

'I'll try to save a day so we can go to lunch together,' Goitia said, making the concession.

'Agreed!' the doctor exclaimed, hastening to accept the offer.

Goitia put out his cigarette on a stone and took his leave. Their conversation in the darkness, from one garden to the

other, a dialogue between two discrete spheres and two different periods of time demarcated by the stone wall that separated them, seemed as though it were the most natural thing
in the world, nothing unusual about it, arising out of the normal course of events, wherein one party was taking a break
from the arid matters covered by competitive notarial exams
and the other seeking to relieve the tingling in a leg which, in
spite of its condition, he had to take for an occasional walk.
The green lamp in the gun room was still on. In the doctor's
house, which was half hidden behind a wall of weeping willows, no lights could be seen, as if the doctor lived in the dark
or economized on electricity, and, curiously enough, both explanations were plausible. As Miguel Goitia walked away, he
rubbed his bare arms under his light shirt. The doctor, well
protected all the way down to his knees by an English overcoat, grasped his cane tightly and, with swaying steps, headed
down the path on which he was wont to make his rounds.
It ran towards the lower part of his property, where the land
belonging to the Las Cruces house separated from the land
belonging to the house called Los Sauces, 'The Willows', and
where both plots were bounded by a high wall, on the other
side of which was another path. The doctor took a turn past
the main entrance and then directed his steps towards his
dark house. He sensed the cat's shadow as the animal shook
itself and followed him, hoping for a saucer of milk. When he
reached the front hall, the doctor turned on the lights and put
his cane in the umbrella stand. His habitual insomnia obliged
him to pay a heavy tribute to boredom, and he spent those
solemn hours sitting in his living room. From there, he could

make out the window of the room where Goitia was studying. The doctor admired the boy's dedication to becoming a civil-law notary without finding that endeavour absolutely ridiculous, and without understanding it, either, because every now and again studious generations arise, and his heart rejoiced that there continued to be physicians and notaries who would be more competent than he had been in his professional life and would not, as evening fell, need to have recourse to the cognac bottle precisely in order to compensate for not having possessed similar determination. However, the tenderest moment of the night would not be long in coming. Old lady Etxarri would rap with her knuckles on the door of the office where Goitia was studying and enter the room carrying a nickel silver tray, a napkin in a mother-of-pearl napkin ring, and a glass of milk for the notarial candidate, in much the same way as the doctor, though with rather less ceremony, offered milk to his cat. It seemed that the old woman, too, was pleased to find that the lad was a diligent young man, and the years after the Civil War had left her with an appreciation for the nutritive value of matches and milk. She laid the tray down, as she did every night, and left the gun room. Enveloped in a woollen mantilla, she stuck her nose out of the door to the garden and turned off the porch light. The Las Cruces house, thus darkened, loomed out of the black lake of the lawn, except for a single spot of light from the candidate's obstinate lamp and the intermittent flash of the Amuitz lighthouse, which cut the chimneys out of the sky. Alone in his house, the doctor confronted the tedious masquerade of his insomnia. At this point, in old horror stories – which depicted feelings very close to his own – a scream would have been heard, and blood would have spattered the glass doors of the Las Cruces house. In any case, dates were needed. Often enough, it's the dead who set dates. At other times, the living set them, but the dates they set are more fluid and subject to changing assessments.

The doctor had arrived in Hondarribia as a recent graduate from medical school. He had a stethoscope, a white doctor's coat, and a case that opened up like an accordion and contained a collection of scalpels, forceps, and cutting instruments. It also included a set of pliers, because in those days, a doctor confronted with a dental abscess had to know how to extract a molar, even though such a case was outside his area of competence. Many physicians went about on horseback and had practices that covered regions of varying size. The doctor settled in Hondarribia, without a horse and without even an automobile. He had a Guzzi motorcycle, one of those with a small engine and robust shock absorbers. It was cherry red in colour, fitted with sturdy tyres, and so well suspended it seemed like the offspring of a more powerful motorcycle that had coupled with a nanny goat. It was to this motorcycle that he owed the ruin of his right leg, but it would be better to say that he owed it not to his motorcycle, but to his youth, and to the rain, and to the somewhat too hastily indulged pleasure of launching himself downhill at full speed on an irregularly paved road. Back then Doctor Castro was not yet thirty years old. When he rode his motorcycle, he wore a pair of welder's goggles, and it's possible that those goggles, which gave him the look of an amphibious animal, contributed as much as or more than the rain or the chaotic paving to his failure to see the parapet of the bridge where he left the best of his knee and his femur. The young physician who had arrived in Hondarribia, clothed in a white coat, armed with a stethoscope and a medical case like bellows, and ready to open an office and take charge of the fishermen's guild's health centre, stayed there beside the bridge. From that time on, the village would have a lame doctor. However, he noticed that people in the village greeted him with less indifference and more respect, because lameness is an affliction that confers a certain prestige, and in any case, unless patients wanted to go to Irún, Doctor Castro was their only choice.

Those were the last days of his youth, but the doctor could not know that at the time. The summer storms succeeded one another like continuous artillery fire in the high valleys, and a dark line on the sea marked the horizon at the place where the open ocean began. The first vacationers of the summer of 1936 arrived, and if the living could set dates, the doctor would choose the day when he lay on his sofa – a young, convalescing invalid, surrounded by various supports, an array of secondary stools, and a panoply of crutches, with aspirin and medicaments ready to hand, as well as a cane, which he was never to abandon in all the remaining days of his life – and witnessed, without leaving his house, a wedding banquet on the other side of his garden. His body now contained a screw, made of steel or iridium or some other precious, rustproof metal, whose function was to hold his fragmented bone together. His motorcycle had been recovered and was now stored in his garage, not unusable, but useless as far as the doctor was concerned, because he could never ride it again. Through his window, he contemplated the leisurely ballet of the wedding guests, who came to the banquet in large automobiles after the ceremony. The descending dusk broke up the music into sudden, premonitory bursts. During that period of his convalescence, the pain in the doctor's leg was excruciating. The difference between the small house of Los Sauces and the villa of Las Cruces didn't only represent a gaping disparity of wealth. Weddings are often sad, but even sadder is the wedding to which one has not been invited, and yet he had to remain there, watching it, and nursing a leg loaded with metal and plaster. That was the date the doctor chose, during the time of his broken leg, so the wedding must have taken place during the first week of June, approximately, right at the beginning of summer. No doubt, there were other people who would remember the date for different reasons, but that was none of the doctor's concern. He could barely move. He got up slowly, leaning on his stools and his crutches. In the years to come, he would learn to use his dead leg as a flying buttress, or as a pillar, and to feel unburdened as it took his weight. Despite the many years that had gone by, he could still hear, through his open window, the music of the wedding and the murmur of the conversations during the banquet. In the end, when night fell and the wedding broke up, he hearkened to the sonorous vibrations of the automobile engines.

So most of what Doctor Castro wished to determine hinged on a question of dates. Not only insofar as what concerned him, but also insofar as what concerned the lad next door, and insofar as what concerned that lad's grandfather, given that the whole complex of events would require but a few leaves of the calendar, and if he dug in his memory a little, he could easily go from the dancing at the wedding, when darkness fell upon the garden and bottles rolled here and there, to the confirmed threat of a military rising.

Several weeks after the celebration of his marriage, as he waited to face a firing squad, Captain Herráiz would remember his wedding trip. The war had intervened in his life, tearing down the curtain of tulle and lace that protected his honeymoon. The first images were white. He could still smell the fragrant incense in the church, and the veil of Isabel's white wedding dress floated over her smile. But before the reality that confronted Captain Herráiz and the knowledge that he had only a few hours to live, his memories kept taking on other shapes. He remembered the two regimental comrades who had served as his witnesses roughly shaking his hand, crinkling the stiff collar of his dress uniform, and swinging their sabre tassels like dancers performing in an operetta. They sprinkled their farewells with crass bachelor jokes, and Captain Arderius made quite a caustic remark: 'Gold digger.'

Captain Herráiz didn't respond. He was unaware that the men of his regiment referred to him in secret as 'Chicken Thigh', and had he known it, he would have taken it as an ignominy. There was something terrible in thinking of *that* as the nickname of a man who was going to be shot. Some said the nickname came from his habit of choosing a chicken thigh whenever paella with chicken was served; others said it was because he always carved himself a thigh when chicken was served. In any case, the nickname alluded to his refined appearance, to the elegant and somewhat affected style of his movements, and to his dandyish way of looking his best in his uniform. All of these were allusions that no one would understand today, and which even then would have escaped a civilian's notice. In the schools for military officers, all the young men received nicknames, and Captain Herráiz had not been exempt from this custom, nor had Arderius, Captain Seven Heads, so called not because of his voluminous skull but because he proved to be alert and shrewd when it came to solving problems in general. And so things could have taken a turn for the farcical during the wedding ceremony, had the nicknames of the groom's witnesses and of the groom himself been used instead of their real names when it came time to speak of them – Seven Heads's intelligence might have been praised, and Chicken Thigh's elegance – but no one would have dared to do that, and in any case, no one was interested in such gems of barracks humour. Doctor Castro didn't know the nickname of the second witness whom Captain Herráiz had brought to the wedding, but given the impression he produced, he might as well have been called 'Seven Sabres' or 'Captain Pistols'. Soon the two witnesses would join the military rising, while Captain Herráiz, on the contrary, without wanting to or without thinking about it, would wind up in the famous Azpeitia column. But none of that could be foreseen. The groom's two fellow officers played practical jokes on him. Everything was about to change, and afterwards, if there had been any grotesque or funereal meaning in those nicknames, no one could have explicated it.

There were no great effusions and no enthusiastic well-wishing on the part of the wedding guests when the newly-weds decided to take their leave. The couple dodged away surreptitiously before the party ended, bidding only their closest friends farewell. After shaking his regimental comrade's hand, Arderius said again, this time into his ear, 'Gold digger.' The newlyweds went upstairs to change their clothes and then got into an automobile that someone had already loaded with two new suitcases, which were part of the bride's trousseau. The bride carried a handbag. Captain Herráiz sat in the driver's seat. The pale twilight of early summer had descended. Lead-coloured clouds edged with gold hung in the distant sky, the kind of sky one sees in prints and commemorative cards, and anyone who saw the bride and groom leaving would have thought they were going to hide someplace where the night was calmer, and where they could finally stop being engaged, after having been so for two years, and especially after such an exhausting day. They crossed the Bidasoa, happy as two truant schoolchildren, and waved in passing to the French customs officials, who wore the Maurice Chevalier–style moustaches that were usual with the Customs Service. Captain Herráiz drove with one hand and slipped his other arm round his fiancée's shoulders – as yet, he didn't dare call her his wife. 'Gold digger,' Arderius had said, and that remark sounded to the captain like an insult, or like a strange form of adultery, in which married love is betrayed by the love of money, a

stronger, more concrete love, and the strange promiscuity that
results is masked by sentimental lies. Then he thought of the
hotel in Biarritz and its wedding-cake architecture, exactly the
right place for a honeymoon. In Captain Herráiz's memory,
the sea was covered with white curls like sheep's wool, and
there was something in that panorama that soothed his soul.
He could still feel his wife's presence, very close to him.
And if he could have done so, or if he had been granted the
fulfilment of one last wish, he would have wished to stand on
the balcony of that hotel again and put his arms round her
waist. Behind him, the contents of the two suitcases were
scattered over the rose-pink counterpane that covered the
big double bed. The hotel manager, knowing that they were
honeymooners, had presented them with a large bouquet
of red roses, accompanied by a gilt-edged card that read,
'*Avec les compliments de la Direction*'. The flowers stood in
a vase and opened slowly, like a choir of little women with
curious little heads. Captain Herráiz had ordered a bottle of
champagne sent to the room. The bottle was chilling in an
ice bucket while they gazed at the sea from the hotel balcony.
Night had fallen. The wind whistled in the rigging of the
flags that lined the seaside promenade, and lightning criss-
crossed the sky over the horizon with short, silent strokes,
as if the storm were still too far off and only wished to
announce its arrival by way of enhancing the wedding night.
The air was like pure oxygen, and breathing it lightened the
heart. Nothing presaged that, within a few weeks, Captain
Herráiz's life would come to an end before a firing squad,
or that memories of his honeymoon would occupy the end

of his life with the fantastic yet intimate vision of that hotel room.

The intervening weeks had been a long nightmare. When the newlyweds returned from Biarritz, Isabel had chosen to stay at Las Cruces, while Captain Herráiz had gone back to his garrison in San Sebastián. Since then, he'd heard nothing from her, and this lack of news gave their relationship an aura of inexistence and fantasy that the captain was unable to distinguish from reality. It was as though she hadn't said 'I do' at the wedding ceremony, or as if she had disappeared into the arms of another lover, or as if she had simply never given herself to him. Things had happened very fast, and he had told her in a letter all that could be told. He saw dead horses. The road from San Sebastián to Tolosa was paved with granite stones. Captain Herráiz heard the sharp clatter of the ammunition wagons' iron wheels and the curses of men whose wagons had overturned, and he saw the fire in a village wedged between a fir forest and a millstream, and in the black building that housed the bakery where he and his fiancée, during their excursions in days of peace, would stop to buy some good bread. The soldiers also passed a wine warehouse that had been sacked, though there was no telling whether the plunderers had been local people or outsiders; perhaps they were the troops who had preceded the unit under Captain Herráiz's command. At the door of the warehouse, a wine cask displayed its broken ribs to the sun. Its hoops had rolled away or lay flaccid at the feet of the splintered staves. There was a fresh reek of fermentation, not completely disagreeable, not completely obscene, smelling as wine usually smells when an excessive amount of it has been spilled. In a certain way, this odour was exciting and pleasant in the nostrils of those weary troops, who had tried marching in step for only a few kilometres after they left San Sebastián. The men made a prolonged halt at the warehouse, unharnessing the mules and loosening their own belts. Some of the troops took off their shoes and socks in order to soothe their blisters with water from their canteens. Captain Herráiz was accompanied by two other officers, one of them a lieutenant in the Carabineros, the frontier guards. This handful of officers formed a group apart, as though they were having a long meeting. Men from all over the region had joined the Azpeitia column, some without weapons or any footwear save espadrilles, others with weapons and military equipment from the barracks that were subjugated after the rising. In front of that wine warehouse, in the shade of the trees that lined the road, the ground was strewn with the strange straw wraps used in those days to cover champagne bottles with a kind of cape or hood that protected the glass. Captain Herráiz and his men had no way of knowing whether toasts had been drunk here to them or to the enemy, or if the troops that had preceded them had carried off the bottles, despoiled of their straw wrapping, in order to slake their thirst on the road. The old, broken barrels showed their insides, dark with cardinal-red vegetation. No other remains of a celebration could be seen. Someone went inside the half-open door, which had been torn from its hinges, and soon came back outside, cursing. There was nothing left in the warehouse. The gigantic shadow of a quarry raised its unpleasant back above the landscape. And

on that slow, suffocating afternoon, entirely shaped by curses
and plans for victory, entirely directed towards the teaching
of a thumping good lesson, to be learned by themselves or
by the deserving enemy, wherever he might be, perhaps on
the heights of Echegárate, perhaps in the menacing cavities
of that enormous quarry – on that afternoon, then, during
a few minutes of repose, the reek of wine clouded the senses
and refreshed the spirits of those scowling, angry troops, still
inflamed by recent speeches and street shoot-outs but languid
and weary after a week of action, and still idealistic, a mixture
of recruits from towns and peasants from farmhouses, soothing
their feet in front of a recently sacked wine warehouse as if
they had found, in the shade of the chestnut trees that lined
the road, a redeemed fatherland.

They had been preceded by troops of Galician militia, who
had fled El Ferrol in fishing boats and landed in Pasajes after
a five-day journey. Then, in more than twenty trucks, they
had travelled the scenic roads to San Sebastián, passing places
where, only a few days previously, summer vacationers had exposed their cleanly persons to the sun; but the Galicians had
been blackened by sea and fire, and having seen their comrades shot, they were hungry for vengeance and life. A portion
of them had split off and gone to defend Irún, following the
secondary route that ran along the coastal cliffs and avoiding
the pocket that Beorlegui had succeeded in consolidating at
Oyarzun. The other, smaller portion, together with peasant
volunteers, had set out for the front, which was beginning to
take shape in the interior of the country. Herráiz had traced
on a map the movements of the past few days, ever since the

fall of the Loyola barracks, but nothing, no map, no plan, no intuition based on topography could give an idea of the scope of the decisions being discussed in the region, some of them as confused as the organization of the column itself, others disparate and heroic, related to the old spirit from which the defence juntas that fought against Napoleon had sprung up of their own accord.

They were carrying two pieces of light artillery, three Vickers machine guns, and a considerable but not unlimited supply of ammunition belts. Herráiz assumed that his troop had been preceded by two armoured trucks transporting the first Galician units. He had sent scouts out along the heights, and although he would have liked to explore the countryside, perhaps even to lose himself a little on the hills, which were thickly forested with fir trees, unmoving and outspread like vegetal armies in the August sun, although he would have liked to wander in the mist that the heat was raising in the deepest valleys, only to drink it afterwards, and although he would have liked to catch a glimpse of the sea between the green lines of the overlapping hills, he had preferred to lead his troops along the secondary branch of the paved road, halting out of prudence or laziness, setting up positions at every curve on the way before continuing the advance through the placid but unending hill country.

The captain moved away from the group and contemplated the splendour of the valleys. The loyalty that was going to be fatal to him, the loyalty that would determine his death sentence, included a bucolic dimension, like a serene, subdued print, where only the accompaniment of military equipment and the smoke rising from a hill could foreshadow a future that would be unhappy, when cowbells would no longer be heard in the valleys, nor villagers' voices, nor woodcutters' axes, and not intense barrages of gunfire, either, and not the explosions that had punctured the past nights and filled them with uncertainty. Captain Herráiz wiped his face with a handkerchief and put it away, stained with sweat and dust. He adjusted the belt with the holster containing his regulation pistol and turned towards the boy who had served as his orderly since the beginning of the march. He was a youth from Beasain, no more than twenty years old, and he had worked as a waiter. He wore blue trousers, a villager's beret, and a military jacket without stripes, a couple of sizes too big for him and probably removed from some corpse after the fall of the barracks. The captain beckoned him with a sign. 'Pen and paper!' the captain cried.

The boy saluted him as though they were schoolboys playing a game and then executed an about-face. Miraculously, bringing up the rear of the column behind a field kitchen like a motorized stove, there was a van filled with all the gear an authentic headquarters might require, including leather folders, untrimmed paper, inkwells, and pens with metal nibs, with which sergeants used to practise calligraphy in peacetime, poking out their tongues as they wrote up their reports. In a few minutes, the orderly came back with what Herráiz had ordered. The captain dismissed the boy and moved over to a rock at the foot of a tree. Men were lounging on the ground with their rifles between their knees. Some were making preparations to eat. Flies buzzed, and from behind the sacked wine warehouse came the sound of a swift-flowing stream. The captain sat on the rock, placed the leather folder on his knees, and began to write a second letter to his wife. He had deposited the first one in a mailbox in Donosti, quite simply, as if he could still believe in a postal service. He had arrived with a detachment to protect the post office building and had dropped his letter into a mailbox. He'd begun that first letter thus: *My Dear Isabel*. But this second letter required other terms, perhaps because Isabel would never receive the first, perhaps because his present situation, poetic in the light that flooded the valleys, rusty and dusty on the roadside where he and his men were resting, called for a more complete commitment of emotion. Any onlooker would have admired Chicken Thigh's composure as he sat under the tree with his pen suspended in mid-air and the leather folder balanced on his knees. Using one thumb to immobilize the untrimmed paper, Herráiz began to write in his fine hand:

My Dear Love.

The captain's eyes grew moist as he slowly and deliberately set down what was supposed to be a description of his stopping place and news of the previous days' events but was in reality the expression of his emotional deracination and of an unbearable nostalgia for the days they had spent in Biarritz. In the military schools, it was said that the most dangerous problems in a war concerned how to get into it in the beginning and how to get out of it at the end. This dictum could also be applied to the captain and his honeymoon. And so his *Dear Love* was still Isabel's happy, embarrassed laughter as she lay between bloodstained sheets in the pitch-black night, with the balcony open to the sea and the bedside lamp turned on, while the last bits of ice chilling the cloth-wrapped bottle of champagne melted in the ice bucket and their two glasses glinted like diamonds and the roses they had received with the compliments of the hotel management bowed their rosy-red heads. They had seemed to be not just a few miles from the border but on another planet, and even more so now, considering what it had been like to return from a honeymoon trip as the entire country was falling into convulsions. Dawn had surprised the captain alone in the bed. Isabel had disappeared into the bathroom, but after a few minutes under the torrential shower she came out again, wearing a brand-new dressing gown from her trousseau. In a few days, they had stopped being fiancés and become lovers, not husband and wife, or at least not exclusively. Although the captain could renounce practices learned in brothels, he wasn't able totally to abandon his experience, while Isabel had dedicated herself, partly with modesty and partly with avidity, to the accumulation of sexual knowledge. It was said that certain women in those years were happy, cautious, and dissolute, and those terms included everything that a judicious and seductive mixture of good breeding and carnality entailed. And had that not been the case, had those certain women lacked any of the three paradigmatic qualities that men both expected and feared, their respective men, if they truly loved them, would have felt cheated, as if their dearest hope were that their betrothed would turn out to be neither so chaste nor so prudent as the bourgeois circumstances of their betrothal obliged her to appear.

My Dear Love, Captain Herráiz continued, gambling on the certainty that his love would indeed read his letter. A rosary of ants marched in procession past his boot. And what had become of his two marriage witnesses? Captain Pistols had gone to Bilbao to join the rebellion, although he would be able to camouflage himself should it fail. Arderius wasn't stationed in the Loyola barracks, and Captain Herráiz could expect to meet him leading an enemy unit once they were through the hills. Was it conceivable that of the three regimental comrades, only one had been excluded from the conspiracy? But that was what had happened, and neither of the other two would hesitate to execute him. While the captain's pen moved across the leaf of untrimmed paper, intermittently seeking the mouth of the inkwell beside him, some of his men raised their eyes. The boy from Beasain, arms folded, leaned against a tree and contemplated him. No one could imagine that the captain had asked for a pen and an inkwell and some untrimmed paper in order to write a poem or a love letter, nor did they think he'd gone mad. Before light fell that day, it was expected that they would reach the crest line, after having cleaned out the shadowy terrain around the quarry, and enter into contact with the force that had preceded them and that was no doubt already deployed, and then they would wait for who knew what events to transpire on the other side. They had stopped near a wine warehouse, a few houses, and a sawmill, all of them deserted, but up ahead, farther downhill, other troops of his unit were reclining in the ditches along the road, and his force amounted to something like 150 men altogether. Some of those farthest off in the twisting line of march took advantage of the rest halt, not to desert – or at least, not as they considered the matter – but to go back to their farmhouses. And all those men, or all those sufficiently close to the captain to see and follow his movements, thought that their commanding officer was writing a note to be transmitted through a liaison to the rearguard or to be delivered by a designated messenger to the advanced positions, but nobody would have thought that their captain was writing a love letter.

The captain prepared to conclude his missive. *Believe me when I tell you that all my love is with you, and nothing will erase the memory of your lips against my lips.* The captain asked for some water. *My heart will beat for you in the difficult days that lie ahead. I shall return as soon as circumstances permit, and in the meanwhile, day and night, my love is with you.* The captain stopped writing. In those minutes, during the brief period of time that had passed since he began his letter, all his pining for his love had been condensed into those lines, saturated and crystallized like some precious chemical solution his heart could hardly identify in words, the same words that kept running through his thoughts, but his men didn't observe this, nor could they, rapt as they were in the trivialities of a rest halt on the march and only occasionally granting their captain's sudden epistolary caprices a distracted glance. The captain raised his head. Then he lowered his eyes and gazed at the rosary of ants that continued to hustle and bustle past his boot. It was the daily hustle and bustle, the barely symbolic image of that long file of men who were following him up the branch road that mounted to the high, wooded,

and still distant crest. Then he looked back at his writing. He
had little to add to the urgent expression of his feelings. With
great care, he again dipped his pen into the inkwell at his side.
He concluded with a simple and tender *Many kisses* and then
signed the letter: *Julen*.

After blowing on the leaf of untrimmed paper to dry the
ink, Captain Herráiz folded his letter in half, then in half
again, and put it, along with another document, into the
pocket of his army jacket. He called the orderly to take away
the writing materials, and when the men saw the captain rise
to his feet, they desultorily bestirred themselves. There was
general motion up and down the long line. Rifles were collected, half-eaten snacks were wrapped in grey paper, and the
wicks of pocket lighters were tied off. The men moved into
place, joking or discussing questions of precedence in the file
or of their respective assignments in the formation's tactical
scheme. The sound of firing came from some distant valley
and the men raised their heads, as if the threat came from
the air at the same time as the staccato crackling of gunshots.
Their halt had lasted a little more than half an hour when the
captain mounted his mule and gave the order to continue
the march. The gun carriages bearing the two artillery pieces
creaked as they rolled over the stones of the badly paved road.
By the end of the day, they had reached the crest line of the
range, but not before a detachment had scoured the inhos-
pitable area around the quarry. The unit had made contact
with the troops ahead of them, already deployed, and Captain Herráiz chose his position in accordance with the ample
terrain and his own intuition. The first column was on his

left, covering both flanks of the main road. On his right, the foothills rolled away towards the horizon of Nanclares, where promontories and chalk hollows formed what looked like the backbone of some great fossil, the grey and golden rock still imbued with the mysteriously tenacious twilight.

The captain ordered the two 75-millimetre artillery pieces set up in the hollow of an outcrop of rock, where they formed half a battery, capable of pounding the first curves of the road on the slope some kilometres below their position. Fifty metres to the rear, sheltered by high ground, the field kitchen and the supply van were stationed. The captain fanned out his three Vickers machine guns so that their lines of fire converged and crossed the most likely approaches to the position. Night had fallen, and the light, limpid air, still permeated by the heat of the day, breathed peace and premonitions. It was said that the troops who had requisitioned the contents of the warehouse were going to distribute the wine later that night, and every unit had to send its quartermaster to fetch it. The lighting of fires was forbidden so as not to give the position away. Thus did matters stand on that fateful night, full of portents, covered with stars, fantastic in its beauty, and indifferent to the destinies of men, its face turned towards the profound panorama of the universe; and at the same time, it was an intimate night that recalled to the heart of every man the memory of other summer nights, when he lingered outside the door of a tavern or stood at the entrance to a smithy or took his leave in darkness after a picnic and an extended excursion in the woods, scenes like illustrations from the same calendar, because all those men retained similar memories of their land

and their condition. In the darkness, the vans seemed to be loaded with coffins. Down towards the plains, it was possible to make out lights, which were said to be the lights of Alsasua or of some other town presumed to be in enemy hands. The sleeping men, the silent, cautious movements of the sentinels, and the mules' bored snorting were elements of the similar ritual performed when agricultural operations had to be carried out with all deliberate speed but within a reasonable period of time, before the arrival of storms or hail. And then the crickets began to sing. The lengthy night was alive with synchronized messages, obsessively and melancholically announcing the approach of September. Nothing in this sector would change for several days, or even for several weeks, apart from the sporadic warning of artillery fire, feeling out positions known to be under solid control, or the laconic crackle of rifle fire between patrols gone astray, because in those days the military rising undertook no large-scale actions, nor had the front yet been marked on any map, nor were any decisions made that could be considered definitive, as if the mutual enemies had made camp and settled in to wait for results proceeding from other districts, other valleys, other regions.

The positions on the heights that the militias and the troops of the Defence Juntas had wished to hold were wiped out in the course of a few days. Some say that the Republicans had sufficient forces to defend the access to all the valleys, and that with a different operational strategy, they could have salvaged control of the frontier and whatever else was still salvageable. At that time, a column of 150 men was a considerable force. But if dates are necessary, it's also true that at the distance of so many years, dates are irrelevant, and the doctor undoubtedly thought about his own situation in those days, newly burdened with a definitively useless leg, and the anguish of knowing himself crippled for life played some part in his forgetful disdain for dates; although if the case required it, the doctor knew how to proceed with dates, in the same way that one knows how to examine a stamp in a philatelic collection or an insect's complex markings. Irún was burned on September 5. Donosti fell on the thirteenth. On the twentieth, Iruretagoyena's troops got through the mountain passes, occupied Monte Andatxa, and thrust as far as Zumárraga. Many years later, a number of commentators would say that the war was lost in the north, and the success of this first onslaught supports their arguments. The Navarrese brigades hurled themselves on Guipúzcoa. The war front stabilized along the banks of the Deva River. It's true that all this took place over a series of long, exhausting, grievous days, but viewed from a distance, they seemed to have flown past as the days do when you run your eye over a calendar. They left behind a feeling of misfortune and uncertainty, like pebbles rolling over the mesh of a sieve, producing an aching, cruel sound, a grinding of teeth, a sign of what hell could be like if eternal damnation were set in those leafy valleys, and poets sang of their grief in the language of the country:

> *Your glory, Mother, has died in the mountains.*
> *How did the heroes fall?*

Disclose it not in Tolosa.
Proclaim it not in the streets of Donosti.
Let not the renegades' daughters exult
Or the traitors' daughters leap for joy.

Others raised similar laments:

Your glory, Euzkadi, has perished in the mountains.
How did the heroes fall?

But there were no hymns, no psalms, no words to sing the bitterness of those two months, which, if you added up the events they contained, were two centuries, and which would remain for many people the only subject of the stories they told for the rest of their lives. Many escaped in boats, and among them were some who, instead of crossing to the other side of the river, pointed their prows towards the west, crossed the mouth of the Deva, and headed for the new front that was forming around Bilbao. But over in the valleys, processions of prisoners were coming back, long-haired, unshaven, their stunned faces hollowed by fatigue. Others didn't come back. Finally, there were others who disappeared a few days after the defeat turned them into suffering matter, rolling around in a sieve. If dates counted for anything, those were, without a doubt, dates on which many destinies were shuffled, even more than could be inferred from eyes aglow with victory or from the bitter taste left in the mouths of the defeated.

A few hours before he was led out to face the firing squad, Captain Herráiz wondered whether his wife would have received his first letter, that is, the letter he had dropped into a mailbox in the San Sebastián post office before he and his troops had moved out, the letter that began with the words *My Dear Isabel*. The second letter, the one that began with the words *My Dear Love*, was still in the pocket of his army jacket. His papers and other documents had been confiscated from him, but he had been granted the privilege – requested by himself – of keeping that letter, and when he raised his hand to his heart and felt the paper crackle against his chest, he remembered his honeymoon again. He was in Alsasua, in the boiler room of the Piarist Fathers' school, which the blast of a howitzer shell had partially destroyed. When he was transferred there, he'd caught a glimpse of the inscription on the façade of the building, right next to the flagpole: COLEGIO DE PP ESCOLAPIOS, and that name had made his fate seem heavier by giving it the character of a schoolboy's punishment. In the semi-darkness of the suffocating boiler room, with its dense network of pipes and valves, Captain Herráiz's face gleamed as if it had been smeared with grease. There was an absent glow in his white eyes. He could hear muffled sounds, like furniture being dragged about or supplies or military equipment unloaded. The court-martial had taken place in one of the classrooms on the second floor, presided over by a school crucifix. A colonel and a major from the Estella garrison, two of those who had joined the rising from the very beginning, constituted the court. A captain from the Automotive Fleet introduced the accused. On the teacher's platform, the extremely summary tribunal conducted a brief deliberation. Those were the days when verdicts were handed down within a few minutes and consisted of two types: thirty years or death. There were men who left the classroom smiling, sentenced to thirty years and therefore safe, if only from execution. For Captain Herráiz, the matter had been resolved differently, and now all he had to hope for as he waited to be executed was the water he'd requested. Over the course of several hours, he examined the place where he found himself. He stared at the thermometers and pressure gauges with a childlike curiosity, and then he furrowed his brow, as though they were oracular. Eventually, he sat on a cement bench, under a window set at ground level, and savoured the painful solace of his remembered honeymoon. Isabel's merry voice came to his ears: 'Julen, hand me my bathrobe!'

And a few moments later, she tiptoed out of the shower and headed for the dressing table, leaving the ephemeral prints of her wet feet on the hotel carpet. The captain, already dressed, had draped his jacket over the back of an armchair. Hands in his pockets, he went out onto the balcony while she finished getting ready. In those days, Biarritz wasn't what it would become in thirty years, or fifty years, nor did it contain many things that Doctor Castro could reveal to his young neighbour if he would accept the doctor's invitation to dine there someday soon, precisely in Biarritz, while the golden autumn came closer. Large commercial areas had invaded what used to be cornfields and meadows, and new hotels had risen in place of the villas formerly owned by rich Jews and Central European princesses, and other disasters or non-disasters of time and city planning had definitively altered the physiognomy of the place that Captain Herráiz had enjoyed on his honeymoon.

But since Captain Herráiz departed this life in front of a firing squad, the question of what he would have thought of Biarritz so many years later was both futile and thankless. Back in his day, the beach still looked as it had looked at the turn of the century, and while he stood on the balcony and adjusted his shirt cuffs, the captain took in the broad and elegant curve of the sandy shore as it received the tide's heavy homage, the tall waves like joyful horses fanning out, the tamarind trees with their fine green plumage, the awnings, the bathing huts with their heraldic stripes in the primary beach colours, namely red, green, and blue. Of all those things, only the tides provided an astronomical clock capable of reducing to its just proportion the insignificance of time past, the tiresome feeling that human memory exaggerates the hold it believes itself to have on time. Captain Herráiz did not imagine that he had attained Saturn's dominion over time, or that, by the power of his memory, he was capable of reversing the universal course of the days, but in those last hours, he consoled himself with the apparent eternity of his visions, nurtured by a lingering doubt that his life was really going to end in a few hours in front of a firing squad. The evocation of the sea was especially welcome in those moments, and that alone soothed his grief. As day was dawning, he heard volleys of gunfire. They repeated similar volleys from the previous day. The beaten-earth courtyard of the school, the captain knew, must be drinking blood, so he fled the thought of the fate awaiting him and returned to the memory of the hotel room.

Throughout the fifteen days of their stay, the hotel management sent up a daily bouquet of fresh roses to replace the ones in the vase. Standing on the balcony, facing the sea, the captain smiled. One might have taken him for a lucky roulette player, particularly cheerful the morning after an exciting night at the gambling tables. Pale and serene, moved as always by the marine landscape, inhaling the sea breeze with delight, surrounded by the triumphantly waving curtains behind him, the captain played with the golden wedding band on his ring finger. He was not yet accustomed to the ring, still an unusual item in his life, like the guarantee of an agreement he hadn't yet begun to evaluate, but which had already taken on the appearance of a good agreement, or a good contract, independently of what fate might have in store. Meanwhile, Isabel was almost ready. The captain stepped back into the room and there she was, tying a green ribbon round her hair, smiling, with raised arms and a sweet coquetry that made her body childlike. She'd put on a green dress, grey-green like almonds, close fitting to just above the knees and then flaring into a little skirt in that summer's French fashion, which was called evasé. Her wedding trousseau included as many as half a dozen fashionable French dresses, almond-coloured, pearl-coloured, honey-coloured, as if chosen to represent the four seasons or the colours of the overcast sky, the clear sky, the frosty sky. A golden wedding band shone on her ring finger, too, and the captain's eye caught a fleeting sparkle, like the confirmation of a consummated agreement. That woman was his dear Isabel, who in the unbearable distress of the last few days had gradually turned into his dear love. That woman was the incarnate form of his feelings and his desires, all mingled together in the euphoria and bashful passion of the wedding trip. The captain stood still, backlit by the light from the balcony and enveloped like an apparition in the billowing curtains. The sea air had dishevelled his hair, and she burst out laughing. There was something formidable in that laugh. And there was something exceptionally painful in recalling it, like an excess of pleasure whose absence torments the mind. Still laughing, she drew near to comb his hair with her own hands, and he took her into his arms and turned her laughter into another kiss and held her close, and then he lifted her in the air as though picking up a doll and laid her on the bedspread, almost in sport, almost without desire, only to see her lying there like that.

'Julen, you're going to ruin my dress.'

'I'm going to dress you in kisses.'

'You're crazy, Julen.'

Captain Herráiz smiled. She wriggled free and rolled away to escape his embrace. He could still see her, free of his arms and laughing.

'You're crazy, Julen. You promised we'd go out for lunch.'

He still smiled at the memory. His eyes shone like hard porcelain in his blackened face, shone in the suffocating semi-darkness of that boiler room, in the sinister and makeshift dungeon where his last hours ticked away. He remembered hours of pleasure, and hours of delight, and silent hours they'd spent hand in hand, gazing at the dark blue sea while storm clouds threatened the horizon. They had also talked about the name they planned to give to the fruit of those hours, for they hoped their endeavours would bear fruit, and if the fruit of their endeavours was a boy, she wanted him to be called Julen, and if the fruit was a girl, the captain wanted her to be called Isabel. They went out to eat at a farmhouse in the middle of a pine forest, at a certain spa located some distance inland, and at the restaurants on the beach, some of which still had the same names and emblems now as they'd had when Captain Herráiz and his bride were there on their honeymoon, as if disaster had spared some reference points in order to illustrate the story better, regardless of whether its protagonists, or those who found a certain kind of virtue in remembering history and celebrating its protagonists, would ever set foot there again. But if Biarritz had changed – and Doctor Castro could testify that it had changed very much – cities and landscapes never change so utterly that one can't recognize them any more. A hotel doorman's features may have changed somewhat since he began as a bellboy, and yet the architecture of people's faces remains unaltered. And the profile of a promontory, which is on geological time, changes very little. The incessant waves never stop performing the cosmic ritual of the tides and submitting to the laws of the moon, and man's only consolation may consist in adhering to those other, insurmountable dimensions of time and by that very means surmounting them, by integrating himself into the movement of the stars and the respiration of the sea and the minutely slow erosion of the cliffs, and seeking in those things the survival of his most ephemeral memories, thus saved from their own condition. In the terrible circum-stances of his last hours, Captain Herráiz remembered Isabel's laugh. With the extraordinary lucidity that those final mo-ments granted him, he realized that the greatest beauty was contained in that laugh, in the naked and simple act of laughing, in the delight of the woman who is beloved and knows herself beloved, even without leaving their luminous room with the windows open to the sea, even confessing, in mutual embarrassment, that they had spent three quarters of their honeymoon without leaving their hotel. The captain thought that perhaps the seed he'd deposited in her womb would prosper, and that someday their child would inherit its mother's charming laugh. Only that laugh could redeem his squalid death. There was nothing to protect him, nothing to sustain him, except the memory of the brief, intense pleasure of his love. And moving his porcelain eyes over the gloomy corners of the boiler room where he was imprisoned, the captain felt that his happiness, however ephemeral, had not been in vain if it provided him some solace in those final moments. The pipes were covered with a thin down, the mould of cellars and neglect. He could sense the inert presence of water in the conduits, waiting for someone to fire up the boilers and for the plutonian toil of the coming winter to begin, of that winter and all the other winters he would not see. Night had fallen. The captain's thoughts flew over different landscapes. A bluish light came through the skylight in the boiler room. Outside that place, he knew, the land lay under the vault of night. In the days when he was engaged to be married, he had dreamed under those same constellations. He heard voices – the changing of the guard – and the sound of engines. But by virtue of his memory, the anteroom to death that he was in could be transformed, and the captain dedicated the better part of his thoughts to that end, as he'd read in history books, as his fortitude and his contained emotion required, for it was almost painful, a painful pleasure, for him to hear Isabel's remembered laugh again.

He had left his golden wedding ring, his wristwatch, his field glasses, and the folded sheet of untrimmed paper, the unenveloped letter that began with the words *My Dear Love*, with a request that they might be delivered to the person indicated. The whole lot, with the exception of the field glasses, arrived at its destination. The war exhibited such caprices, saving certain small objects with the tactile delicacy of a blind giant and devouring property and people like the same giant in a fury. Half a city could be destroyed, bridges could explode and viaducts collapse, and a piece of paper, a gold wedding ring, and a watch could be saved. When dawn came, the walls around the Piarist Fathers' school stood like tall shadows. The impact of a shell had opened a gaping hole in the façade. Captain Herráiz couldn't raise his eyes to the poetic and serene brightness of the day. He crossed the schoolyard with rapid steps. The basketball goals were still standing. A watering hose was connected to a bronze tap. The bell that ended break at the school hung unmoving in a corner, above the waste-paper baskets. Some ammunition cases covered with a tarpaulin were stacked next to two vans. But he saw none of this nor even intuited it, because his thoughts were elsewhere. He was executed next to a union member, a metal worker from Mondragón, a man as tenacious and faithful as a forest warden, who had been among the captain's troops. Three privates and two civilian volunteers constituted the firing squad, which was under the command of an officer from the Estella garrison, like the two members of the court-martial. The captain could have requested for himself the honour of giving the order to fire and could have assumed that the said honour would be granted to him, and he could also assume that the members of the firing squad would present arms to his corpse after the volley, to his corpse alone, that is, and not to the mortal remains of the unionist from Mondragón, in accordance with some section of the military regulations. But the captain didn't believe that it would be a heroic privilege to give the squad the order to fire at him, nor did he think that the honour paid to his corpse could be, in the circumstances, any sort of consolation. He would have liked to suppose that he was the only one of the three regimental comrades – the others being Arderius, the intelligent and caustic Captain Seven Heads, and the enraged Captain Pistols, his two marriage witnesses, who were both, no doubt, celebrating their victory somewhere along the front – well, he would have liked to suppose that he was the only one of the three who didn't deserve to die a few weeks after returning from his honeymoon. That was how the doctor had always imagined the captain's feelings, and in fact, he was right.

The doctor shook his arm in the shadows and tried to follow the laboured flight of a nocturnal butterfly with his eyes. He'd gone out into his garden to smoke a cigarette. The street-light at the entrance to the property was on, and all around it a frantic cloud of bugs and moths were risking their lives. The doctor sat down on a wooden bench. The clump of hydrangea shrubs displayed its pale, monstrous flowers, as large as a child's head. In daylight, their colour was a washed-out blue, but in the darkness they seemed to accompany the doctor with a livid, phosphorescent glow. It was probably past midnight. The doctor wasn't sleepy, and in any case, it had been many years since he'd had a set time for going to bed.

'Satan,' he murmured.

He'd served his cat a saucer of milk in the kitchen, but now the animal had come out into the garden, and the doctor could feel him gratefully rubbing himself against his leg, the good one. As is usually the case with cats, the doctor's had three names. He was known as Satan, but in moments of great tenderness, the doctor called him Pichi. The cat's third name was known only to the animal himself. Satan was docile and young, and his fur was black, very black, although it seemed to have silken stripes in the light from the street. Satan lifted his tail in an arabesque and rubbed his body against the doctor's healthy leg again. Then he moved away and sat with his face to the night at the edge of the light circle, on the border between the still-warm flagstones and the shadow of the grass, next to the immobile congregation of hydrangeas. The doctor's dead leg, as stiff as a piece of wood, was propped up on a low stool, and in this position, in which the great bulk of his heavy body rested in shadow and cast a shadow even bigger than his body, the doctor remained for a long time, until the lights in the neighbouring Las Cruces house were turned off. His long, corpulent silhouette had a Caesarian profile. Intermittently, he lifted a cigarette to his lips. Bored by his nocturnal contemplation of the garden, the cautious, prudent, and jet-black Satan withdrew from the illuminated edge of the flagstones and jumped up on the stool. He walked briefly along the doctor's rigid leg as though it were a roof beam before finally settling in his lap. The doctor stroked the cat's black fur and sighed.

Satan. Maybe it wasn't the devil who had plotted Captain Herráiz's destiny. There were surely grounds for the doctor to consider that the bad luck that had descended upon him so cruelly, destroying his leg in a motorcycle accident, was the same bad luck that had descended upon the country in general and upon the captain in particular, although the doctor would have been embarrassed to place his accident with his Guzzi on the same plane as the outbreak of the Civil War. However, the dates did coincide, give or take a few weeks. That September, while smoke from the burning city of Irún clouded the sky above the estuary, spread a thin veil, the colour of tobacco and cinders, over the ocean, and altered the delicate grey cloudscape, fugitives were streaming across the international bridge or setting out in boats to cross over to the other side of the water. Former combatants, those who had not fallen back to the line of the Deva, those who were all that remained of the ephemeral army formed by the Defence Juntas of Guipúzcoa, fled by tens, by hundreds. Before jumping onto rafts, armed men buried their rifles and ammunition cases in the sand of the shore. Ashes rained down on the beach for some time after the artillery in the San Marcial fort fell silent. As the first detachments from the Navarrese columns were occupying the frontier, the doctor, a young man in the prime of his life, was taking his first steps in the garden at Los Sauces with a leg that seemed to weigh 150 kilos, and the young widow in the Las Cruces house was caressing the taut skin of her belly with an attitude of expectancy, like the young wives in medieval paintings who feel the fruit of the Annunciation growing inside them. Maybe she hadn't yet unpacked the suitcases and the trunk from her wedding trip or placed her honeymoon souvenirs on shelves, and maybe the news that she was a widow had not yet reached her. There were gunshots and executions on the Hondarribia beach, before the very eyes of the fugitives who had reached the other shore. Far from there, in the yard of the Piarist Fathers' school in Alsasua where Captain Herráiz had departed this life, the various administrative sections of the rearguard's quartermaster corps settled in to wait for winter to pass and spring to come, when the final offensive against the city of Bilbao could begin. As the doctor recalled, it was later learned that the captain had been buried in the cemetery of Alsasua, in the corner known as 'the Reds' cemetery', where his body remained for some time, until it was reclaimed, if that was the way to put it, or recovered, and then transferred without too many bureaucratic setbacks to the modest mausoleum of the Herráiz family in San Sebastián. As often happens in such cases, Isabel was never completely convinced that the recovered body was Julen's. The young widow's fantasies nourished a melancholy, delicately irrational doubt, which allowed her to interpret death in terms of non-existent possibilities of escape from it. And the blood spilled in front of a firing squad was now beating in her womb. Her imagination remained like this, filled with memories and expectations, and that was the bitter cup and the sweet sugar of her days. She thought that her wedding had been a sumptuous celebration in the garden of love, and she compared it in her memory with a painting by Rubens that she had seen in an illustrated book. She thought that her honeymoon had been a period of romantic rapture, like that of the lady, seduced by an officer of dragoons, whom Isabel had discovered in the same book, in a mediocre reproduction of a picture by a famous French painter. And finally, she thought that the body buried in Donosti wasn't Julen's, despite the fact that a discreet military department had sent her his papers, a letter, and a few personal objects, including a golden wedding ring and a wristwatch. In her mind, his tomb was a stranger's tomb to which she would never bring flowers, and she never did. Julen was probably a fugitive somewhere on the other side of the border, on the other side of the estuary spreading out before her eyes like the River Styx, and with such a thought one can live a whole lifetime, even though the years take what is simultaneously cruel and hopeful in the beginning of solitude and absence and make it lose its gleam and its intensity of feeling, shuffling and recomposing images that sanctify life's portion of unacceptable grief.

During those months, the fruit conceived in Isabel's womb was thriving. The woman would lower her eyes and caress the mystery she harboured inside her as if it were the fruit of the Annunciation. At other times, nurturing the fantasy that her husband was alive and a fugitive, she would remember the book of Sacred History from her schooldays and imagine the illustration of the Flight into Egypt. The seed thriving in her womb had been deposited there by the loyal, somewhat affected, somewhat unthinking Captain Chicken Thigh, he who returned from his wedding trip to go to war. But – and this was what concerned the doctor just then – what did the lad next door know about all that? And did he care? How much of that story would be news to young Goitia, shut up over there in his late grandmother's house, thoroughly dedicated to preparing himself for the solid, peaceful, and upright destiny of a civil-law notary? But there was a mystery, and the youthful notarial candidate could not possibly suspect it. Those first months of the war contained an enigma that concerned young Goitia's very blood, affected his red corpuscles and perhaps his fortune, and perhaps even the way he envisioned his life, such an enigma as could reduce to rubble the common sense and good judgment that had led him to prepare for his famous notarial examinations in his deceased grandmother's tranquil house; but the words that could help the youth decipher the mystery would not come from the doctor's lips, and if those words were uttered, it wouldn't be to unleash a new tragedy, but to resolve the game, as one adds pieces to a social jigsaw puzzle. Should the doctor talk, the mystery would become as clear and miraculous as a liturgical investiture. And if he opened his lips, it would have to be with a view towards constructing the scientific version of the facts, for such a version can best help a man to understand his own situation and to recognize his own blood in a way compatible with real circumstances, whether sordid or sublime; if the doctor opened his lips, it would have to be with a view towards ascertaining historical truth. A good while had passed since young Goitia had turned out the light in his study on the other side of the garden and gone to bed, leaving to his dreams or his nightmares the great volume and number of topics he had yet to work up. A good while had passed since the old Etxarri woman had finished bustling around her kitchen, and now her lights were out, too, so that the Las Cruces house was an architecture of shadows. Old and corpulent, the doctor initiated the obligatory movements in the process of getting to his feet. Visiting the basements and cellars where memories are stored could be a horrific experience, and the doctor knew a great deal about that sort of thing. His disability had kept him at a sensible distance from the war, but the price paid for this exemption, the heavy, crippled limb he dragged about with him, was no compensation for the passionate furore of youth, no matter how dangerous. He expelled Satan from his lap, moved the stool aside, and amid a mechanical creaking of joints placed the foot of his dead leg on the ground. Then he seized his cane and stood up with the uncertain delicacy of giants. Satan meowed at his side. The doctor tried to make him enter the house, but the cat ambled away, lifting his elegant tail, exhibiting the little pink button of his backside, and stealthily disappearing into the night. The melancholy giant, feeling rather weary and thinking that perhaps he would indeed be able to fall asleep, closed the door of his house and went to bed.

Seen from the Los Sauces side, the Las Cruces house had been asleep for a good while. But seen from the Las Cruces side, it was conceivable that the old Etxarri woman had the same difficulties as the doctor in finding any sort of repose with her head on a pillow. Before going to sleep, she would drain a glass of dark cinchona wine, as thick as syrup, from one of the bottles she'd saved from the Etxarri inn and kept for herself. And it was also conceivable that the old woman listened to the sound of the woodworms in the wood and the unlocatable creaking of the parquet floors and awaited the intermittent suicide of a drop of water in the bathroom sink, as if those were all clues that might awaken her memory, for she was the memory of that house in its rawest state, as much as or more than Doctor Castro was, as much as or more than the deceased grandmother had been; she was, so to speak, the deep mirror, somewhat clouded by cinchona, of the doctor's keen memory. Between them, the doctor and the old woman could awaken the inexistent memory of young Goitia, assuming that young Goitia had any interest in the stories the old woman and the doctor could tell him.

Some days later, the doctor and the lawyer, having run into each other on various occasions in the village, had an encounter in the garden. Doctor Castro reiterated his invitation to have lunch in Biarritz. 'I'll drive the car,' he proclaimed, his dead foot anchored in the grass. 'I'll drive any one of those jalopies I've got in the garage, or I'll drive the Morris Oxford if the old woman will let us borrow it.'

'She won't let us borrow it.'

'The old witch.'

Young Goitia made no reply. Seen from Las Cruces, his gigantic, lame neighbour occupied the entire garden with his urgent presence. As is often the case with older people, there was something obsessive about him. He insisted on arranging the excursion to Biarritz as if his status depended on it. Maybe the doctor's solitude bored him. Or maybe he was crazy. The young lawyer stared at the ground while the doctor braced his bad leg. With such a leg, it would be impossible to work an accelerator. Maybe his car was equipped with a manual accelerator. None of that was important. With a yearning gleam in his eye, as if he longed to get behind the wheel of a large automobile, the doctor insisted: 'I'll do the driving.'

'That's not the problem,' Goitia said. 'The problem is that I have a lot of studying to do.'

'The hell with studying,' the doctor said. 'There are more important things in life than notarial topics.'

'Not for a future notary.'

'Right, not for a future notary. But I'm a good neighbour, and I have certain neighbourly duties. One of those duties is to invite you to lunch.'

Goitia smiled. It was the middle of the afternoon. What old-style summer vacationers used to think of as the lunch hour had been reduced to a fifteen-minute, time-wasting break in the notarial candidate's well-organized study plan. The doctor raised his big blue eyes. He was sure he knew the routine: The lad would take a fifteen-minute turn around the garden to breathe some oxygen and clear his head, while the old Etxarri woman, faithful to the customs of the past, would fix him an afternoon refreshment of coffee with milk and biscuits, or a sandwich of quince jelly or puréed chestnuts, or some other traditional snack. Obviously, the old woman knew that study is exhausting and that the boy needed to recover his strength and keep fit until the dinner hour. The doctor paused and considered the lawyer's flesh. The youth's visit was not yet ten days old, and already the doctor, with his fine, clinical eye, could estimate that his new neighbour had put on a couple of kilos. If his strict study plan didn't produce a civil-law notary, at least it would produce a lawyer somewhat fatter than the slight, pale, recently graduated lad who had arrived in Hondarribia almost ten days ago. The doctor smiled brightly. If there was one quality of the old Etxarri woman that you could count on, it would be her ability to fatten up a future notary, adjusting her budget accordingly and spending the necessary amount of time in front of the stove.

'So we'll go tomorrow, all right?'

'No, not tomorrow. In two or three days.'

'All right,' the doctor said.

Pivoting on his axis, he turned away from the garden wall and cast a glance at the sea, which was visible between the trees. The estuary was a grey sheet, hardly altered by the capricious, fan-shaped designs the currents made on its surface, which rippled with striations that looked immobile from a distance. The tide was at its highest point. It was a moment of fullness. The ocean seemed to overflow onto the shore in a melancholy satiety, as if it concealed a ruminant animal with waves for a snout and a longing to graze on the unreachable meadows. On the opposite shore, the coastline was fading into tones of grey shot with gold in the light of what promised to be a splendid sunset. Four black points remained unmoving in the middle of the estuary. They were fishing boats, waiting for the tide to recede so that they could fish for baby squid. The doctor turned to his neighbour again. 'All right, we'll go in two or three days,' he repeated. 'You won't be sorry for letting me have a little of your time. I'll take you to lunch in the hotel where your grandmother and grandfather spent their honeymoon. I suppose you'd prefer me to call them your grandmother and grandfather, rather than Isabel and Julen.'

'That doesn't bother me,' the lawyer said.

'Are you interested in the subject? Or are you not interested at all?'

The lawyer made no reply.

'I suppose it doesn't interest you,' the doctor went on, in an ample, generous voice that suited the sumptuous contemplation of the ocean.

He paused and stretched out his hand. 'Look at this landscape,' he said. 'Look at the estuary and the sea. Something seems to be saying that the other side of that estuary is the kingdom of the dead, even though the idea's refuted by the vehicles crossing the international bridge in both directions. It's all a matter of knowledgeable presentation. This is the landscape that your grandmother contemplated during the more than forty years of her widowhood. You could say it's the same landscape I've been contemplating all that time myself. Does that have any importance? Does it? Maybe it doesn't interest you, because the connection with that landscape has been lost. But if, on the contrary, it interests you, maybe there's something that could interest you even more. Someday after we have lunch in Biarritz, I'll take you to Vera de Bidasoa.'

'Do you think I'll have any time left for studying?'

'You don't have to stand on ceremony with me.'

'It's no joke,' Goitia protested. 'I'd be glad to go on an excursion to Biarritz or Vera de Bidasoa or wherever you'd like to take me, but I came here because I wanted to spend a quiet time studying for my exams.'

'I know.'

'Don't take it the wrong way. We'll go out to eat together.'

'In two or three days?' the doctor asked suspiciously.

'In two days. I'm sure I'll need a break by then.'

'All right.'

The sound of a voice made them both look up.

'Excuse me,' the lawyer said.

The old Etxarri woman appeared on the porch with a napkin draped over one forearm and a tray in her hands. On the tray was the afternoon snack. The servant didn't leave the porch, and young Goitia turned back to his neighbour to take his leave. The gap that yawned between those two men, between the young lawyer and the old doctor, included something vaster than just the distance between different generations. It appeared that they lived within distinct frames of reference, as was no doubt the case. The doctor was afraid that a lunch would resolve nothing, because the transmission of memory – if one considers that it may be indispensable at some point – has a great deal to do with one's own solitude and with the need to keep conversations going as a weapon against boredom, and simultaneously, the act of transmitting one's memory responds to a pernicious notion that doing so guarantees some form of immortality.

As the youth moved away, the doctor said, 'We'll talk it over again.' Then he repeated his words, lifting his cane in the direction of the fugitive: 'We'll talk it over again in two or three days.' Lowering the cane, he struck at the blades of grass next to his leaden foot. His smile grew broad and secret, as if he were hiding treasures he'd be able to reveal only with extreme caution.

The youth walked up the sloping garden to the house, obeying the servant's call like a schoolboy. There was a wicker table on the porch, and there the old Etxarri woman placed the tray. Goitia unfolded his napkin and sat down to eat the small repast: quince jelly and a glass of milk. It could have been his deceased grandmother's afternoon snack. From the height of the porch, the lawn seemed to roll away, undulating in the tardy light. The old woman withdrew. Then she turned in the direction of the doctor, retreating there in the distance, moving along the garden wall, and she gazed at him for a few minutes with her hands on her hips, as if she were demanding that he give an accounting, from down there, of what he'd been talking about with the boy. Whatever it was, the boy belonged to her, she was the one who fixed him his meals and his snacks and watched over his sleep, and apparently she would have liked to watch over his thoughts as well; it was as if the old Etxarri woman, aware that she was coming to the end of her days, had no other desire than to appropriate the blood and the life of her incomprehensible and studious guest, who was in the flower of his youth. The doctor limped away from the garden wall and continued his walk under the trees. Long columns of shadow crossed the lawn, and in the backlight of the gleaming sea, above a thin cloud of mosquitoes, the sky received clouds of gold, as in the ancient iconography of a burned village or a sacked and looted city. The old Etxarri woman remembered other golden skies, too, but in her thoughts, twilights succeeded one another with the mysterious and profound unconsciousness of animals, and her sensibility, only slightly stimulated by the generous play of gold and grey in the sky, responded to other instincts. She went back into the house while the boy finished his snack on the porch. At that very moment, the doctor disappeared.

For years now, the doctor's territory, like his cat's, had been confined to the two or three thousand square metres of his garden, not counting his obligatory visits to the village, and it's possible that the cat's territory was bigger. With a glance, he recognized the boundaries of the garden wall and the shadows. He took walks out there because exercise made his leg feel better. He stopped at the top of the small hillock and gazed at the rooftops. Then he went inside to read and smoke. The boy didn't go out into the garden that night to take the air, or if he did go out, he went through a door on a side of the house where he couldn't be seen. Or maybe he'd decided to go down to the village – who could imagine what free lives boys lead? The doctor went outside to keep watch and remained in wait, sitting on the wooden bench between the clump of hydrangeas and the streetlight, with his leg propped up on a stool and Satan in his lap. All his thoughts brought him back to the years of his youth, when he was recently settled in Hondarribia, and recently crippled, as if the presence of the young lawyer in the Las Cruces house had served to conjure up the tragedy whose repository the doctor considered himself to be and of which the boy himself knew nothing, because a gap of two generations, by its very extent, induced forgetting. Shadows of memory rose up in his mind, the gold

and blood-red of countless sunsets accumulated in the inde-
fatigable lushness of the garden, in the indecisive memory of
shadows. The doctor sighed. The placid Satan was asleep or
pretending to be asleep across his legs, and in the doctor's
forced immobility, since he didn't want to disturb the cat, the
damp night air began to make his back wet. The intermittent
beam from the Amuitz lighthouse kept cutting out segments
of darkness on the hills and igniting sudden, brief flashes in
the treetops. Somewhere in the night, the sea was breathing
with a strong undertow. Fishing boats hung burning yellow
lamps over a sheet of black ink. And above everything else, as
if to attach a broader significance to his sense impressions, he
could hear the whistle of a locomotive in the distant railway
station of Irún, and that rent in the night, that heartrending
lament, made Satan jump off his lap, and the long, melancholy complaint made the doctor shiver, too. He attributed
his trembling to the dew, but also to the memory that the
train's complaint had succeeded in awakening.

Three

THE STILLBORN FRUIT

A S SATURN DEVOURED HIS CHILDREN, so had time devoured María Antonia Etxarri's memories, leaving behind only a tormented and confused accumulation. She recalled her years as a young girl in the Etxarri inn with her mother and stepfather, until the war came, with its events and its consequences, or what the old Etxarri woman considered, in the burning guts of her individual experience, to have been the consequences of the war. She remembered her time as a maid in the house of the rich man of Vera, Don Leopoldo, like Leopold, King of the Belgians, when Don Leopoldo was confined to a wheelchair after suffering a stroke. And she also remembered the time after she arrived, still a young girl though not exactly a maid, in the villa of Las Cruces. Each of those periods had left a trace, sometimes insignificant and sometimes profound, in her memory. They were three large, clearly defined segments, which marked her life like broad furrows. The smell of the Etxarri inn perfumed her feelings and the warmth of the stable awakened primitive emotions as she wielded a pitchfork with sharpened prongs to turn the hay. In the house in Vera de Bidasoa, the wheels of Don Leopoldo's wheelchair were wooden, two big wheels with metal spokes and rubber tires and two smaller wooden wheels like the wheels of a toy wheelbarrow or the wheels

of a cradle. And in the most spacious parcel of her recollection, the one that went back to those very days, her memories nourished deeper mysteries and awakened other feelings.
Those days were from another era. Back then, the trees on the
Las Cruces estate had yet to attain the state of growth they
had reached now, except for some century-old specimens that
didn't seem to have increased in size or undergone any fluctu-
ations in magnificence, as if their imposing dimensions were
part of some ancient record in which human memory was
unable to detect the imperceptible development of their cir-
cumference. It happened that way with some old memories,
solider and better defined and more emphatic than recent
ones, which always seemed to be in a process of elaboration.
At her age, at María Antonia Etxarri's age, the consistency
of life was starting to lose its sharpest contours, but it wasn't
losing either force or heat. She got up at seven in the morning. She put on her big rope-soled sandals or her rubber clogs
and started shuffling around the service area, moving like a
bear. She was as punctual as the cat that belonged to the doctor on the other side of the garden wall. The cat spent the
night outside. He would be looking for a way into the Los
Sauces house around the time when the old Etxarri woman
in the Las Cruces house stuck her head out of the kitchen
door. Satan distrusted the old woman, but he wasn't afraid of
her. Three or four generations of Satans had succeeded one
another, roaming back and forth between the two gardens. If
the cat was close enough, the old Etxarri woman would chase
him away before returning to her kitchen. Her breakfast was

an enormous bowl of coffee and milk, which she had to hold with both hands. Then, with the fragrant steam in her nostrils and her eyes blurred by the turmoil of some bad dream, she would linger over breakfast for a while, adding up her accounts and cogitating.

If doing accounts and cogitating took her no more than half an hour, her day would be simple and propitious. But it sometimes happened that her thoughts were more complicated, more sinister, more confused, and then her breakfast would take longer. In the more than three weeks that had passed since young Goitia's arrival, his presence in the house had complicated María Antonia's thoughts and prolonged the time she spent over her coffee and milk. But she couldn't change her feelings, or pretend that in fifteen days her soul had been soothed, or that she had managed to block sudden accesses of tenderness towards her young guest. The boy was going to stay in the house for six weeks, or two months at the most. He'd given himself this period of time to go over the topics for his competitive examinations, which meant that María Antonia's joys and desolations would be drawn out for at least another three weeks. Satan, the doctor's cat, had gone back to his own garden, but Saturn, god of time, continued to devour the old woman's entrails. And therefore, María Antonia lingered longer over breakfast.

The songs that were sung in the Etxarri inn after the frog-fishing competitions sounded again in her ears:

> *Go Mendieta,*
> *You're the greatest.*

And she could also hear the strange song she'd heard a smuggler from Vera singing:

Your glory, Mother, has died in the mountains.

They weren't happy memories, not insofar as they evoked the war, nor insofar as they evoked the frog-fishing competitions, and so the old woman thrust the songs out of her memory with a brusque movement of her hand, as one who hears a bothersome buzzing shoos it away. She put her nose in her steaming breakfast bowl and with a long, noisy slurp drained her milky coffee to the grounds. She had only a distant memory of her rape during the war, but that's the wrong way of putting it. María Antonia set the empty bowl aside. Then she wiped her lips with a green-and-blue kitchen cloth.

If it was a bright day, the old Etxarri woman would stand on the threshold of the kitchen door after breakfast and contemplate her domain, but if the day was dark or threatened to be overcast – and on the day in question, the sky had been overcast since dawn – the old woman would remain seated with her elbows on the table and carry out some prolonged interior contemplation. The curtains of rain or the distant, dull-grey clouds bursting over the open sea filled her with nostalgia, because for her, the weeping of the heavens was the ultimate poetic sensation, and nothing compared with the lyrical emotion of abandonment and dispossession that the rain promised. She wasn't a sad woman, but she saw in the never-ending grey clouds of autumn, whose approach was heralded by the sudden storms of September, a confirmation of the life cycle, which was an experience she understood in meteorological terms – inevitable, not destructive – and the powerful north-west winds of winter received from her a certain kind of triumphant consecration. And if the day looked like a watercolour, her emotions were more distrustful, as happens in persons who think that gentle sensations, like bright colours, are not made to last. Saturn was devouring her entrails. But who could have imagined that the old Etxarri woman was capable of working out such feelings? She rose from the kitchen table and walked over to the sink, where she left her breakfast bowl. Young Goitia would be getting up at eight. His breakfast had to be ready. He would take it in the drawing room.

The boy cared about nothing but those examinations of his. He was marking off the days on the calendar. Other than that, he cared about nothing, and so it had to be if the boy really wished to become an upstanding man, the old Etxarri woman thought, and that was why he had come, not for any other reason, not to resuscitate ghosts or make deals with the past, and not to revive Saturn's wound in the old woman's entrails. She didn't like the fact that young Goitia wasted precious minutes every afternoon conversing with the doctor over the garden wall. But the boy had other things on his mind. That morning, while the old woman was fixing his breakfast, Goitia had gone to have a look around the garage. Later, sitting down to his coffee and toast, he'd asked about his grandmother's car.

'Was that my grandmother's car?'

'I suppose it was your grandmother's car,' the cautious old woman replied, as if she really wasn't sure whose car it might have been.

Goitia insisted. 'Was it her car?'

'I suppose so.'

The young man, correctly supposing that the old woman was going to keep saying 'I suppose', asked no further questions. The automobile, its tyres deflated, was resting on four wooden blocks. A threadbare blanket covered its hood. Did the doctor want to go to Biarritz in that relic? Young Goitia believed that either the doctor's memory was failing him or the old man had gone crazy. María Antonia went back to the kitchen so that the lad could have his breakfast in peace. She didn't know whether his enquiries about the car and his grandmother sprang from good or bad motives, but in any case, it would be highly exceptional for her to feel obligated to speak about those matters or to give explanations. Once she was in the kitchen, she closed the door and burst into tears. Her eyes wept for all that they hadn't wept for when she was a girl, but her sobs were weak, not the same now as they would have been then. Before the placid landscape visible from the kitchen window, her deep, bloodshot eyes clouded over for a few minutes. She wiped her face with the dubiously white handkerchief she carried in her apron pocket. Making sure that her eyes were dry, she returned to the drawing room to collect the breakfast tray. The boy had shut himself up in the gun room to study. Before washing the dishes, she examined the bottom of his cup for a few moments. The coffee grounds offered no great revelations, and besides, María Antonia Etxarri had grown sceptical of all predictions except those made by the television weatherman. She raised her eyes skywards once again, looking through the windowpanes with her hands still under the tap. The following day would bring some morning downpours, followed in the afternoon by sheets of steady rain. Maybe that September day was the first day of autumn. Young Goitia was her guest, but Saturn was devouring her entrails, just as Saturn had devoured the engine of the automobile that had been sleeping for so many years in the garage.

After breakfast, Miguel Goitia shut himself up in the little gun room to study for two and a half hours. His programme was unvarying. Two and a half hours of studying and a ten-minute break, then two more hours of study until lunchtime. Behind him, in the spacious kitchen, he could hear the tap, weeping torrentially into the sink, but soon the pipes stopped their coughing and sighing. The depths of the house resounded with the silence of a mausoleum. There were gloomy cavities in the house, spaces nobody had ever inhabited or explored, but the mystery of that resonance, had Goitia been interested in uncovering it, was limited to the well in the cellar and to the empty cistern that had been used until twenty years previously, when the house was connected to the municipal water supply and the plumbing system renovated.

Every two days, Goitia telephoned Madrid from the village to speak to his mother or his girlfriend. The doctor imagined the conversations, or wasted time imagining conversations he probably wouldn't understand, because he was a man who didn't understand the telephone, much less the affectionate or sentimental conversations people had on the telephone. But he would have been surprised to hear young Goitia speaking, not like a young lawyer, but like a boyfriend, or like a son, with the inquisitive and tender inflections of a son's or boyfriend's voice, speaking over many kilometeres of distance but with the intimate closeness of shared feelings. And the doctor might have thought that young Goitia would have used the same inflections and the same affectionate tone to speak to his grandmother Isabel. The question, however, was whether he used the same tone and inflections to address the old Etxarri woman, courteously playing the role of the guest while the old woman silently played the role of his grandmother. That was what the doctor would have imagined.

Rain or shine, the doctor was the last to arise, generally around ten in the morning, at which time he would open the door for his cat. The animal would be on the wooden bench on the porch, waiting for him. The doctor made his appearance, unshaven, leaning on his cane, and wearing slippers and a robe, under which his striped pyjama bottoms were visible. His hair formed a dishevelled crest on his head, and there was something deranged in his appearance, as though he were drunk, and what he really looked like was a man who had spent the night slumped in an armchair, drinking instead of sleeping. Satan slipped between his legs and headed for the kitchen, where some tinned meat and a saucer of milk were usually waiting for him. When the doctor looked outside, his eyes went first to the neighbouring garden, to the placid and studious silence of the Las Cruces house, while he could feel behind him the ominous silence and disorder of the Los Sauces house. In Doctor Castro's life, there had been not only a succession of cats. There had also been a woman. Her name was Hortensia Fiquet, and to honour her given name, the doctor had planted the big clump of hydrangeas – *hortensias* in Spanish – in the garden, although he might just as well have honoured her family name by planting a fig tree. She was from Perpignan, and something that was nobody's business had happened to cause them to break up after only a short time. They may have stayed together six months or a year, and if the details of their relationship were nobody's business, the amount of time it had lasted was even less so. It must have been during the 1950s. She had been a professor of French, but no one could remember whether she had taught at the state high school in Irún or in a convent of nuns. In any case, the story of that affair had little to do with the story that now involved the doctor and young Goitia. Of Hortensia Fiquet, all that remained were the blue hydrangeas – the blue *hortensias* – which later turned pale or drably pink. Crippled men are often solitary men, people declared in the village. No one could be certain that the disorder in the doctor's house, as well as in his life, was due to the absence of a woman. There are men who subvert order because they carry a deep-seated, centrifugal inertia that destroys the space as well as the feelings around them, and that may well have been the case with Doctor Castro. No one could know what the doctor owed his solitude or the grand total of the invoices solitude had submitted to his life, no one could know that, not even those who knew the significance of the clump of hydrangeas and remembered, fleetingly, the attractive, elegant ease, the Catalan or Cerdanyolan neatness of Hortensia Fiquet.

Moreover, one couldn't say that the doctor had maintained a relationship with his neighbour in Las Cruces, with Isabel, the grandmother, although men have always been suspicious of neighbourly relations between a man and a woman, especially those between a man and a widow, and perhaps more caustic imaginations would have been particularly suspicious of such a relationship between a crippled man and a young widow. Insofar as anything the villagers understood was concerned, none could be so categorical as to aver that the two neighbours had shared a deeper connection, an unimagined, mystery-shrouded bond. And indeed, what did they know about all that, the merchants, the old summer vacationers, or the members of the fishermen's guild? What did the teeming humanity of Hondarribia, decimated by war and exile, know about all that? Hondarribia was no longer a village; it was a little city, with its prosperous cooperatives and its influx of new visitors. Irún had been raised from its ruins, and everything, except for the doctor's centrifugal and destructive activity, seemed to have been born again after the brief pact with the devil and fire. The grey mists of the estuary had veiled other memories, perhaps more romantic but not always pleasant to scrutinize. The hydrangeas remained, all that was left of the single amorous relationship the doctor was known to have had, but not sufficient grounds for declaring that the man had truly possessed the feelings attested to by the flowers. Similarly, he could have ordered the hydrangeas, the *hortensias*, pulled up, and forget-me-nots and daisies planted instead, without necessarily suggesting that he couldn't forget some woman named Daisy, but this was the sort of thing that the gardeners of Hondarribia – that is, those who knew or believed they knew the doctor – could not always thoroughly understand.

The doctor cast a glance at the neighbouring garden, gazed for an instant at the melancholy clump of hydrangeas, and went back inside the house. The cat was waiting for him in the kitchen, impatient for his tinned meat and his platter of milk. He reiterated the eager, pitiful meowing uttered down the generations by all cats demanding food, not demanding affection or attention, and that was precisely what the doctor loved about cats. While Satan was eating, the doctor prepared his own breakfast. Coffee and toast. Although the day threatened rain, he went out into the garden to have his breakfast there.

At the end of a minute, with his coffee in his hands, he felt a sudden desire for conversation. He wondered why, as the years passed, he increasingly felt the need to have a living creature at his side, some interlocutor other than the cat and the hydrangeas. No, that wasn't it. His solitude wasn't opting for that solution. The question the doctor asked himself as he raised his eyes to the cloudy sky that morning, examining the band of wan light that illuminated the horizon and would, perhaps, disperse the midday clouds, set the afternoon afire, and end in a biblical sunset – that question had nothing to do with the recurrent paradoxes of his solitude; instead, the doctor was wondering what were the chances of an excursion to Biarritz that very day. He settled into the big wicker chair with the cup of coffee in his hand, laid his cane on the ground beside him, and stretched out his leg. When the cat finished eating, he came outside and joined the doctor in the chair.

Once again, Doctor Castro felt an irrepressible urge to seek human company, and such weakness of character irritated him. He had sufficient patience to hold out for another ten minutes. He distracted himself by contemplating the bar of yellowish, rather ghostly light that widened and rose between the clouds on the other side of the estuary, on the other side of the border. Then his desire for conversation became too strong. He got to his feet without picking up his cane and limped into the house, swaying like a bear. Soon he appeared at the door again, tottering on the threshold with a telephone in his hand and the cord untangling behind him. He placed the telephone next to the coffee cup on the garden table and sat down once more in the wicker chair. From there he could see the office, or the sewing room, or whatever it was, where the lawyer studied. He could have sworn that the boy could see him, too. The windowpanes reflected the leaden sky, and behind them he could make out a studious silhouette. The doctor leaned forward and seized the telephone. He put the apparatus on his knees and dialled the number for Las Cruces. There was probably a telephone in that office, or in that sewing room, or whatever it was, and the boy himself would answer. And so he did. At the end of the second ring, the boy picked up the receiver without even rising from his seat. The doctor endeavoured to sound jovial.

'Goitia? Good morning. It's your neighbour calling. I see that you're a diligent man, and an early riser to boot.'

The lawyer didn't understand who the caller was. The telephone beside him, a black Bakelite device that had been silent until that moment, had rung, he had answered it, and now he failed to recognize the doctor's voice.

'It's your neighbour,' Doctor Castro repeated. 'I can see you through the window. If you turn your head this way, you'll see me in front of my house.'

The lawyer turned his eyes towards Los Sauces with the receiver pressed to his ear. He moved a few books that were on the table and thrust his nose close to the window glass. Beyond the garden, about thirty metres away, it seemed to him that he could make out the doctor, installed on the little terrace in front of the door to his house and half submerged in the luxuriant mass formed by the hydrangeas. The doctor cheerfully raised an arm above the circle of flowers and said, 'Do you see me?'

'Yes, I see you,' Goitia mumbled, somewhat disconcerted by the sight of the doctor, whose voice was in his ear.

'Good morning, my boy,' the doctor repeated, with even greater enthusiasm.

'Good morning.'

Doctor Castro solemnly settled back in his chair. Visual and telephonic contact had been established. The unbearable solitude of his breakfast had been resolved. There was still some tepid coffee in his cup. With the telephone receiver in one hand and the cup in the other, he took a sip. Satan had occupied the other chair and was staring at his master with dilated eyes, admiring the telephone and human inventions.

'Today's the big day, my boy. We're going to Biarritz for lunch,' the doctor said.

'Today?'

'Come, come, Goitia, don't make me beg you. We agreed that I would take you to lunch today.'

'I didn't remember that.'

'That's why I'm calling to remind you.' The doctor waved his arm again, sending a grand signal to the villa of Las Cruces. Seen from the villa of Los Sauces, Goitia's silhouette shifted behind the window. 'Do you see me? I'm reminding you.'

'Yes, I know we talked about that,' Goitia said. 'But it wasn't clear that we said today.'

'We said today. Think what you will, but today you're going to give your notes a rest. This won't stop you from becoming a notary someday.'

The doctor let a minute of silence pass. He knew that the boy needed time to reflect. It couldn't be easy to accept an invitation to dine with an old, solitary bear like him. That was all right, though. A boy decides to shut himself up for a couple of months so he can study, so he can prepare for his upcoming competitive exams in the most eccentric corner of north-eastern Spain, and an impertinent neighbour invites him to lunch. The doctor sat up a little in his chair to check on his neighbour. On the other side of the garden, behind the window of the office, or the sewing room, or whatever it was, the air was thick with hesitation. At last, the lawyer replied, remembering what the doctor had said about the Morris that was in the garage at Las Cruces. 'We can't go in the car that's in the garage,' Goitia announced. 'It's undriveable.'

'Undriveable?'

'It's up on some wooden blocks, it's covered with dust as thick as your finger, and there's an old blanket over the hood.'

'The Morris is undriveable?'

'That's what I said.'

The doctor burst out laughing. 'Come on, my boy. You can't think I'm going to trust an old relic to take the two of us to lunch in Biarritz.'

'You had suggested—'

'Put that car out of your mind. The old Etxarri woman will wind up selling it to me, and then the Morris will be a real collector's automobile.'

'So what are we going to do?'

'I'll go and rent a car.'

'I don't know if that would be prudent.'

'Prudent?' Once again, the doctor was quite surprised.

Goitia remained silent.

'All right. It would have been more pathetic to go to lunch in the Morris,' the doctor said, pretending not to have grasped the allusion to his disabled leg. 'That's what I had imagined – going to the hotel where your grandmother spent her honeymoon, and in the same car she made the wedding journey in. Magnificent, right? But I think it's better not to add too much pathos.'

'I don't understand.'

'Just an old bear muttering. Anyway, if you're referring to another kind of prudence, don't worry, I'll let you drive.'

'I don't want you to think that I don't want to go to lunch with you,' Goitia stammered.

'I don't think that for a minute,' the doctor declared emphatically. 'I'll come to fetch you at twelve noon.'

The lawyer sighed and surrendered. 'All right.'

'And now you've got more than an hour to study.'

Before hanging up, the doctor sat up straight, so that his whole bulk emerged above the hydrangeas. Bracing himself on the back of the chair, he signalled to Goitia by waving his hand. Behind the window of his study, the lawyer replied with a vague gesture. The doctor smiled. 'Do you see me?' he asked.

'Yes, I see you,' Goitia repeated, with a hint of irritation.

'You won't regret coming to lunch with me, I can assure you of that,' the doctor said. 'Now, I'm sure the old woman's listening to you on the other side of the door. You can tell her that you and I are going out. She won't dare acknowledge what she owes me. Much more than you can imagine.'

The lawyer hung up the Bakelite telephone. He sat for a few moments looking at it, a contraption from another time, as black and heavy as a telephone made of stone and painted black. Then he raised his eyes to the neighbouring villa again, but the doctor had already disappeared. Or he had submerged himself again behind the hydrangeas. Then Goitia stood, went to the study door, and opened it to see if the old woman actually was behind it, listening. There was no one. The hall was plunged in darkness, and all that could be heard was an indistinct, metallic sound. The old Etxarri woman was in the drawing room, cleaning dishes and polishing silver. She cared for the cutlery in the house as if it were her own, which in fact it was. The lawyer closed the door again and sat back down to his books. He felt a vague desire to be in Madrid or in some other place, but not in the place where he was.

He couldn't concentrate. After a while, he abandoned his books and went to talk to the old woman. He assumed that she'd been listening at the door. But why did the doctor care whether she'd been listening or not? The servant was in the drawing room with a vinegar-soaked rag, polishing a set of several dozen pieces of flatware, an entire service except for the little coffee spoons, which were in a different set. The storage chests, lined in maroon velvet, lay open on the table. Flatware for fish, for meat, for dessert. She supposed that the cutlery was all sterling silver. But it might have been silver plate. She had dissolved some aspirin in the vinegar. Vinegar with aspirin made the pieces shine. Goitia stopped in the doorway of the drawing room, unable to articulate a word. The old Etxarri woman had obviously been listening at his door, because she'd listened at many doors over the course of many years, and in all kinds of circumstances. Besides, that house, the villa of Las Cruces, was her house, just like the silver cutlery. Goitia babbled an apology: 'I'm having lunch with Doctor Castro today.'

He seemed to be asking permission, not so that the old woman would grant him her indulgence, but by way of observing forms whose neglect might arouse jealousy. What was he thinking? Had he come to this place in order to go crazy? The old woman looked at him with an old woman's tender, watery blue eyes. She thought that the lawyer wanted to examine the cutlery, perhaps even to count the pieces. The old Etxarri woman knew how to calculate their value. If they were sterling silver, their weight would come to more than four kilos. Four kilos of silver. She knew about silver. But maybe the flatware service was not silver at all but rather the alloy called pewter, and that was a doubt that couldn't be resolved, and so the old woman had calculated the service's value that way, too, taking into account the loss she would suffer if the service turned out to be pewter. The service could be melted down, and she would still have the kitchen cutlery at her disposal. When she saw Goitia in the doorway of the drawing room, she placed herself between him and the flatware chests. The vinegar cloth was still in her hand. While making a piece of cutlery shine, she had indeed been listening at the door, because she was distrustful, and because she was afraid of what the boy might learn from the doctor.

The doctor appeared at twelve sharp. He apologized to Goitia for having set their appointment for such an early hour, but the lawyer had to understand that the French ate their midday meal at twelve-thirty, or one o'clock at the latest, and the doctor could do nothing to change the customs of the French, nor could he persuade them that, since they were so close to the border, they should adopt Spanish customs. The reverse was also true, but that was another question.

He'd rented a white car and driven it to Las Cruces himself. He accomplished this by crushing the accelerator with his crippled leg, making the clutch howl, and by stamping on the brake pedal, when necessary, with the same fury. He had brought along his cane, which was lying next to the gear-lever.

When Goitia came out of the front door, the doctor got out of the car, leaving it running, circled the vehicle, and got back in on the passenger's side. The cane remained where it was and now lay next to his left hand. Goitia adjusted the driver's seat and tested the various controls before backing up onto the villa's circular driveway. Then they went down the Las Cruces road towards the village, driving along the seashore. They skirted the village on a street lined with chestnut trees and joined the highway leading to Irún and the Hendaye bridge. The doctor turned towards his companion and asked, 'Have you ever been to Biarritz?'

'No.'

'You can't imagine what it feels like for me to be going to Biarritz with you. Finally. Any excuse for going to Biarritz is a good one.'

'Do you go there often?'

'No, I don't go often. I meant that I'd use any excuse to go there. But I rarely have an excuse as good as this one. I mean, going to Biarritz with Isabel's grandson . . .'

After they crossed the border, the doctor brought out a flask of cognac from the inside pocket of his jacket and took a swallow. His lips were wet as he screwed the nickel-plated cap back onto the flask and returned it to his pocket. Then he turned towards Goitia again. Out of the corner of his eye, Goitia could see the doctor's smiling face, and he could smell the cognac on his breath.

'Do you speak to your mother often?'

'I've talked to her on the telephone several times since I've been here.'

'A good son.'

'Why do you ask?'

'Simple curiosity. It's been many years since I last saw your mother. She wouldn't recognize me.'

'She asked me to give you her regards.'

'She remembers me?'

'So it seems.'

'Ah, little Verónica. Her husband kidnapped her and took her away to Madrid.'

'My father's from Bilbao.'

'It amounts to the same thing. If your mother ever comes this way, I'll invite her to lunch in Biarritz, too. But I don't think she'll come here. She doesn't get along with the old Etxarri woman, and it's her house. That's what your grandmother Isabel wanted.'

'I'll tell her that we talked about her.'

'Very good. The delightful Verónica. Many a time, she jumped onto my lap. And sometimes, when she was afraid, she'd hold on to my bad leg as if it were a telephone pole. I taught her a Basque song: *Pipa artuta aita naiz.* . . . And now she has a son who's going to be a civil-law notary. Has the old Etxarri woman told you that little Verónica used to jump onto my lap and cling to my bad leg like a pole?'

'She hasn't spoken to me about my mother.'

'I'm not surprised. That woman comes to us from the glacial era. Even though I'm older than she is, she's got half the feelings I have, and she looks twice my age.'

Goitia didn't reply. They had driven past the farmhouses on the outskirts of Hendaye, and the doctor told him to follow the coastal road. On their right were the new highway and the ongoing construction of the motorway. Over the sea, the sky had opened up to reveal a strange flowering of high cumuli and rain clouds. At that moment, rain was streaming down on the line of the horizon. The sky above the Bay of Biscay was like a living being of changeable character, with attributes lighter and more delicate than the turbulent, choppy presence of the sea. The road went past country estates and farmhouses. Big commercial centres were gradually gaining territory at the expense of cornfields. Before they reached Saint-Jean-de-Luz, the doctor suggested that perhaps it would be a good idea to stop there and drink an aperitif, but the lawyer preferred to go on directly to Biarritz. Then the doctor took the cognac flask out of his pocket again. He felt the need for an appetizer to accompany his drink – peanuts, olives – but then again, cognac could hardly be considered an aperitif.

The doctor slapped the pocket where he kept his flask and said, 'It's the only thing that soothes my leg. You see that cloudburst out there?' he added, pointing at the cloud that was emptying itself of its water. 'My leg detects it. I've got a twenty-five-kilogram barometer attached to my hip.'

The lawyer turned his eyes to the sea, where the cloud continued to pour down rain. A second, more distant formation of clouds was lowering over the horizon. The sea was iridescent with the pearly tints of diesel fuel. Goitia lowered his window slightly and the storm's strong, oxygenated odour came through the chink. The interior of the vehicle smelled of new plastic. There was also a light whiff of cognac in the air. Goitia handled the car smoothly. He'd decided to enjoy the excursion, and every now and then when he reached for the gear-lever, his hand closed round the doctor's cane, and the mistake elated him. He was trying to change gears with a cane, an old cripple's cane. The doctor remained silent for some minutes. The road ran on past summer villas, many of them already closed because the season had come to an end. There were some tiny gardens, cut back with the meticulousness of a hairdresser, others more lavish, and still others transformed into car parks or supermarket parking, where only a single decorative tree, a row of tamarinds, or a gigantic monkey puzzle tree indicated the former presence of a garden. The doctor pointed out a bar, vaguely intending that Goitia should stop. The lawyer's eyes kept searching out the sea between the succession of country houses and villas. The doctor interrupted his thoughts.

'What did your mother say when you told her you were going to come here?'

'To Biarritz?'

'To the old Etxarri woman's house.'

'She didn't say anything. Should she have said something?'

The doctor heaved an aromatic sigh. 'No, there was nothing she should have said. That's just it. The thing is, she didn't say anything.'

'I don't understand what you mean.'

'What's there to understand?'

Goitia struck the steering wheel. His good mood had evaporated. What were these riddles? He stopped at a red light while a file of children with short trousers and multicoloured rucksacks walked across the zebra-striped crossing zone. The doctor's cognac odour wafted to the young man's nostrils again, further irritating him. He said, 'I'm here so I can have lunch with you and take a break from my studies, not so you can break my head with questions. All right?'

'All right, my boy, all right. I only wanted to know what your mother thought about your stay here.'

'What does what my mother thinks have to do with anything?'

'Probably nothing.'

'Well, then?'

'Then nothing. I'll phrase the question differently. Didn't it surprise your mother to learn that you were coming precisely *here* to study for those damned examinations?'

'No, it didn't surprise her. Why should it surprise her?'

'Frankly, it's been years since anyone expected your mother to come here, or you, either.'

'I'm sorry.'

'The old Etxarri woman doesn't seem to be sorry.'

'No, she doesn't. Is all this going somewhere?'

The doctor unscrewed, as before, the cup-shaped, nickel-plated cap of his flask. Goitia opened his side window. The doctor made no reply to his question. In an access of impatience, Goitia struck the steering wheel again, this time with both hands. 'Besides, I didn't know I was going to lunch with someone who's constantly reaching into his pocket and pulling out a flask of cognac, as if it were some kind of tonic,' he continued ironically.

'It is. In a certain way, it is. Your grandmother gave me this flask. It was the flask your grandfather used when he was on campaign.'

'I don't think my grandfather drank when he was on campaign.'

The doctor thought this a valid conjecture and dropped the subject. The line of schoolchildren had finished crossing the intersection, and Goitia reached for the gear-lever. The cane had rolled towards him, and he roughly pushed it aside. The doctor put it between his legs. The boy was getting irritated, all right, and he was getting irritated, too, and that wasn't advisable, because they were supposed to be having a good day and a good lunch together, and maybe they might take a walk afterwards and the doctor could exercise his leg a little on the seaside promenade, rainstorms permitting, or maybe they could go to a café and talk and return home in the evening with the feeling of having spent a good day in each other's company, the young lawyer in the old doctor's company, or vice versa, the solid, solitary doctor in the company of an irritable lawyer with no time to waste, or at least resigned to wasting only that one day. As they entered Biarritz, the doctor indicated the sign BIARRITZ – BEACHES, which the lawyer would have followed in any case. It had rained a short time before, and the tyres hissed on the wet asphalt. Tiny droplets of rainwater still hung on the elegant, feathery foliage of the tamarind trees. The road ran along the beach. The sand was a dense, uniform colour, as if the tide had just receded. The terraces of some cafés and restaurants had been cleared, but others had remained exposed, and their pedestal tables shone wetly. The doctor pointed out the Grand Hôtel. The lawyer made no comment. The doctor concluded that he was going to have to apologize.

'I'm sorry I upset you.'

'It's not important.'

'I'm a curious old man,' the doctor said, striking the floor of the car with his cane's rubber tip. 'And that sometimes leads me to commit impertinences. Park wherever you want. I've invited you to lunch, and I promise not to bother you with any more damned questions. What's wrong with me? Why do I have this stupid rage for asking questions? It's over. I promise you, it's over.'

'That's not it.'

'Damn it, your mother's opinion interests me. Your mother should have come with you to Hondarribia, damn it, and then she would have joined us for lunch. Between the two of us, we could have told you some things.'

'Why? Is there something I should know?'

'That's a stupid question. You've asked the last of the day's stupid questions, and I'm not going to answer you.'

They continued in silence. Goitia parked in front of an ice-cream parlour. The doctor recognized the establishment. In recent years, it had changed names three times, always Italian names. Now it was called Fregoli. Who was Fregoli? An opera composer? A tenor? The storm had brightened up the colours of the awning. The doctor had a thought for Hortensia Fiquet, the educated, refined woman with whom he had shared a little less than a year of his life and his feelings and who without any doubt would have known who Fregoli was. A nougat-maker?

The doctor savoured the sweet sensation of being in France. Goitia locked the car and joined him on the pavement. The doctor checked the time and made certain Goitia was on his left side so that he himself could walk without obstruction. The hotel restaurant was on a terrace with a balustrade, just above the beach promenade. The threat of another storm made them request a table inside. Deep wall-to-wall carpets muffled their steps. It was around one o'clock when the doctor elegantly shook open his napkin, the lawyer meticulously unfolded his, and they settled in for lunch.

'I, too, was a man in love,' the doctor said in the course of the meal, and then he went on to recount to the lawyer the story bruited about by the old gardeners of Hondarribia, that is, the one about the clump of hydrangeas – of *hortensias* – and the woman of that name to whom those flowers were dedicated, and about the doctor's ephemeral romantic relationship with her. But had the doctor continued to expatiate upon his emotional life, amid the knives and the forks and the succession of dishes, his young companion would have thought, 'This man is an idiot,' and that was obviously not the doctor's goal, if indeed he had one other than the goal of acting like a proper host in that hotel restaurant. He prided himself on controlling his thoughts. With age, his desire to explore memory and acquire the discipline of knowledge had taken on dramatic aspects, like a theatre production whose director reveals only the seductive and advantageously lit sequence of events going on downstage and leaves the shadowy nightmares of the

backstage area for themes never to be expressed. Isabel had
spent her honeymoon in that same hotel and eaten lunch,
with everyday banality, in that same dining room. The carpets and upholstery had surely been changed since then, and
the waiters weren't the same, because otherwise they would
have looked as mummified and crippled as the doctor himself. There had been no change in the lamps that hung from
the ceiling, the ones called 'spiders', with tear-shaped crys-
tals and bronze arms and hundreds of pieces of many-faceted
glass, which was at that moment mingling the rainy greyness
reflected from outside with the brilliant sparkle of the wall
lights. The arrangement of tables and chairs was different.
Back in those days, great hotels had become the cathedrals
of the *haut monde*, performing the function that cathedrals
had provided in centuries gone by, centres of pilgrimage and
enjoyment and boredom where visitors were served by canons or maîtres d'hôtel. And if a new cloudburst pelted the
windows of the dining room with rainwater, Doctor Castro's
thoughts would become even sadder, although they were already sad and guilty about what concerned him. He would
have liked to tell the story as though he'd found it written
down in pencil, in some impulsive, passionate, immediate
form, like the outpourings in war diaries and in letters from
prison, and – why not? – in diaries written by women, subject
to every sort of distress and disinclined to take the trouble,
in times of shortages, to find pen and ink, which, however,
Captain Herráiz had not lacked when he wrote his two letters, the first from San Sebastián, and the second when he
was on his way to the front. And had those letters never been

received, perhaps a school notebook would have turned up, written in pencil, with a record of the distress suffered by the addressee in wartime, but the letters arrived, the first because it had been deposited in a box in the main post office and because of the absurdly good postal service, which continued even in the darkest moments of the rebellion, and the second because it was delivered after the captain's execution with his belongings, that is, a watch, a souvenir of Loyola, a hip flask, and some other knick-knacks of the kind that the executed always seem to have about them, but not including his field glasses, which had been confiscated as military equipment. The doctor had to place himself on the near side of suffering, at the moment when a recently married woman receives two letters and a handful of trivial objects with the news that her young love is dead, and she lays both hands on her stomach as if to support the treasure she carries inside her, and she refuses to believe and weeps, but afterwards, those letters and that handful of objects are put aside, like evidence too painful to be borne. Another woman, firmer or more serene in her grief, would have seized a pencil and recorded all that in a notebook, like a prayer, or like an act of revenge against fate. As he entertained these thoughts, black clouds gathered over the doctor's brow, because Isabel's love had been a tragic love, not a faded love, and that was a horrible privilege, not like his love affair with the queen of the hydrangeas or the figs, the sweet, late-blooming Hortensia Fiquet.

Some say that the honeymoon and the loss of virginity mark a couple's relationship forever, but neither Isabel nor the captain had much time to verify that assertion or to determine the significance of the drops of blood dribbled onto a hotel bed sheet. She had been a virgin, of course; all brides were virgins back then. In the following weeks, we can assume that she, too, like her husband, recalled her honeymoon, and therefore we must believe that her memories were made even more vivid when she read the aforesaid letters. Her happiness had been brief. Little or nothing in writing remained of those weeks, or of those days, or rather of those moments when the captain's living eyes glazed over, permanently crystallized by death into an inert, mineral gleam, like a trace of eternity that she had been unable to contemplate, that she would not have recognized, and that even then, with the evidence of his death in her hand, she still denied. And even so, the memory and the intensity of the young husband's love belonged to a register deeper and more mysterious than death itself, deposited in Isabel's memory of her love for him. The letters that Isabel had received from the captain were there. Nobody had destroyed them. In some part of the house, in some folder, in some desk's secret drawer, those letters lay sleeping, as they had slept for so many years. The doctor would have given a great deal to hold those letters in his hand and to be able to add them to his store of knowledge. Not out of some unseemly curiosity, but out of the immense respect that all human feelings related to death elicited from him and which, he thought, would somehow have been reflected in a posthumous reading of those letters. He would have liked to interpret the young widow's melancholy without having recourse to the kindly smile of the psychiatrist when faced with slight or inoffensive forms of madness. Given the opportunity to read them, he would have expected that mail between two lovers would grant him, like something out of a novel, the privilege of gaining access to their lives shortly before one of them learned that he was going to die. Isabel no doubt read the letters every night, and they made her feel once more like the beloved woman she had been, the one to whom the letters had been addressed, or rather, she felt she was that other, beloved woman, the one she had been and would never be again. . . . *Dear Isabel* . . . *My Dear Love* . . . Her favourite of the two letters was the second, more tender and more tragic, perhaps because the captain had sensed that his death was near when he wrote it. And when she read it, she murmured a song of her childhood that the letter suggested to her, as if somehow, when she held before her eyes the love those words contained, she became a child again. . . . *The blue afternoon on the path* . . . Perhaps it was the memory of a romantic walk the two of them had taken. Perhaps it was what the psychiatrist, in his kindly way, would call a regression. Perhaps it was the refuge of childhood for a soul in pain. But even though grief deranges the reason and makes one return to childhood years and songs, she was strong in herself, and she knew how to separate nostalgia for lost innocence from the present, brutal introduction to sorrow.

It's possible that she received messages from her family in Bilbao over the radio – that wasn't so rare in those days. Separated families sent messages to their loved ones across the battle lines. On the banks of the Deva, the country had turned into another country, and the land into another land. Isabel may have received news, but probably the indifference to which her terrible melancholy had reduced her was stronger than the desire to find out what had happened to her family, to those of her blood who had remained on the other side of the front. The last immediate memory she had of her previous life evoked the unreal and now almost grotesque whirl of the dancing at her wedding. The house had acquired inhuman proportions. It was inhabited only by those ghosts. On some nights, the doctor would hear the sound of music. By then, he'd already laid aside his crutches, and every evening he'd go out into the garden to take his invalid leg for a walk. So it was: From then on, his indispensable companion would be his repaired leg. Cane in hand, silent under the stars of that first autumn of the war, the doctor would hear music in the night, music coming from the villa of Las Cruces, and it wasn't the music of the phantom orchestra that played in Isabel's memory, accompanying the incessant carousel of the dancing at her wedding, but real music, though seeming unreal in the night and in the midst of war. It was the music that Isabel was playing on a gramophone, and it was produced from one of those Bakelite discs that spun and crackled as if the gramophone were a little mill, and what it was grinding was sand. At that time, she was not yet visibly pregnant. Her pregnancy was known only to herself. Captain Herráiz's seed was pulsing in Isabel's belly, and no one knew it. And the most important thing was not to know it, so that she might bow with greater fascination before the terrible void the captain's death had created around her and preserve the ignorance of her state, so that no hope, no future life, would come to change the sumptuous contemplation of her solitude. One night, the doctor saw her step out onto the porch. She was carrying the two letters in her hand. In the dimly illuminated house behind her, the gramophone was spinning out a waltz or a melody from the wedding music in *Lohengrin*, accompanied by the inevitable sand-grinding. Still unsure of himself with his cane, the doctor halted. For some days, the Amuitz lighthouse had stopped sending out signals, because it had been blown up. The moon was sailing across the heavens. It was the September moon, the moon of vigorous tides, and one could hear the muffled sound of the sea pounding the breakwater below. The shadowy outlines of the cliffs grew larger. Scattered lights could be seen on the other side of the water, and far away, up the French coast, a twinkling: the Biarritz lighthouse, intact but weak, like a glint of peace among dark shadows. The lighthouse was so far away that its beam could not be made out. Maybe she took those signals for a call, or for a repeated but indecipherable message, summarized in two brief twinkles and a pause, and then a somewhat more pro-longed twinkle, followed again by two brief twinkles and a pause, as if insisting on the message might conduce to its interpretation. She knew that the light came from Biarritz. She stood there, hypnotized by the distant twinkling, until the record was over and the gramophone needle was running round in an empty groove. Then she turned towards the house as if something had interrupted her fantasy or her dream, as if that waltz or wedding march were meant to be unending, and perhaps she was irritated, like children interrupted in their daydreaming. The doctor, fearing that she might discover him, retreated. The gramophone needle kept scratching in the stupid Bakelite groove. She stopped. She seemed to hesitate. Abruptly, she threw down the two accursed letters she'd been holding, hesitated again for a few seconds, and then stooped to pick them up, and in that violent gesture the doctor recognized that she wasn't deranged; the only delirium she was suffering from was that of her grief. And he deduced more than that, because the rebellion against fate that her demeanour implied was a sign of strength. It always happens like this, when a person is able to dominate the melancholy that forms the border of madness and gather up the reins of suffering again. And thus, after throwing them on the ground, she gathered up those letters. Then she entered her house. Almost at the same moment, the noise coming from the gramophone ceased, and a few seconds later, the lights went out. Then the doctor emerged from the shadows. There was nothing sordid in his spying on that scene. There was nothing obscene or murky in his curiosity; on the contrary, the doctor felt protective and affectionate towards the woman, even though misogyny and his physical state prevented him from showing his feelings, and there was a certain grandeur in satisfying his curiosity, because someday that curiosity could be illustrative, could enable him to delve into the roots of the story. Many situations need to have been witnessed by someone. Many things are comprehensible because someone felt the blade of curiosity like a knife and slipped it into the story at the right moment. Perhaps pride hindered Isabel from asking for help, or from asking for company. The doctor hadn't considered that question. Autumn, sad and miserable, was stripping the trees. The north-western winds combed white tufts into the waves. On certain days, one could make out the silhouette of a destroyer on the horizon, probably the *Velasco*, part of the friendly fleet or the enemy fleet, according to which radio stations the doctor was able to tune in. The front lines of the war had moved away, but in his neighbour's house, the intimate, irreconcilable tremors that the war had caused were still being felt like a secret cataclysm, perhaps more pathetic because it was more private. The doctor was a witness to those events, and maybe it was his mission – his only mission – someday to find an explanation for them.

Other things happened. On some nights, poor wretches were executed down on the beach, and the shots could be heard in the village. Then all that stopped. It's said that a few tuna-fishing vessels still transported fugitives to the other side of the estuary, but that may not be true, because there were no ships or even boats, for almost all of them had fled. Guns were mounted on two barges that had remained in port. Fresh troops arrived. Some people remember the coming and going of trucks in the night, driving with their lights off through the crossroads at Irún and along the old San Sebastián road, and lines of roped mules loaded with cases of ammunition – the whole train of that war, which started without knowing that it was really a war. A signal station was established on the heights of Mount Jaizkibel. In those days, the road was barely practicable, and beasts of burden carried the material for the station up the mountain. Through the Velate Pass, the Navarrese columns received a good part of their supplies of weapons and men, who were sent to garrison the frontier or to reinforce San Sebastián or to cover the seaward flanks of the troops in the passes as they made their way down to the line of the Deva. Behind the shelter of a concrete slab, under the lighthouse platform, a coastal battery was set up. The guns were of such heavy calibre that no mule could carry more than two of their shells. No one could say whether or not the battery had ever opened fire. There are some people who remember all that, and also some who remember a village strangely deserted in the midst of the hectic movements of troops and supplies, as if, paradoxically, the same circumstances obtained in overcrowding as in solitude. There had been little destruction. And the people, that is to say, all those who were fleeing the war, the women and children, or the men who hadn't fought, or those who had thrown away, before it was too late, a rifle too rashly taken up, along with a belt and some bands of ammunition, or those who had nothing to fear from the victors – all those people were prowling around like beggars or panhandlers, waiting for the army field kitchens to finish distributing food to the troops and to deliver the leftover bacon, potatoes, and bread to the civilian population.

An officer came to the doctor's house. Some weeks previously, the bulk of the unit that had occupied Hondarribia after the assault on Irún had moved on to other positions, leaving a small garrison in the village. A squad with reserve supplies had remained on the Alameda, and a powder magazine for the rearguard was established in what had been an automobile repair shop. The officer who appeared at the doctor's house belonged to a communications section. The doctor opened the door but didn't step over the threshold. The officer saluted. He was a young man, wrapped in a raincoat with his lieutenant's stars on the inside of the upturned collar, and bareheaded, as he was carrying his military cap, protected by his raincoat, under his arm. The lieutenant was about the same age as the doctor, perhaps a little younger, and it should not be forgotten that the doctor, at the time, was a young man. He examined the lieutenant's bearing before stepping aside to let him come in. Yes, they could have been about the same age, neither young nor mature, although in terms of the calendar, they were both still young, because a few events had served to prolong time and age indefinitely. A light rain was falling. The lieutenant ran his hand through his wet hair. An orderly on a motorcycle with a sidecar was waiting for him beside the garden gate. Before entering the house, the officer shook off the rain, removed his raincoat, and slung it over his shoulder. He was wearing calf-length leather boots, which tracked in a little sandy mud from the garden and crunched on the floor tiles in the entryway. When he reached the living room, the boards of the parquet floor creaked. The lieutenant dried his hands on a handkerchief. He drew a sheet of paper from the pocket of his uniform jacket and addressed the doctor: 'Doctor Félix Castro?'

The doctor replied in the affirmative. The lieutenant folded the paper with the doctor's name and returned it to his jacket pocket. The pocket had no button. There were problems to be resolved that didn't concern the doctor directly. Because of his dead leg, nobody was interested in enlisting him for military service, not even for a rearguard hospital. The officer cast a glance around the interior of the house and asked another question. A corporal and two privates operated the

signal station on Mount Jaizkibel. A second lieutenant and six
soldiers under his command had been assigned to the coastal
battery. For all those men, the lieutenant had to find lodging
that would allow them to remain close to their posts. The
path that climbed to the station on Jaizkibel passed behind
the villa of Los Sauces and traversed a portion of the meadows
in the rear of the Las Cruces property. The road leading to the
battery and the lighthouse passed lower down, in front of
the two villas' garden walls. Four of the soldiers assigned to
the battery were bivouacked in a shelter set up near the guns.
Two more had moved into the living quarters attached to the
lighthouse. The second lieutenant had found accommodation
in the village. One man was permanently on duty at the signal
station, and lodgings were needed for the other two.

'Who lives in the neighbouring villa?' the lieutenant asked.

'A woman – a widow. I'll put your men up in my house,'
the doctor hastened to add.

The officer reflected for a moment, stroking his chin. He
had left his cap on a little table when he entered the living
room. A few droplets of water oozed from his hair and ran
down his cheeks. His eyes were yellow, as if he suffered from
a liver disease or had gone several nights without sleeping. He
seemed not to have heard the doctor's offer.

'Is she young?'

'She's the widow of an officer,' the doctor said.

The lieutenant assumed that the doctor meant an enemy
officer. 'I understand,' he said.

Then he looked around, as if he were thinking of taking
up quarters there himself. In those days, the house had the

same arrangement as it did now, and in that the doctor gave proof of his constancy, his attachment to things, his laziness in introducing innovations or in getting rid of certain pieces of furniture. He didn't know whether those factors, which shaped his character, sprang from slovenliness or existed because having certain constant reference points enabled him to value his life more, even if the reference points were nothing but furniture. The little table where the lieutenant had left his cap was still in the living room, because the years pass with greater ease over furniture than they do over men. The lieutenant stepped over to a window. For a few moments, he gazed out at the villa of Las Cruces, on the other side of the garden. A silhouette glided past the window facing him. It's possible that she had heard the motorcycle arrive. The doctor moved a chair out of the way and limped closer to the window where the lieutenant was standing. The silhouette passed again behind the gauzy lace curtains. The officer drew his head back, as if the doctor's proximity bothered him.

'Does she live alone?'

'She lives alone,' the doctor said. 'The gardener does some odd jobs for her.'

'Many people live alone,' the lieutenant grumbled.

The doctor refrained from making any comment. Then, carefully keeping his tone free of the least hint of reproach, he said, 'Her husband fell in Alsasua.'

The officer turned round abruptly. 'Is that my fault?'

'That's not what I meant,' the doctor said, making a cowardly apology.

'Is it my fault that there's a widow woman on the other side of that garden?' the officer retorted, pointing a finger at the doctor's French doors.

The doctor made no reply. He moved away from the window and looked for a chair. The lieutenant walked to the foot of the stairs and raised his eyes to the upper floor. There was a great weariness in his movements. He assumed that the bedrooms were up there and no doubt thought wistfully about a bed with a double mattress, dry sheets, and woollen blankets. Then he turned to the doctor, who had managed to reach an armchair and was sitting with his leg outstretched next to one of his crutches. The visit was surely nearing its end. The lieutenant had not come to chat but to transmit a notification. Nevertheless, he stayed a while longer at the foot of the stairs. Anyone who had been on campaign and lived through the events of the last months would have felt the attraction of a home, a comfortable living room on a rainy afternoon, the silence in the other rooms, books on the bookshelves, some maps, and a fireplace where winter fires would soon be burning, and perhaps he wouldn't have imagined that the person living in the house was an invalid who would have preferred to be an officer on campaign, so that he could experience those events differently; for without admitting it, the doctor had always carried some regret in his heart for not having lived the war the way those men lived it, both victors and defeated, perhaps with more enthusiasm for the losing side, because of the poetry attached to defeat, but also with some feeling for the side represented by the yellow-eyed lieutenant, wrapped in his wet raincoat, who could

just as easily have been, say, a civil expert as a military communications officer, but whose good health and intact bones
gave him the opportunity to participate in the war. Was that
what the doctor would have wanted? Was that really what he
would have wanted? Over the course of his life, he'd indulged
in some fantasies about what might have been. Probably, he
would have been mobilized and posted to some medical services unit, or if he'd thrown in his lot with the other side, he
might have followed the refugees to Vizcaya, or to the other
side of the Bidasoa, or who knows, his life might perhaps have
come to an end on the beach, or against a wall. In civil wars,
there's nothing more dangerous than their beginnings. If you
can survive that, it's easy to stay alive afterwards. No one could
say that doctors who had been so unlucky as to treat enemy
casualties would be spared. Yes, Doctor Castro thought, the
really dangerous enterprise is to survive the early stages of a
civil war, and thanks to his ruined leg, he was doing just that.
The lieutenant returned from the foot of the stairs and cast a
glance into the kitchen and at the door that led to the cellar.
Then he turned to the doctor.

'Has there been anyone else in this house?'

The doctor shook his head. Why was he being asked that
question? Again he felt cowardly and cautious, as if unimagin-
ably fateful decisions lay in his visitor's power and depended
on the doctor's reply. He said, 'There hasn't been anyone here
who has anything to do with politics.'

'I'm not asking you that,' the lieutenant said with a smile.
'It's a question of finding accommodation for two men. That's
the only question.'

The doctor gave a sigh of relief. 'I'll put up those two soldiers, Lieutenant,' he replied.

'All right,' the officer said brusquely.

He patted the pockets of his jacket, looking for the paper
with the quartering assignments, but he was obliged to recognize that he'd forgotten it. He hesitated for a few moments,
calculating that nothing was keeping him there any longer
except the appeal of that comfortable home, and perhaps a
game of cards and a good nap, which would help him forget
too many days without any rest at all. He picked up the cap
he'd left on the little table and thrust the headgear under his
arm. He directed his eyes to the window again in a long gaze
that passed over the garden wall and the neighbouring garden
and sought to determine whether the silhouette of the young
widow the doctor had talked about would cross the window
once more. Then he turned round, wrapped himself in his
raincoat again, and left the house without saying goodbye.
A trail of sand from his boots remained on the floor tiles in
the entryway. The smell of his wet coat remained in the living
room. When he got in the sidecar, the orderly who had been
waiting for him beside the garden gate started the motorcycle
and drove up the road a little way before turning round and
heading back down. With the aid of his cane and one crutch,
the doctor propelled himself out of his front door in time to
see the motorcycle go by.

When the men from the battery walked down to the
village, they passed in front of the villas, singing as they went,
and returned a couple of hours later, often rather drunk and
unsteady on their feet, and if it rained, they returned in a

cluster, huddled together under a canvas sheet. Those assigned
to the signal station on Jaizkibel went down the back path.
The two men who were to be quartered in the doctor's house
presented themselves two days later. They were Carlist *requetés*,
volunteers from Cizur, on the outskirts of Pamplona. One
of them was an electrician whose surname was Fuentes. The
other was a farmer or a farmer's son, and the doctor didn't hear
his name, but it seemed that his comrade called him Severo.
They showed the doctor the quartering orders their officer
had given them. They each carried a bedroll, a blanket, a
canteen, and some personal items, among them a strange
folding stool, which Severo had picked up somewhere and
which was of great importance to him. Their helmets were
attached to their belts, as were their blankets. No doubt
their red *requetés'* berets were among their personal items.
When they entered the house, they felt uncomfortable,
like teenagers caught with an embarrassing object, and
didn't know where they should put their rifles. Some days
later, by which time they had gained more confidence,
the electrician explained that he'd been assigned to the
communications section because he was an electrician, and
that his friend, the farmer's son, had come with him. The
doctor had already confined himself to the lower floor, as
he didn't yet dare to climb the stairs with his crutches or
his cane. The two soldiers each chose a room on the upper
floor. Soon the electrician stopped coming to the house
because, it seemed, he had found other accommodation in
the village, unbeknownst to his superiors. The other soldier
remained, the boy named Severo, who gave the doctor to

understand that his comrade liked bars, some of which were now open in the village, and that he was involved with a woman. Then the young man began to spend his evenings on the lower floor with the doctor, who gradually came to feel some affection for him and accepted his company like that of a big, docile dog. He was a lad of twenty-two or twenty-three, with thick peasant's hands that gripped his rifle as if they were holding on to a hoe, a rake, or a wagon shaft. He held his spoon the same way when he sat down to eat with the doctor, balancing his plate on his knees, refusing the table, and it was the doctor who prepared their dinner, believing that his obligations as host went beyond offering the fire and salt required by the ordinances of war. The youth had not participated in the bloody assaults on the fortified convent of San Marcial, or in the firing from both ends of the Endarlatza bridge, or in Beorlegui's daft manoeuvre through the mountains, or to put it another way, the only actions he had taken part in were the occupation of the ruins of Irún and the establishment of the communications post in Hondarribia, well behind the front lines. In short, for whatever reasons, Doctor Castro was growing increasingly fond of him and even appreciated his name, Severo, which the doctor would not have hesitated to give to a dog. At nightfall, the soldier would come down from the signal station, lurching about on the path because of its many twists and turns. Soon it was necessary to light the fire in the hearth, and in the course of those evenings spent before blazing logs, the big kid from Cizur came to seem like an oversized companion animal, hypnotized by the fire, with his elbows resting on his knees, his head inclined, and his large hands clasping his rifle, which he held between his legs as he sat on the collapsible stool he'd confiscated in some small-scale pillage and for which he showed great esteem, with the unmistakable admiration that denizens of the rural world feel for folding things. The doctor, installed in his armchair, stretched out both his legs to the blaze, feeling the heat moving up his good leg and sensing a slight tickling in the rigid one. The electricity had been cut, or it functioned only intermittently, because the turbines in some of the power stations along the waterfalls of the Bidasoa had been damaged and some cracked dams had lost volume. One must envision the living room, illuminated by a candelabrum or by burning candles stuck in bottle necks. The glow from the hearth put fire in the cheeks of the boy from Cizur, whose expression was as severe as the name Severo implied, and the same glow lit up the doctor's nose and sparkled in the glass of cognac he had at hand, the last glass from the last bottle of his cognac reserve, one of those brandies from before the war that were later so greatly prized. That was the sum of those wartime evenings. One must remember – and the doctor remembered – the long nights and the short days. The boy had been witness to half a dozen horrors, not all committed upon humans; some of the victims had been animals, one of them a pig, hacked to death by the bayonets of the group from Cizur in order to carry off the quarters and the slabs of meat for their provision. Nobody had felt sufficient compassion to kill the pig with a knife before they began to cut it to pieces. And the human horrors and the memory of the dismembered pig's screams darkened the boy's face and opened up long pauses of silence between him – by nature a man of few words – and the doctor's unembellished questions. One must consider those evenings, with the crippled doctor and the sombre Severo, who broke into an imitation of the doomed pig's shrieks every time he told the story. He didn't say *cerdo*, the usual word for pig, he said *gorrín*, in the Navarrese way. And with lugubrious irony, the doctor thought that the dozen and more names given to the pig in Spain illustrated the country's diversity as well as all its misunderstandings. The boy declared that, in his opinion, the unnecessary cruelty to that *gorrín* had been a sin. He kept quiet about the human horrors. But in the end, he described one of the atrocities he'd witnessed, without saying that it was typical, or rather hiding the fact that it was. They had handcuffed a man, tied his feet, and thrown him into the middle of the road, so that their unit's entire convoy, consisting of two trucks and three wagons loaded with the munitions of half a field battery, passed over him. The unfortunate wretch's bones cracked like chicken bones. That was how things had been. But if he assumed that Severo wasn't the most sensitive of the forty volunteers from Cizur, then the doctor had to think that a couple of them must have put an end to their remorse by getting themselves killed, or they must have succumbed to the long melancholy of guard duty, nearly apathetic, nearly numb to the emotions of the senses, or in some other state of clinical balance imposed and established by the war. The big northwest wind forced its way down the chimney and blew smoke back into the living room. A little later, the wind seemed to suck up the air, provoking a whirl of burning embers. The gusts raised the roof tiles and made the joists shudder. From the signal station, one could watch the endless procession of sea squalls, week after week, and that unremitting sameness clouded the boy's head. Soon the season of Christmas nougat and chestnuts would arrive. In the middle of December, the soldiers received their Christmas rations.

The doctor had a few tins of asparagus in his pantry. That might seem ludicrous, if looked at from this distance, but it's possible to imagine what a tin of asparagus represented in those days, not because of its nutritional value, but because it was special, it evoked a party, a celebration, and it helped one forget the long-standing diet of potatoes and chickpeas. He had run out of cognac, but there was still some asparagus. Then he remembered his neighbour and decided to give her a tin of asparagus and half a pound of the nougat the Cizur boy's family had sent him. He had coffee – which, for some reason, was readily available in Hondarribia – and sugar was coming, because sugar beets were being boiled on the banks of the Ebro. There was no oil, and if by chance his neighbour had run out, there was nothing the doctor could do about that. If other people were running out of oil, he grumbled to himself, well, he had run out of cognac. The doctor paid her a visit, but he did not undertake this operation without taking serious precautions. He walked down from Los Sauces, aided only by his cane. After reaching the road and walking past the garden wall, he stopped at the gate of Las Cruces to catch his breath. Up to that point, nothing had gone awry. His leg was responding – that is, though it seemed to hang down dead from his hip, it nonetheless obediently executed the manoeuvre of dragging its foot and then stiffly thrusting it

forward, after which the good leg joined it, and so on succes-
sively. After a few minutes' rest, the doctor stepped through
the gate and walked up to the porch. A rucksack with the provisions – the tin of asparagus and the nougat – was slung over
his shoulder. Before knocking on the door, he adjusted the
rucksack and assumed the most dignified posture he could.
His neighbour answered the door herself. The gardener came
only occasionally to perform various chores for her, and it was
still some time before María Antonia Etxarri would arrive to
serve in that house. Isabel hadn't stepped outside for months,
both because of the interminable succession of squalls and
because of the horror of open spaces that often accompanies
great grief. It was an exceptionally calm night. Isabel had a
fire going, too, and when she showed him inside, the doctor smelled the hot aroma of burning firewood, overlying
the humid, wintry atmosphere of damp carpets and cold furniture. Isabel looked at him without recognizing him. Her
hands were in gloves made of coloured wool. In the darkness
of the porch, her figure had reminded him of the silhouette he
often saw passing behind the window, with the same mystery
and the same intensity.

'I'm your neighbour in Los Sauces, Doctor Castro.'

'Yes, I recognize you,' she said.

Very good. The doctor had been mistaken. She recognized
him. A low garden wall, thirty metres of garden, and half a
lawn stood between them, and it was as though they were separated by a continent. There was electricity that night, but the
little entrance hall the doctor stepped into was very dimly lit.
He leaned his cane against a chair and opened his rucksack.

'I've come to bring you a few provisions. In times like these, neighbours have to help one another. The war involves us all.'

'What are you saying?'

The doctor hesitated, unable to repeat his words. Of course the war involved everybody, especially that very woman. She had barely avoided being obliged to receive a couple of soldiers into her home not long after losing her husband. She had escaped the outside world by remaining shut up in her house. She had managed to reach some kind of equilibrium between the winter and her solitude, and at that moment, at that stupid moment, her Los Sauces neighbour appeared at Las Cruces, reminding her that everyone was involved in the war, beginning with those who had shot her husband dead and ending with the intrusion of a neighbour who rooted around in a rucksack and extracted a tin of asparagus and half a pound of nougat. The sequence of events passed through the doctor's mind. It was pathetic. Exceedingly pathetic. Conscious of his accursed stupidity, the doctor babbled an excuse, holding out the package with the asparagus and the nougat. She extended a gloved hand and took the package. Then the doctor met her eye. 'That's some asparagus and nougat,' the doctor said.

'Thank you,' she said, uncertain whether she should open the package or do something else. Finally, she decided to put it on a console table. 'Would you like to come in and sit down?'

'Sit down? Oh, no. I couldn't sit down with this leg,' the doctor said, slapping his bad leg like a horse that had made an admirable effort and obtained good results. 'If I sat down,

I'd have to stay seated for two hours. I think I should go back home. I've done my good-neighbourly duty,' he added with a smile.

'Thanks again,' she said. 'If you need coffee, I have coffee.'

'Oh, I've got coffee, too,' the doctor exclaimed, overjoyed that the conversation was taking a good turn. 'What I don't have is oil.'

'I don't have oil, either. I'm sorry.'

'No, that's not what I meant. I don't need oil,' the doctor said, correcting himself rather nervously. 'I'm not exchanging asparagus and nougat for coffee and oil. It's a gift.'

She smiled. 'Very well,' she said.

'I've got a soldier quartered in my house, and I depend on him for my supplies,' the doctor said, gently patting his crippled leg. 'I can send him to the village to get what you need. Or what he can find.'

'Thank you. I have my gardener. Really, wouldn't you like to come in and sit down?'

The doctor pondered the question for a moment. 'No. No, I won't come in.'

She smiled again, a little disconcerted. The entrance hall resembled a chapel. Her hands were folded on her chest, enveloped in the coloured gloves, which let her fingertips show. The cold was penetrating her body. The fireplace heated only the big drawing room. A memory came to the doctor's mind, a recollection that went back only a few months but seemed to come from another century or another age. To see her like this was very different from seeing her on the day of her wedding. Her face had lost colour and looked pallid in the semi-darkness.

She had matured, in the sense that suffering brings on maturity. Her pupils were dilated, and her eyes had increased in size. Her hair was gathered on her shoulders, and as he remembered the scene at the wedding, it was difficult to imagine the elaborate hairdo that had crowned the beauty of the bride. The doctor had probably expected a tragic vision, not sweet but not completely unsociable, of suffering. Isabel was a domestic vision, not even aloof from oil shortages and problems with provisioning, for those were not what tormented her mind. Her strength didn't come from outside her. Then the doctor lowered his eyes and noticed her condition. Under her folded hands in their coloured gloves, her stomach was swelling with the bulge that gives females their true strength. How could he have failed to notice sooner? That was where her force came from. She looked about five months pregnant. The doctor was so surprised that he couldn't be certain. Five months pregnant, yes indeed, the doctor thought, making the calculation, at least five months, and it couldn't be otherwise, he couldn't suppose that her pregnancy was the result of the Annunciation. The doctor raised his eyes from his neighbour's fascinating stomach and asked, 'Five months?'

'A little more than five months.'

'You can't stay alone in these circumstances.'

'I think I can deal with them.'

'Can you?'

'I think I can.'

'You should go inside and sit down,' the doctor said abruptly, recognizing the signs of fatigue in her. 'Maybe I should go in and sit down, too. Somebody has to stay here with you.'

'I don't need anybody,' she insisted.

'All right. You don't need anybody. But the time will come when you *shall* need someone, and that time is coming soon. . . . May I suggest that you call me?'

She made no reply. She probably hadn't given the subject much thought. Did she plan to give birth alone? He imagined her situation, between the winter and the darkness and the war, and with all her attention fixed on the growing bulge in her belly.

'I'll call you if it's necessary,' she said in a firm voice.

'My leg prevents me from going beyond this garden wall, but as long as I'm the only doctor around who's not treating war wounded, it's my duty to deliver a baby or treat a toothache.'

She made a gesture of impatience.

'Especially with a first parturition,' the doctor went on. 'And let me express my sympathy. I imagine that a posthumous child . . .' He stopped himself in time. 'Forgive me.'

She gave him a withering look, raised her hands to her stomach, and clasped her bulge. 'I don't need condolences. Do you understand?'

'I imagine that bearing a posthumous child is not the best way to become a mother,' the doctor said, thinking that he had to complete his sentence.

Then he looked away from her intense eyes. He had an absurd thought: What was that solitary woman going to do with asparagus and nougat? Music came from the interior of the house. She had the radio on. They were playing patriotic *pasodobles* ahead of the news bulletin. The doctor wouldn't have dared to suggest that they should spend the evening together, that evening and other evenings, and in any case she would have refused, just as the doctor had at first refused to go in and sit down. Neither of them felt cordial enough for that sort of thing. It seemed to the doctor that Isabel was wearing scarlet lipstick. No, not scarlet, but violet or indigo. It was an illusion of the semi-darkness, which lent her lips that colour. They were prominent and fleshy, what men would have called a young woman's 'bee-stung' lips, and they gave her pale face an allure of which she was not completely oblivious. So perhaps there was another reason not to enter that house or not to prolong his visit there. It was said that in the city there were still people hiding in cellars or creeping around in attics, fugitives from Irún or marked men and women from Hondarribia, but it was a novelistic or romantic idea to imagine that this young widow with the blue lips and the bulging stomach was harbouring fugitives in her house while they waited for a launch to take them to the other side, and in fact neither the doctor nor Isabel had enough kindness or courage left to expose themselves to other people's dangers. The doctor was supporting himself on the back of an armchair. He looked around for his cane, which he had left leaning against some piece of furniture. 'In any case,' he said, 'I'm sorry for the misfortune that has fallen on this house.'

'I don't need condolences,' Isabel repeated.

'I understand, I understand. Nevertheless, you're going to need me to assist you, and it had better be clear to you that I'm prepared to do so,' said the doctor, seizing his cane and positioning his leg for a pivot. He didn't wish to act against this solitary female's will. Female animals gave birth that way, and the doctor knew that he was confronting the instinct of one such female. 'There's a young soldier quartered in my house,' the doctor added, ignoring her silence. 'He's a good lad. And I'm an invalid. I'll tell him to be alert for whatever may happen.'

She didn't reply. The doctor turned his back on her and headed for the door. His leg responded with renewed strength. When he reached the door, she hadn't moved from her place. With his hand on the door handle, the doctor turned round to take his leave.

'Good night.'

Before he stepped outside, she abruptly raised her chin and said, 'Doctor!'

'Is there something else?'

'Thank you for . . .'

'The asparagus and the nougat.'

'Exactly. Thank you for the asparagus and the nougat.'

'Think nothing of it. Happy holidays,' the doctor said, without irony, almost mechanically, on the assumption that the tradition of well-wishing proper to the season was ingrained in everyone's unconscious. He opened the door and received the cold December air in his face. Then he closed the door gently, as if he and the house had established some degree of complicity. He was wrong, or at least he wasn't completely right, and not because of her, not because of the distrust her grief threw up around her, but because of himself, because he was irresponsible and insecure, without any more notion of how to attend a birth than what he'd learned in medical school, that is, not much, and just as he trusted his crippled leg to do its part on the way home, he also trusted that the natural process of birth required nothing but patience and tenacity. The doctor closed the door behind him and felt the astronomical peace of the night on his face. Without a doubt, it was freezing in the mountains. She, for her part, had not moved. She was still standing in the middle of the entrance hall, holding the bulge in her stomach, near the package of asparagus and nougat that the doctor had brought her. As he returned home, the doctor looked over the garden wall and saw a light in the living room at Los Sauces. That meant that the boy from Cizur had arrived. The waxing crescent moon shed a sterile light on the estuary, the same indifferent moon as in peacetime. A fine, cold fog enveloped the bare trees. Those were the days when it snowed on the mountains of Lesaka and the frontier of France was covered with white, and later the snow froze. The winter of 1936 was like that, cold and bright, as people say all winters were in the old days. The doctor set out for the villa of Los Sauces from the villa of Las Cruces with renewed determination. He'd begun to think of his ruined leg as a solid support, and he believed it could be a guarantee of longevity, like the freeboard of certain ships. With the passage of time, his prediction had looked more and more accurate, and now it was confirmed. The doctor had survived long enough to be old as well as crippled. He could still boast a little about his good shape and strong constitution to Goitia, his young lawyer neighbour.

On the day when the doctor took young Goitia to lunch in Biarritz, María Antonia Etxarri seized the opportunity to make an inventory of all the table linen in the house. She knew that there were four sets of embroidered table linen in Las Cruces, along with another three sets of ordinary table linen for everyday use. Nonetheless, they had to be verified, much as the doctor verified the state of his health by patting his leg. She opened the drawer in the chest of drawers where the embroidered table linen was kept and counted the folded tablecloths without taking them out of the drawer, as one might run a hand over the spines of some notebooks. Then she knelt down to count the napkins, spreading them out on the carpet on the floor, twelve napkins per tablecloth, except for a set of reduced size, embroidered with saffron-coloured thread, of which there were only six. The three sets of table linen for everyday use were in a different chest of drawers, located near the kitchen, and she didn't bother to count those. She usually carried out this operation every few weeks, just as she regularly examined all the flatware in the house in an attempt to resolve the mystery of whether it was sterling silver or pewter or silver plate. She liked to be alone when she took out the cutlery and the table linen. Since the guest had been in the house, she'd been able to do it only once. And that was already weeks ago. So in order to do it again, she took advantage of young Goitia's absence when he was having lunch with the doctor.

María Antonia Etxarri had lunch early, in her kitchen, at around one o'clock. She had stopped doing any serious cooking, and she'd come to like tinned food. She liked tins of already cooked dishes, the ones she'd been used to preparing herself. She found the tinned versions neither better nor worse, perhaps because she'd begun to forget her own dishes, her own stews. Tinned stews tasted more acidic to her. But she also thought that the fault might be hers for getting old, and that the acid taste was in her gums and on her palate. Moreover, tinned stews had turned out to be much more economical. She would never have to take out any portion of the eighteen million she had in the bank or pawn the pewter or silver flatware. And so it was that on that day, after having inventoried the table linen, she opened a tin, heated its contents, and sat down in the kitchen to eat. There was an oilcloth with blue and white squares covering the kitchen table, and there had been other oilcloths, but no tablecloth had ever covered that table.

Occasionally, she cooked *bacalao*, salt cod, because she hadn't learned whether it was available in tins, and also because the people at the *bacalao* shop knew her, and they always gave her the piece on the bottom of the pile, the piece that was the tastiest, because it had absorbed the tasty juices from all the other pieces of *bacalao*. She felt great respect for codfish. She believed the fish that Jesus distributed to the crowd in the miracle of the loaves and fishes was cod. That was why she had heard people at the carnival in Lesaka refer to the fish as Santo Bacalao, Holy Cod. Once in the last three weeks, she had cooked *bacalao* for young Goitia, but the lawyer hadn't seemed to notice that it was *bacalao* from the bottom of the pile, the tastiest piece. María Antonia Etxarri thought that she had an acidic palate because she was old, but she also thought that young Goitia had no palate at all. While he was having lunch in Biarritz, she heated a tin of broad beans with red *chistorra* sausage, like all tinned foods rather acidic to her taste, but that was her taste now. Later she'd go back to counting the table linen, and maybe she'd count the bed linen, too. The sky had cleared up after the midday storm. A faint light came through the kitchen window and revived the oilcloth's satiny sheen. The house was an empty space filled with voices and weeping from the past. There was music on the radio. It was a group performing the hit song of the moment: *Quita tus sucias manos del volante de mi camión*. As a person who had no driver's licence, María Antonia was interested in anything that had to do with driver's licences, so she paid the song some discreet attention. Then her thoughts swerved off in other directions. Thrusting her spoon into the steaming plate of beans, María Antonia Etxarri considered that getting old was worth it, if only because it meant she could enjoy a plate of beans like these.

The doctor and the lawyer finished their lunch at around three-thirty. By inadvertent coincidence, the lawyer, like the old Etxarri woman, had eaten a dish of broad beans, but his were very tender and served with foie gras. This choice was not the best the restaurant had to offer. By dessert, he was repeating the foie gras. The sky had cleared over Biarritz, too. In the middle of lunch, the doctor got up and went to the lavatory. Left alone, the lawyer had a look around. The stucco-work on the ceiling appeared to have been executed by some branch of the pastry-making profession. Except to attend fancy weddings, no one but old people frequented such hotels any more. Nevertheless, in other times, those had been the fashionable salons, inexplicably subject to the caprices of fashion, as any fashionable bar today is subject to current fashion, and in those days, it was the decorated-pastry look of the Second Empire or the rigid art nouveau furniture, doubtless introduced during the last renovation. There was a porcelain figure, a Chinese mandarin the size of a watermelon, on a draped stand. Whenever a waiter passed nearby, the vibrations of the floorboards caused the mandarin's movable head to nod in greeting. But the lawyer's eyes were drawn to the elegant, bevelled-glass doors. They gave access to other reception rooms and to a sumptuously furnished and no doubt suffocating interior, and if the company that owned the hotel hadn't reacted to one of its periodic crises by selling off the furniture, the sofas his grandmother had sat on would be back there, along with the little tables at which the newlyweds of half Europe had played cards during the interludes allowed them by their passion. The lawyer smiled. Someone at a table near him had ordered a soufflé flambé for dessert. The blue flame of the rum made him think of a crematory oven. At that moment, the doctor returned, making his way among the tables. Goitia wondered how many of the old folks who were staying in the hotel now had spent their honeymoon in those rooms, and how many might come there to celebrate their antique love with a flaming soufflé. The doctor sat down and shook out his napkin with an aristocratic gesture. The lawyer turned his gaze to the big windows. Except for the line of the horizon, where the colour was more intense, the sky was a pale blue, streaked with unmoving bands of white clouds. The storm clouds had shifted eastwards, and it was raining in the mountains. In the intervening time since Goitia and the doctor had arrived, the restaurant had almost emptied out. Two or three people remained at a few tables. The tablecloths were littered with breadcrumbs.

The doctor had eaten he no longer knew what, because the conversation had diverted his attention to other times and other circumstances, nor did he know whether or not that had been his true objective, as he was repeatedly torn between what he could talk about and what he couldn't say. And although it seemed like stretching the truth to call a conversation what had in fact been a monologue, and not even a moral lesson or a history lesson or a disquisition on genealogy, nevertheless, when all was said and done, it seemed to him that he had eaten well. With a sad gesture, he fanned breadcrumbs off the tablecloth. A waiter observed his movement and arrived at the table with a silver-plated device consisting of a comb, a brush, and a kind of small hopper for collecting crumbs from the table. This activity jolted the doctor out of his faraway thoughts, and he asked for the bill. He ordered no cognac, even though he was thirsty for cognac. He intended to wait, and when they were in the car again, he'd drink the rest of the supply in his flask. He paid in francs and left a fifty-franc note as a tip. He didn't know whether that was a stingy tip or a generous tip. He didn't care.

'I had several good reasons for asking you to have lunch with me here, over and above all the things I told you,' the doctor said, taking it for granted that the after-lunch lingering, which at least in his opinion had gone on too long, was over.

'What reasons?' asked Goitia.

'Listen to me. If I had been married, I would have liked to spend my honeymoon in this hotel, too.'

He leaned on the edge of the table and stood up, inadvertently letting his napkin fall to the floor. The table shook. Goitia rose and moved his chair aside to help the doctor. The waiter brought them the doctor's cane and their raincoats. Music came from inside the hotel. A wedding was being celebrated in one of the reception rooms. When the waiters entering and leaving the dining room opened the doors, the vaporous melody of an orchestra could be heard, only to be muted again when the doors closed. At the end of the night, wedding receptions like this generally wound up in a nearby casino, the doctor said. Had he had such a wedding, he thought – but this thought remained unspoken – he would have liked the celebration to end with the guests losing a fortune at the casino gambling tables. But that was another matter. And damned if he knew whether a cripple even ought to get married. Or whether it was a defective character or unusually powerful feelings that caused a crippled man to remain a bachelor, bound to his leg the way Ulysses was bound to the mast of his ship, unresponsive to all siren calls that didn't come from a brothel. But that was indeed another matter, and the doctor suspected that it had nothing to do with the real matter at hand. The awareness of how alone he was and of how careless it had been for him to seek out company sufficed to put him in a bad mood. They left the hotel arm in arm. The lawyer went ahead of the doctor in the lobby to stop the revolving door from crashing into him and then returned to take his arm. The doctor tried to free himself, pushing the young man away so that he could rely solely on his cane.

'I know a marvellous place to commit suicide around here,' said the doctor, whose digestion had made his mouth sour.

'Far?'

'No, not very far.'

They reached the place where they had left the car, and the doctor pointed out the road that led to a lookout tower. The powerful incoming tide struck with great force. A few shirtless teenagers were risking themselves on the little bridge so they could get doused by the spray of pulverized water that rose to a great height every time a wave broke. It seemed they were risking their lives, and perhaps they really were, for a game, for a dare, jubilant and drenched by the golden mist that suddenly covered them. Out beyond the breaking waves, the sea rippled with white patches like fleeces of wool, the sheep-scattered sea, tended by the winds, carrying in its bosom the uncontainable force of the tempest that could break out in a few hours, or on the other hand, maybe the wind would die down at dusk and they would be granted the dark sea of night, thick and placid as a muscular animal, brimming over at high tide as if the exhibition of its power had filled the basin formed by the land and the continents. A line of incandescent light marked the horizon. Goitia and the doctor stayed in the car and looked at the breaking waves for a long time. The doctor finished off the contents of his cognac flask. Great quantities of water leaped over the parapet and covered half the road. The spectacle repeated itself monotonously, the muffled explosion of the waves following the tall spew of white foam. The windshield misted up. The wine-dark sea disappeared from sight, and all that could be heard was the shower of pelting water when the trajectory of a wave reached the car. The young people who had been playing on the bridge seemed to have been snatched away by the tide. They suddenly appeared on the other side of the road, playing with a ball. The doctor wiped off the clouded windscreen. 'I think we should go back,' he said.

Goitia started the car, and they drove to the coastal highway on the same road by which they had come. The bands of clouds that had streaked the sky were spreading and merging. The surly ocean stretched out before the doctor's eyes, like the saturnine fields of time. When they reached Hondarribia, the doctor asked the lawyer to drop him off at Los Sauces. The automobile rental company would come to fetch the car, but Goitia offered to return it himself and walk back to Las Cruces. The doctor watched him drive away and patted his pockets, looking for his house keys. It was not unpleasant to find himself alone again. He appreciated the silence. He appreciated the presence of the cat. He appreciated the experience that life had given him in that house, guilty or not, distressing or indifferent over the long course of the years, but which at least allowed him the company of his ghosts. He was thirsty. He thought it must be around six in the evening. After changing his clothes, he sat in an armchair in front of the window and poured himself a glass of cognac. Then the sky began to darken, and although it wasn't yet the season for lighting a fire, the doctor shifted the armchair round and turned his eyes towards the hearth.

The fire of the winter of 1936 was burning there, but it was lit only by his memory, and that was enough; it was like fixing his eyes on a real fire, because there's nothing more atavistic than the contemplation of a fire stoked by human memory. During the first winter of the war, firewood arrived from Irún, not just any firewood, and not firewood from the mountains around Irún, but wood from beams and roofs that had not been totally consumed when the city was burned. At the time when the rubble of Irún was being cleared away, those beams and joists and planks were cut into pieces to be sold as firewood. There was a business whose sole purpose was to sell scorched wood. And so, from the ruins of the burned city, at least enough material was extracted to keep the survivors warm. That winter was a harsh winter. It's said that winters during wartime are always harsh, or so they remain engraved in the memory, as though winter had to add a portion of cold and chilblains to the sufferings caused by the wrath of men. The doctor ordered Severo to chop firewood for his neighbour. The boy from Cizur obeyed the doctor as if his orders came from an officer. Every two or three days, he cut up some wood into logs and kindling, filled a basket with it, carried it over to the villa at Las Cruces, and returned with news. He would say that he'd seen Isabel looking bad. Or that he'd seen her, and she was well disposed. On another day, Severo brought her three quarters of a salt pork loin, taken from a piece the boy had managed to subtract from two pieces salted for his captain. The day of the Epiphany had already passed when he brought her some chocolate. In those days, chocolate came in half-pound bars. Each bar was divided into one-ounce portions, so two bars contained sixteen ounces. Severo brought the woman eight ounces. Chocolate was good for pregnant women. The boy knew about women who were on the point of having a baby, because he had watched three of his sisters give birth. When it came to parturient females, he had a good eye, and he let the doctor know it, not bragging about his knowledge, nor suggesting that he'd be coming back someday soon with news of a birth that, in the doctor's opinion, was not at all imminent, but with the simple naturalness of someone who talked about mares and women in the same way, the only difference being that mares weren't offered chocolate. He felt no more implication in the tragedy of that unhappy woman than what he would have felt for one of his sisters in the same condition, to wit, widowed and pregnant, a situation that the boy from Cizur had no difficulty in understanding, after what he'd seen in the war. He sat in front of the fire without taking off his overcoat and held his rifle between his knees. Sometimes his face swelled up and seemed to become big and round. His mouth split open like a red wound when he smiled. He'd made his own calculations, and even though the doctor might think that he'd counted wrong, what he'd seen his sisters go through and what he knew about female animals convinced him he was right. One night when he came back from delivering firewood to Las Cruces, he made an announcement to the doctor, in the same considered tone he would have used when talking about a calf: 'That woman's going to have her baby any day now.'

And indeed, that was what happened. No midwife would have predicted what the boy from Cizur had announced. It

was the middle of February. Rain fell in powerful gusts. The
sky showed black, the colour of stormy nights, but in this
case an unmitigated, thick blackness that not even lightning
flashes could tear. Indian ink had been spilled on the universe.
Humans had been shut up in a box of rain, in a contraption
invented by God to test his creatures' patience, and their fear.
It was one of those black nights that are recorded only in the
Bible and the sacred books, precisely the kind of black night
that only unlucky women choose for giving birth. The Bay
of Txingudi looked black, blacker than the hills on the other
side. The water was a pool of tar, as if the sea were sending a
black tide into the interior of the land. The massif of Jaizkibel
rose against a sheet of black in the night, which was black
with rain, as if it were raining tar. Nevertheless, on that night,
there was a supply of electricity. The forty-watt bulb on the
porch at Las Cruces was on, and more light could be seen in
the drawing room. Rain was falling in disoriented gusts that
came from every direction. It lashed the westward-facing windows, just as it drummed hard against the glass panels of the
kitchen door. When a nocturnal wind howls, people say it's a
'dog night'. That night was a dog night and a baby night, too.
The boy from Cizur had gone over to the villa of Las Cruces
to deliver some firewood and light the Señora's stove, or to
bring her some chocolate or some meat or whatever little supplies he was in the habit of bringing. He came back, wrapped
in his soaked overcoat. He opened the door all at once, and
the rain blew in all the way to the floor tiles in the living
room. Then he tossed back the hood of his overcoat, revealing
his red face, and shouted, 'Doctor! That woman's dying.'

The doctor turned round with a start. 'What's happening?'

'She's dying.'

The doctor sat up. 'Go back over there and put some water on to boil.'

The door closed with a crash. 'No! Come back!' the doctor shouted.

The door opened again. 'Get some towels and sheets. Tear the white sheets into strips.'

She had two months to go. That meant that her baby would be two months premature. Giving birth after a pregnancy of only seven months wasn't generally a fearful prospect, but it could be in those circumstances. And even if things were different from what he thought, even if he'd guessed wrong and the woman was keeping the secret of her own calculations and nine months had in fact passed, that didn't make the circumstances any less fearful, and the Cizur boy's shout had sufficed to announce them. The doctor didn't know why he'd told the kid to tear white sheets into strips. Births don't require bandages. He should have asked for cloths. That was a first sign of incompetence, but it was nothing to get alarmed about, and anyway, his alarm had made itself evident when the boy burst in and announced the imminent birth. The doctor hastily crossed his living room and went to his office. His leaden leg had never seemed so heavy to him as at that moment. He filled his medical bag with what he thought he'd need, namely alcohol, cortisone, aspirin, a syringe, a case with a pair of scalpels, the stethoscope from his days as an intern, a pair of forceps that could perhaps be useful, and a tin containing sterilized gauze, none of which reflected any incompetence, either, since it was the humble sum of what he had. Then he went back to fetch his cane. He had walked the several metres from the living room to his office without crutch or cane. An impulse had prompted him to haul his leg after him as if willpower alone could make it work. His step was surprisingly sure, and with a similar act of will, he thrust himself into a raincoat and opened the garden door. The wind whipped his face. He went down the path leading through the trees, skirted the low wall, and crossed the neighbouring garden, passing among the shadows of the tormented bushes, covering his head with his raincoat, holding the medical bag in his left hand, struggling with his cane as with a pivot to get himself up the slope, and finding his way by the glow of the lightbulb that was swaying on his neighbour's front porch. Severo was waiting for him and opened the door.

'She's upstairs. When I got here, there was nobody down-stairs, and I found her upstairs.'

'Is there hot water?'

'I'm heating it.'

'I'll need washbasins full of hot water.'

The house was practically in darkness. There was some light coming from the upper floor. The doctor took off his raincoat and threw it over a chair. He cast a glance upwards and began to climb the stairs, clutching his bag in one hand and mak-ing sharp sounds with his cane. His body's enormous shadow spilled out over the stairs, step by step. When he reached the top, he paused and caught his breath. The source of the light was in one of the bedrooms. And there she was, having been there, no doubt, for several hours, maybe for more than twelve hours, or maybe for a day and a half, because it had been two days since Severo had last brought firewood and food to Las Cruces, and they didn't know how often her gardener came or even if she ever let him inside. The doctor had to think of a way to make sense of her actions, to find some human reason for them. He had to think that she had wanted to give birth like that, alone, trapped in the syndrome of her accursed solitude, a condition too real and too substantiated ever to be discussed.

'Hot water!' the doctor shouted.

At that very moment, Severo entered with a steaming washbowl. The boy looked scared. He left the basin at the foot of the bed and withdrew into a corner. He'd seen three of his sisters give birth, and he'd seen some atrocities in the war, but he'd never seen a woman who wanted to have her baby alone, voluntarily alone, clinging to her solitude and to the fruit of her womb as to a piece of timber in a shipwreck. The doctor approached the bed. The woman was bathed in sweat. She was breathing forcefully, as if a weight were pressing on her lungs. When she sensed the presence of the doctor at her side, she opened her eyes. For a moment, she held the doctor's gaze without blinking, and then she closed her eyelids again. Her tight, weary breathing continued. The doctor delicately examined her. The woman had thrown the covers to one side of the bed. She was wearing a long nightdress that covered her stomach, a stomach so swollen that it seemed to have acquired a position of pre-eminence in her physiognomy, to be more important, more silently alive than the body it inhabited. The lamp on the night table was turned on. Its light was sufficient. The doctor palpated her stomach with an uncertain gesture and then abruptly withdrew his hand. The woman was clutching the bars at the head of the bed, and her whole body was shuddering. Women died in childbirth from exhaustion or haemorrhages, and the question was how long this woman's heart would be able to hold out. She had expelled the mucus plug that blocked the opening of her cervix, and the whole bed was soiled and soaked. It had doubtless been some time since she'd begun to lose fluids. Everything in the bed felt damp and cold, like a deathbed.

'A towel!' the doctor shouted.

When the boy came out of his corner and handed the doctor a towel, he delicately slipped it under the woman's body. Then he raised her nightdress and started washing her legs. Yes, she had indeed expelled her mucus plug, and her amniotic sac had broken as well, but something didn't look right. The doctor felt the perspiration running down his forehead. Now he was sweating, too. Individual cases differed, he knew that, and he thought he should stop assessing his incompetence and his fear, assume them, and hide them from the eyes of whoever could judge them; besides, nobody in that room was in any condition to notice anything of the sort. Gently but firmly manipulating his patient's belly, he set the baby in the right position. It was like making a ball turn inside a taut stomach. Once again, the woman expelled a stream of liquid and mucus and shapeless fragments of tissue.

'Hot water!'

The boy returned with another steaming washbasin in his hands. The woman's panting was no longer audible. But her shaking continued, as if she wanted to get rid of some foreign object that was occupying her body, which was in fact the case, the natural situation, the doctor thought, regaining confidence. He had no need even to open his medical bag to determine that her heart was beating like the rocker arm on a hydraulic pump, at risk of giving two or three more good strong strokes and then stopping altogether, and it would be even less necessary to bring out the scalpels and split open her womb to free it of the foreign body; birth is indeed a natural process, he thought, and in it two lives are at stake, or one life and one death, and all within the course of a few hours, as if nature placed its highest bet on the timing of a childbirth.

'Cloths! I need cloths, damn it!'

Something was beginning to come out. If the woman's heart could only hold out a few minutes longer . . . He'd forgotten the storm that was raging outside. The boy handed him another towel and a torn sheet.

'A little more. One more push,' the doctor said, certain that she was in no condition to hear him.

He had rolled up his sleeves, and the new expulsion of fluids had made his hands dripping wet. The light from the bedside lamp flickered. The baby had moved again. The doctor stopped the flow with one hand and with the other forcefully manipulated the patient's stomach. The inert form inside it seemed to turn round and settle into the right position, or at least that was what the doctor thought he felt when he risked applying pressure to her sides. Sweat rolled down his forehead. He asked Severo to wipe him off with a cloth, and the boy obeyed. For a moment, the doctor turned his eyes away from the chaos of fluids and excrement and contemplated the woman herself. Already a widow, she hadn't imagined that she could be a victim, too, and nevertheless so she was, with the special kind of victimhood that pertains only to women sacrificed in childbed, amid amorphous debris and the ejaculations of their entrails. Maybe her heart wouldn't hold out, and then her sacrifice would be resolved into the chaos of what had been a thwarted existence. The doctor thought about the cortisone in his bag. He wasn't sure whether injecting her would be the correct thing to do. His fears and his wretched, unjustified sense of incompetence played their part in the calculation, and before he could decide, a weak rasping and a new effort, made in short, monotonous, indifferent waves, drew his attention back to her womb. A suspicion had begun to form in his mind. There was something frighteningly passive about what that womb contained. The boy put his face close to the doctor's ear and murmured, 'We have to give her some air.'

'What did you say?'

'She needs air.'

The doctor made no reply, and Severo began to fan the woman with the corner of a towel. Her eyes were closed or rolled back in her head, and her undone hair lay on the pillow in a big, soaking mass, like a clump of ferns or wet seaweed. One of her hands groped the mattress beside her, as if she were looking for something, while the other still clasped one of the bars at the head of the bed. At that moment, the lamp on the night table teetered. Some minutes passed. Her shaking was intermittent, almost like that of a dying person. The doctor decided to force the issue. With one hand, he assisted her dilation, and with the other, he applied pressure to her stomach, as he had been doing for some time. His suspicions were being confirmed. There was something inert and passive in there. He couldn't perceive the slightest beating or any movement distinct from the mother's effort to eject the object inside her. Perhaps half an hour had passed since the doctor's arrival. During his long pause, he observed that a small but continuous trickle of blood had soaked the towel. Then he turned over the cloth he'd put under the woman's body to absorb the fluids that did not cease to flow out of her. The doctor took out his handkerchief and wiped his brow again. He looked at the watch he carried in his pocket. Another quarter of an hour had passed. There was no way of predicting how long a birth might take. The woman's body suffered a new contraction. Like a piston stroke, the movement expelled blood, mucus, and a kind of white drool. She also expelled a piece of the placenta. The doctor felt a sudden anguish, and cold sweat ran down his forehead. At some births, it was the custom to pray. There were ancient prayers for childbirth, but they were not what the doctor had learned in medical school. He didn't want to impose his own anguish on the woman's suffering, and he tried to calm himself with small, immediately accomplishable tasks, asking the boy for another cloth, wiping away the steady discharge of fluids, assisting the effort and tension of the womb with continuous pressure on the stomach, helping the organ to evacuate its contents. And so another fifteen minutes passed, maybe more, or maybe there was no way of measuring the length of the woman's suffering, the unremitting agony that seemed to be tearing her body apart, as if an enemy had impregnated her in order to end her life. He couldn't know if her life was on the line, but everything depended on the slow, strong beating of her heart, whose very strength was an affliction. The doctor closed his eyes for a moment. He felt the liquids from her body running over his hands. The biblical curse on woman, condemned to bringing forth children in pain, came to his mind, and that pain seemed to him unbearable, a punishment inflicted by an unjust divinity that she had not sought to bribe with prayers in the crucial instant of her life. The woman started. The lamp, its light filtered through parchment, swayed on the night table. Either God or the devil clasped her body in his fist. The doctor opened his eyes in time to see the kid from Cizur making the sign of the cross on the other side of the bed. Then the doctor found that it was absolutely necessary for him to leave the room for a moment and breathe. Wiping away the bloody flux with a towel, he asked the boy to take his place and got to his feet, leaning on the bed as he rose. He went out into the hallway, where the air was fresh and healthy. Rain beat against the windows, and the storm whistled in the roof, as if a fully rigged mast were standing up there. The downpour began to slacken a little. The air smelled like rain and nitrogen. The long hall extended into darkness. At the last turn, a mirror glinted, cutting the darkness like a knife blade. The doctor inhaled the frigid air with all his might and returned to the bedroom. The boy from Cizur welcomed his presence with relief and passed him the cloth he was holding. The doctor leaned over the bed again, kneeling on one leg and stretching out the other. His brow was dry, his mind clear, and all his attention fixed on whatever was about to happen.

Another half-hour went by. Successive waves of pain shook the woman's body, and from between her clenched teeth came a groan that was not human. Someone wanted to take away her life amid a vile flux, but the horror of that image gave rise to a moment of placidity. The woman unclenched her lips and gasped for air. She appeared to be summoning all her strength. The doctor put both hands on her stomach. Then he placed his left hand on the bulge and held it there so that the baby wouldn't get turned round again, and he slipped his right hand between her bloody thighs. Her body jerked twice, weakly, and then once again, harder and longer. Her bleeding became profuse. The doctor was sweating. He could taste his sweat, salty in his mouth.

Then came a contraction stronger than the rest, and the doctor gently received in his right hand the baby's little head, which he held up, clear of the soaked towel. Once the head was out, the rest of the body followed in two or three brief convulsions. The body was well formed, beyond doubt premature, and frighteningly inert, with something stubborn and monstrous in its passivity. Its colour was the purple of plums. It was a girl. It would have been a girl. The doctor cut the umbilical cord with a pair of forceps. Then he tried to revive the diminutive corpse. At that moment, no doubts about his competence occurred to him, no questioning of his ability to perform the operations necessary in such a situation, for he knew he had in fact performed the necessary operations, he'd followed clinical protocol without error and done nothing but assist the natural process, so that his responsibility was dissolved in the irreparable error of nature itself, an error that had preceded the delivery. These considerations didn't occur to him at that juncture, nor was there leisure for him to evaluate his skill or his clumsiness. She had lost consciousness. The doctor had no time to get out his stethoscope. He put his hand on the woman's chest and ascertained that her heart was beating. Cortisone. He wrapped the lifeless infant in the cloths that had been meant for her first nappies and thrust his hand into his bag. He let Severo take charge of the poor baby and hurriedly gave the woman a cortisone injection. After a few moments, her heart reacted again.

'Take that away,' the doctor said.

With the little package in his arms, the boy from Cizur looked disconcerted. 'Where?'

'Put it in another bedroom.'

The haemorrhage became more intense. It seemed as though all the woman's blood was going to drain out of her. The doctor remembered from medical school the two causes of women's deaths during childbirth: heart failure or loss of blood. He applied a few layers of gauze and changed the towel, dropping it onto the parquet floor at his feet, where there was a scattered heap of soiled and soaked towels. Then the flow decreased. A strong but contained surge, like a residual stream, expelled the placenta. There was further loss of blood. Not excessive. The uterus had contracted, and the capillary vessels had closed. The residual haemorrhage was light. Steps must be taken to avoid septicaemia. The doctor applied sterilized gauze again in the best way he knew how. Then he picked

up the remains of the placenta with the forceps, placed them
in a washbowl, and finished washing her. She had recovered
consciousness. Everything had happened in half an hour,
maybe three quarters of an hour, not more, perhaps not much
longer than it would take him to remember it, because the time
he'd need to recall those events wouldn't surpass the real time,
so precisely were they fixed in his memory, so incandescently
bright were his gestures and his actions, although the
remembered circumstance could be recollected and repeated,
and the time gone over again and again, until it ended up out
of proportion, with all sense of real time lost. That was what
it had been his lot to live through. That had been his penance
in the war. But the cruelty unleashed on innocents was now
falling on that mother who had proved unable to become a
mother and making her its victim, multiplying her solitude
by a solitude a thousand times more unbearable than the first,
because after a delivery with such disastrous consequences,
to be still alive was both a stroke of luck and a punishment.
The doctor gazed at the woman for a few moments. Her belly
had lost all its volume. He bent over her, passed a fresh towel
over her body, and covered her modestly with her nightdress,
as he imagined a midwife would have done. Then he covered
her with the blankets on the bed. She was still panting. Her
young body looked as though she'd survived a shipwreck and
the sea had tossed her up on some beach in the middle of the
night. He thought he should put her in another bed. There
was another one in that same room, a smaller bed against a
wall. When Severo returned to the room, the doctor asked the
boy to help him move her, but then he changed his mind. It

would be better to wait for her to regain some of her strength, better to let her rest where she was.

For the first time since he'd entered the bedroom, the doctor took stock of his surroundings. Two hunting engravings hung on the wall. An antique crucifix spread its arms above the bed. The storm had died down. Through the black window came the gentle, steady sound of the rain. He bent down to collect his bag and started to put away the instruments he'd used. When he got to his feet, he felt the ache in his leg. He'd forgotten about it. Severo approached him and murmured something in a low voice.

'What's that?'

The youth repeated his question, and the doctor replied loudly, 'You'll spend the night here. I'll come back early tomorrow morning.'

The woman opened her eyes. The doctor bent over her. She was about to ask about the baby. That was the question she had on her lips. But no wailing could be heard, not a single cry, nor was there the sound of footsteps or whispering in that silent room, and no one had handed her a small, trembling package to cradle on her bosom. The black and gentle rain provided the tragic or indifferent background music, and the woman understood that she had been delivered of a stillborn fruit; perhaps she'd understood that some time ago, but only the silence and the rain had convinced her that she wasn't mistaken. She raised her head slightly, as if she wanted to make sure of something. Her efforts had hollowed out her cheeks. Soon she let herself fall back onto the pillow. Her very sensitive ears told her that her hopes had come to an end, and when she knew this and understood it, she sealed her lips.

'I'll come back early tomorrow morning,' the doctor said.

She made no reply. The boy from Cizur placed the dead baby in a shoe box and made preparations to spend the night in the house. On the following day, he went to the cemetery with a package under his arm. Nobody asked him to do it. He offered to perform this service, because he had no guard duty that morning, and because to a certain extent, he'd grown fond of the tiny corpse he'd held in his arms. It looked as though that was going to be his tenderest memory of Hondarribia, and that his gesture would redeem the horrors in which he'd participated or which he'd witnessed in the war. He left the shoe box there, in one of the holes dug for stillborn babies, not entirely formed and not malformed either, but on the point of being formed, babies unbaptized and therefore nameless, the seraphim with oversized heads and fish eyes who cluster together in groups and go to limbo. Then the boy from Cizur walked back to Los Sauces with empty hands, with hands that were more than empty, because he didn't know what to do with them.

Some weeks passed. The unit of volunteers from Cizur received orders to move out and join the second company of the third regiment of Carlist militia, *requetés* from Navarre, which had suffered casualties at Eibar, and the signal station was transferred with the unit. From loaded troop trucks, the soldiers said their farewells and shouted, 'To Bilbao! To Bilbao!' And others sang to God and their dead in juvenile voices, for they were little past the age of innocence, and it was as if they weren't heading to the front but rather going on an excursion and leaving behind a winter too inclement and too boring. And off they went. Severo took his leave of the doctor with a rustic's plain and simple affection. The offensive against Vizcaya was being prepared. Bilbao would fall that spring. Thanks to the ruins of Irún, there was more than enough firewood to last the entire winter. But it was of no use to the doctor to remember the days and weeks that followed, when the awful night he'd lived through was already beginning to crystallize in his memory. It was of little use to him to remember the elements that were shaking around in his life back then, or to recall his bitterest emotions, or to weigh up which proportion he should assign to chance and which to his reiterated consciousness of his fault, because he didn't believe that there had been a fault, though indeed there had been misfortune, and it was the irreparable consequence of a delivery carried out in those circumstances. He couldn't deplore his incompetence or drown his memory in cognac for a whole lifetime, even though the subject of his incompetence inflamed his mind, as if he doubted the judgment of not guilty he'd rendered in the case of himself. Had he been at fault? These hands of his had assisted the woman in her childbed – that was indisputable – but nature was at least equally at fault, because nature had so dealt the cards. It didn't seem likely that much had changed in the bedroom over there at Las Cruces. Probably no one had taken the hunting engravings down from the wall. Probably no one had thrown the crucifix into the nettles by way of getting rid of Him or judged that there could have been a higher responsibility for what happened. It was possible that the beds

were still where they had always been, because the furnishings
in such houses always have more longevity than the people
who live in them. Perhaps a leak surrounded by an aureole
had appeared in the ceiling. Perhaps young Goitia, who was
so conscientiously preparing for his notarial examinations in
the former gun room, slept in a bedroom near that other bedroom. The doctor hadn't dared ask him. But back there, in his
memory, the black rain of that night had remained, and the
circle of light around the parchment-shaded lamp, and the
bloody towels littering the bedroom floor, and the rustic boy
from Cizur, holding the dead baby in his arms, gazed at the
doctor with astonished eyes over the exhausted woman's body.
She had lost a great deal of blood and her labour had taken
almost all her strength, but it was even more frightening to
contemplate her now, immersed in the silence that seemed
to have usurped her whole existence. Yet from her very grief,
from her very silence, the woman would acquire increased
strength, whereas what remained to her that night – the black
night, because there was none blacker for many years – might
not have been enough.

Four

THE WRONG WOMB

'THE DAY AFTER TOMORROW?' the old Etxarri woman asked, narrowing her eyes in incredulity.

'Yes, that's what I said,' the lawyer replied, not absolutely certain that she had understood him.

The old woman frowned. Young Goitia had entered her kitchen with the intention of asking her for a glass of water, or with some other intention, but instead he'd suddenly announced that he would be returning to Madrid the day after tomorrow. The old woman hadn't been prepared for that, and the lawyer was unable to understand the perplexity provoked by his announcement. Perhaps he should have phrased it differently. Perhaps the woman hadn't understood the meaning of his words, that is, perhaps she hadn't realized exactly which day he was talking about. He'd figured she should already know his plan, or else she should remember it, because Goitia had first announced it to her a week previously. But it was very possible that the old woman had forgotten all about it. She probably didn't live according to the calendar. In any case, the lawyer underlined his meaning: 'Tomorrow I'm going to get my books together and pack my suitcases,' he said, making packing gestures with his hands, in case the old woman still didn't want to understand him.

She pondered for a few seconds. Then she reacted with a strange show of pride that disconcerted the lawyer. 'The day after tomorrow,' she said in an oracular voice, 'the day after tomorrow, I was planning to make *bacalao*.'

'*Bacalao*?'

The old woman nodded. She'd prepared *bacalao* for him once before. It was ten-thirty in the morning, and because she planned to dust that day, she'd bound up her hair with a handkerchief tied into two tight knots. The handkerchief gave her even more of a countrified air. She passed her tongue over her gums, as though a remnant of her breakfast had remained behind. After dusting, she intended to put half a salt cod to soak. She would soak it for thirty-six hours and change the water three times. A woman of her acquaintance put her *bacalao* to soak in the toilet tank for only twenty-four hours, changing the water every hour by pulling the flush chain, but in María Antonia Etxarri's opinion, that was no way to proceed. She planned to use one of those holy cods that bear the image of Christ visible on their back skin, on the grey parchment of their scales, as on Verónica's veil. She knew that a good *bacalao* could be recognized by the way the spots on its back figured the Holy Countenance, but to avoid overwhelming the lawyer, she kept that information to herself.

'Well, in any case, I have to go back to Madrid the day after tomorrow,' Goitia concluded.

María Antonia Etxarri didn't insist. The lawyer scratched his head and left the kitchen without risking further comment. The old woman had been washing dishes, and she dried her hands on her apron. The chessboard floor tiles gleamed in the morning light, and there was a vague smell of bleach in the air. It was a sunny day, and the pots and pans hanging on the wall shone in all their glory. Backlit by the French windows, the old woman appeared transfigured for an instant. The autumn light enveloped her robust body. But that radiant-edged silhouette, practically haloed in sanctity, concealed the surprise and the affront caused by young Goitia's announcement. She hadn't imagined that the boy would stay there forever, she had even known that he'd be going before long, but the very thought filled her with a dark rancour. She considered Goitia a black-hearted ingrate for the small enthusiasm he'd shown at the prospect of *bacalao* – the lawyer hadn't postponed his trip immediately upon hearing the jubilant news that she was going to cook *bacalao* – but the source of her rancour, the reason she felt affronted, might have been deeper in origin, almost indiscernible, proceeding from the old woman's blood and entrails, as if from a very old and still unpaid debt. She moved away from the glass-panelled door, and the pale sun once again invested the floor tiles. The kitchen was illuminated with the geometrical innocence of a Flemish wood-panel painting. The old Etxarri woman opened the door of a dark room and disappeared inside it. When she re-emerged, pushing the door with an elbow, she was armed with a feather duster, various cloths, and a tin of wax polish. Then she exited the peaceful, melancholy kitchen area, passed in front of the gun room without granting the lawyer so much as a glance, and headed for the dining room. Life moved, soft and grey, among the plumes of her feather duster and glided, smooth and satiny, under the determined buffing of her polishing cloth, because that, for her, was life and dedication, and she kept glory and rancour only in her guts. And while she dusted and polished, she had songs in her ears, songs like the music of the spheres, songs from her childhood and young girlhood.

> *Ay, Miguel,*
> *Miguel, Miguel,*
> *Mikeltxu . . .*

She hadn't known anyone called Mikeltxu, but a woman who's been raped at the age of sixteen by a stranger ends up considering her rapist a kind of malicious ghost, and that ghost acquires a name, upon which falls all the bitterness and melancholy of old age. However, there was no need of any song to illustrate that María Antonia's entire life had been conditioned by that distant event, back then as well as now, the present, when the luminous, real morning blended into the ashen and no less real twilight of her existence. Nothing had a name any more. And so the songs gave a name to what she would have been unable to name otherwise. She could be seen through curtains, loaded down with her heraldic panoply: peacock feather duster, polishing cloth, and tin of wax. She could be heard singing to the quick rhythm of her cloth as she polished the furniture. Anyone would have forgotten about her after that, and the lawyer, absorbed in gathering his papers, forgot about her.

Around midday, Goitia saw the doctor coming along the asphalt road that led to the village. First he saw the doctor's hat above the garden wall. Then, where the built-up road reached half the height of the wall, he could see the doctor's head and shoulders. The lawyer hadn't moved from his study in some time. He'd spent half the morning collecting and sorting his notes. He stretched out his arms and pushed his chair back, and then he went out into the garden of Las Cruces to chat with the doctor when he opened the gate of Los Sauces.

'Good morning!'

'Good morning, my boy. You see how splendid autumn days can be,' the doctor said, describing a semicircle in the air with his cane and indicating the pale effect of the sun on the dead leaves.

'It is a very fine day.'

'Indeed.'

The doctor had taken a walk to get the stiffness out of his lower back, and he was returning with a newspaper under his arm, because he wasn't too old or too crippled to go down to the news-stand in the village and buy himself a paper. But he was breathless from the effort, and he had no desire for conversation.

'I wanted to tell you that I'm going back to Madrid the day after tomorrow,' the lawyer said.

'Ah, yes?'

'Yes. The time I've spent here has been very profitable.'

'I'm glad to hear it,' the doctor said.

The doctor slowly closed the gate. He was wearing a long raincoat and a scarf knotted under his chin. The day was clear and luminous, with one of those skies that autumn consecrates to celebrating the splendour of bare trees and dead leaves, leaving a pale veneer on the surface of things and robbing them of colour. The doctor saluted his young friend by raising his cane towards his hat. 'I'm glad to hear it,' he repeated as he went up the road to his house, on the other side of the stone wall.

'I'm going to score high on those exams,' Goitia said.

'Of course,' said the doctor, already some distance away.

Then he turned round. 'By the way, have you told old Antonia?'

'Yes, I've told her.'

'And what did she say?'

'Well, I don't think I'll be able to enjoy the *bacalao* she's planning to cook.'

'Have you ever tried it?'

'I certainly have. She served it to me two or three weeks ago.'

'You should stay for that reason alone.'

The lawyer burst out laughing. 'No, I won't do that.'

The doctor saluted with his cane again and hesitated for a few seconds. Then he shrugged his shoulders and set off towards Los Sauces. When Satan saw him approaching, he came out from among the flower boxes. It was a beautiful day, and the bare branches of the trees drew a zebra skin on the grass and the fallen leaves in the garden. That afternoon, the old Etxarri woman was moving around the kitchen, as she often did of an afternoon; but this time, perhaps, she was nervous or upset because of the lawyer's announcement, or perhaps she was agitated by some obscure project, or perhaps she simply felt shut up or about to be shut up in her solitude. The night frightened her, the autumnal night, which came on too early, reducing the hours of daylight, and was filled with new constellations, the ones that hide behind the mountains during the summer, the Ass, the Goat, the Man with the Club, and the others whose names she didn't know because she hadn't been able to interpret them. Before nightfall, she went out into the garden, and the fermented air, thick with rotting grasses and flowers, tickled her nostrils as if it were cider air, or cider gas. Then she shut herself up again. The boy would have dinner in the village. Beyond the garden of Las Cruces, she saw the lights in the doctor's house go on.

When the war passed near the Etxarri inn and left it in ruins, María Antonia went to Vera de Bidasoa and had the good fortune to be taken in by the rich man of Vera, Don Leopoldo, the King of the Belgians. At that time, Vera de Bidasoa was a village with blackened walls that had not suffered in the war, because it had offered no resistance, and the columns proceeding from Pamplona had passed through Vera without a fight on their way to the Endarlatza bridge. A garrison stayed in Vera and sent up detachments to guard the passes, watch the border with France, and maintain calm in those mountains, the same in Vera as in Elizondo, where the garrison was larger. But María Antonia Etxarri knew nothing about the course of the war. Her period was late, very late, and she didn't know whether the cause was the stress of events or the humiliation of having been raped. This hadn't happened to her with the two men she'd known before, the one who had been her boyfriend and the one who had taken advantage of her, but those men had acted with her consent, even though she wasn't certain that she'd actually desired them. In any case, she'd resigned herself to her punishment when her stepfather beat her with his belt buckle and called her *txona* and dirty whore, maybe because he hadn't dared to take advantage of her himself, and whatever had happened to her with those two men, her periods had continued to come regularly. But when three months had passed since she'd been raped in the inn, she had to recognize that she was pregnant; that was what she got out of the war. The King of the Belgians, as everyone called him, received her in his house. This was a building of two floors, with a patch of grass where a walnut tree stood. Moss and lichen and little ferns grew on the garden walls. Don Leopoldo was confined to a wheelchair, and someone pushed him to the dining room, where the girl was waiting for him. The wheels clattered over the joins in the parquet floor.

'Your parents have run away, and you can stay here until they return,' he said. 'Do you understand? They have nothing to fear. Eventually, they'll be back.'

María Antonia didn't reply. She was looking at the wheelchair, which seemed to have served another generation. It had two big wheels like bicycle wheels and two smaller wooden wheels. The King of the Belgians was grateful to her stepfather, because Don Leopoldo had suffered his embolism in the inn some days before the outbreak of the war, and the stepfather had been the first to take care of him.

He patted the girl's cheek with his right hand and then sat back in his chair again. A blanket covered his knees. The stroke had left his visage slightly askew, but his expression wasn't disagreeable. He had a high forehead and prominent cheekbones, and the mishap hadn't altered the strength of his face. A shiny, plum-coloured blotch had spread across his forehead. He was a generous, affable man, and in spite of his stiff mouth, he smiled. He cleared his throat – swallowing saliva was difficult for him – and turned to the person who had accompanied him. 'She'll share a room with the cook. This girl has suffered, and someone has to take care of her.'

'Very well.'

'Careful with the boys,' the King of the Belgians added, addressing María Antonia, for he knew what had happened to her. Someone had told him about it. Maybe he thought there was nothing else he could do. Then he turned his wheelchair round by himself and rolled away, click-clack-click over the broad pine parquet floorboards. He stopped for a moment to glance out of the window and then left the dining room. Ever since his mishap, his life had been confined to the main floor, where he'd had his bedroom installed. Outside on the patch of grass, there were three cows around the walnut tree. An old bathtub served as their water trough. That patch of lawn was no garden, and Don Leopoldo's house, for all that he was the rich man of Vera, didn't have a garden, because he was a man of industry. He had an interest in a paper factory, as well as a business in Vera and, in Irún, a big hardware store that had been looted. Years before, in what had been the garden, he had ordered the building of a warehouse for the paper factory. A convoy of two trucks loaded with military equipment was parked on the lawn with the cows. The vehicles belonged to the garrison's quartermaster corps. María Antonia Etxarri could see those trucks through the window, and she could also see them from the window of the room she shared with the cook. There were executions in Vera, too, against the walls of the cemetery. And among the atrocities that she could have recounted, there was the one concerning the two bound men whose floating bodies had appeared in the river. First they had been made to blaspheme – *I shit on Christ* – and then drowned so that they would go to hell. Or so it was said. The people who had seen the two bodies after they were fished out of the river said that their mouths were black for having dirtied the name of Christ and their heads swollen from the blows they'd received. One of the dead men was missing an earlobe. A rifle butt had squashed it, and a fish had eaten it away.

María Antonia climbed the stairs of the house behind the cook. In the big, rambling houses of Vera that she'd known, the attics were as vast as meeting rooms, with enough space for bedrooms, for storing trunks, and for a granary. The cook bent her head to avoid the big beams above the turning of the stair. María Antonia's hair barely grazed them. There were three rooms. Amid the complicated carpentry of the roof, the rest of the attic served as an attic.

When they entered the room, the cook said to María Antonia, 'This will be your bed.'

'Are there sheets and spreads?'

'There are. This house has everything, and there's no shortage of linen.'

Then the cook gave her some clothes, because she'd lost hers when she left the inn. Later, when her pregnancy became visible and her stomach was growing, she was given clothes appropriate to her condition. The cook gave her two skirts, some bed linen, and a shawl. And so María Antonia, in those difficult months, had food and clothing, and she helped in the house with whatever there was to be done and learned many good things from the cook. It was in that house that María Antonia first thought about having her own house someday, and it seems that she launched her imagination very far into the future with that thought, leaping over the years, the lustrums, and the decades, until one day she found herself the owner of Las Cruces. But back then, as always and with everything in her life, she could evoke her obscure desires only with the words of a song:

> *I want a pretty little house*
> *With flowers around it, and trees,*
> *Where you can touch the stars with your hands,*
> *Where you sleep with the sound of the sea.*

And apparently her imagination had indeed made a jump in time, past tragedies and premonitions, and come to rest in Las Cruces, under the autumn constellations, facing the sound of the tides, in the villa that was definitively hers, because Doña Isabel had bequeathed it to her. But back then, in Vera de Bidasoa, in the house of the rich man of Vera, she was still a girl who'd been raped, and she still saw shadows moving in the night. Sometimes they were soldiers coming down from the mountain passes, frozen, wrapped up in their overcoats, back from patrolling the well-patrolled frontier with France. And on other occasions, the shadows were fugitives,

men on the run, seeking the protection of the mountains and
a chance to cross the border, shadows trying to evade the other
shadows, the ones wearing overcoats, and some shepherds had
been executed for serving fugitives as guides, and some smug-
glers left over from peacetime suffered the same fate, or else
they made a fortune doing business in the war.

In any case, María Antonia looked out of the window of
her attic room, which faced north, and watched winter come.
When dawn appeared, there were icy flowers on the windowpanes. The nights spilled an offering of frost onto the roofs,
and the cold entered bodies as if it wanted to inhabit them,
like a foretaste of deathly cold, a cold all the more fearful and
unbearable for residing in the living, lingering in joints, leaving long, scarlet lines on legs and hands, and numbing fingers
with a filigree so painful that the cold seemed to be tracing
the circulation of the blood with a steel needle. The dining
room, the bedrooms on the lower floors, and the kitchen were
heated, but the cold took possession of the attic rooms. Why
was she remembering all that? Certainly not to complain. Not
even the shadow of a complaint crossed her mind. The old
Etxarri woman accommodated the cold and the winter darkness in her memory, and she was able to compensate for them
with the grateful recollection of a good fire, one of those fires
that make the blood beat in your temples, a hearth fire in the
stone fireplace of a real home. And at the time, she was an
ignorant little girl, far from an adult, and already a woman,
compelled to go to bed with a sergeant in the Carlist *requetés* who had been without his wife on the night of their first
wedding anniversary. But what she'd felt then had not been

sorrow, nor was it sorrow now. Why not? She didn't know. Sorrow has hidden forms and manifestations that pretend not to be sorrow, but they can weigh down a whole life, like a load of charcoal in the soul. And in the space between those two figures, between the pregnant young girl and the uncouth old woman, her entire existence had transpired, so that the two were linked only by memory. But as for the intervening years, considering that tragedy and suffering and premonitions are the very school of life, the old Etxarri woman couldn't complain. She'd had her part of suffering, just as the cows had their portion of grass, and from it they took their nourishment, since that was what strong girls and healthy cows had to do. She'd known other winters before that one. There was a washbowl filled with water in the room, and in the morning it was covered with a thin sheet of ice, but no one in that house experienced the misery of the war.

There was no lack of blankets. The cook slept in the same room, under three blankets. She was a big, white woman, with hands like her body, big and white. She was a good cook. She knew about cooking, and she knew about other things as well, and before María Antonia's stomach started to show, the cook had suggested to her a poultice of abortifacient herbs. She also thought that something could be accomplished with a knitting needle. All that awakened dark fears in María Antonia, not fear associated with inducing an abortion — she wasn't much tempted by that idea — but the even greater fear that the baby she was carrying in her womb would be a monster, with a black mouth and a swollen head like the corpses that had turned up in the river, because of having been conceived in the greatest evil that could be inflicted on a girl, evil that was bound to have consequences. As for an abortion, she could never do such a thing, it was beyond her capacity, and even if she had to give birth on the threshold of the church, she would give birth, because that was her instinct. She felt strong where others would have felt weak, and before she went to sleep, she would gather her forces and curl up, knees touching elbows and fists clenched under her chin, protecting her stomach, and then she would stare at the window with wide-open eyes, contemplating the sumptuous blue of the night. Those were terrible, icy nights. She slept under two blankets. The cook's great bulk lay in the other bed, snoring away. From her, María Antonia learned how to prepare stews and also how to choose the best vegetables. That house lacked for nothing during the war. The cook's white, chubby hands, the ones that had offered her herb poultices and knitting needles, played with potatoes and fashioned big round loaves of bread. Having first severed a chicken's crest in order to bleed it, she'd held it under one arm and finished it off by smothering it in her other fist. And while they were in the kitchen, and since María Antonia's stomach was getting heavy, the cook whispered to her about the greater evils that it had been María Antonia's good fortune to escape.

'You're lucky you didn't wind up a soldiers' whore in a tent brothel,' the cook said.

The girl made no reply.

'Do you hear what I'm saying?'

María Antonia nodded. The cook pressed the chicken, whose wings were still flapping, more tightly under her arm.

Some Moroccan units, which had been among those repulsed in the attack on San Marcial, had spent a little time in the village before being relieved by fresh troops. Some even more frightening thoughts occurred to the cook. The light from the fire lit up her hair.

'Do you know where Moors stick it in women? In both holes.'

'Is that true?'

'Of course it's true.'

María Antonia shivered. After the experiences she'd had in the course of her brief existence, she could imagine that she'd escaped some atrocious things. The cook lifted the lifeless chicken by its long neck, holding it high, like a trophy, gave it to María Antonia to pluck, and then went out to the coop for another chicken. María Antonia held the dead chicken between her legs and began to pluck it. There was a bucket filled with hot water at her side. From time to time, she dipped the chicken in the hot water to loosen the quills of its feathers and make plucking it easier. In the house of the King of the Belgians, food was never in short supply. Two chickens were to be cooked for Christmas Day. By María Antonia's reckoning, five months had passed since the events, that is, since that detachment of troops had arrived at the inn, and with them the sergeant who had raped her. And four months had passed since she'd first come to the house in Vera, after wandering the highway – which was crammed with soldiers moving up to the front – for an entire month, on foot and alone. And in those five months, her stomach had grown round and strong, a pregnant girl's healthy belly, on which she rested the chicken she was now plucking. A fire was burning in the hearth. The kitchen fire had also been lit. The cast-iron back of the fireplace sent out blue and orange flashes. Water was boiling on the stove. There were other servants in the house, including two women of the cook's age and a man who had neither been called up by the army nor run away from it. But María Antonia found herself alone in the kitchen at that moment, assiduously yanking out a chicken's feathers. The cook came in from the yard, holding the second victim by the legs. The animal flapped its wings desperately. This chicken, like the first, had red feathers. Its open eye, round and bright, was the colour of wine, and its legs were yellow and shiny, a sign of good health. The cook smiled with the ludic, ferocious expression of a gladiator. So is the existence of animals and people, too, María Antonia thought, so it is and so it ends, cut off by a blade or by sickness, whether that existence has been long or short, and the old Etxarri woman, thinking about what the girl she once was had been thinking, could not but approve her thoughts. Nor could she recall, as her memory scanned the past, any other kitchen as big as that one was, none so luminous and ardent by the hearth, or so cool and gloomy in the depths of the pantry, abounding in pots and casseroles, well stocked, with a stone floor, with white tiles above a granite sink, a wooden draining rack where plates and dishes were lined up like books in a library, and a small iron tank, the house's central source of hot water, which was heated in pipes in the cast-iron stove and collected in the tank, and a calendar with a hunting scene on the wall, and under the print a little cardboard box for the needles and spools of thread used to sew together stuffed meat rolls, and the calendar page, which in her memory always indicated the month of December 1936. The cook clamped the chicken under her arm just as she'd held the previous chicken, and in order to bleed it, she sliced off its crest with a knife, as if she were shaving its head. Then she clamped its beak in her fist to smother it. The animal beat its wings even more violently. María Antonia turned away her eyes and concentrated on her task. She bent her head over both her bulging stomach and the chicken she was plucking, over the two things occupying her lap, the chicken and her swollen belly, as if they were the same thing or the same destiny, and she occupied her mind by thinking that her life would be more miserable than the lives of those chickens if she had wound up in a tent brothel, where Moors would be having their atrocious way with her. But she would have liked to explain the essential thing, and she figured that nobody in the house would be interested in hearing it. The essential thing was to sense what she was carrying in her womb, to sense how it was suspended inside her. It was something strong, something at once blind and sensitive, and it made her feel the way a robust tree might feel just before spring, assuming that a tree could have female feelings, which was not, to María Antonia's way of thinking, a sure thing. Nevertheless, she could be certain that her swollen belly contained part of her and part of the anonymous sergeant who had made her pregnant, but it was more — almost totally — a part of her, even though, during the course of the past five months, she hadn't forgotten the face of the man who'd impregnated her or the circumstances in which her impregnation had taken place.

Don Leopoldo, the King of the Belgians, sent for her. He was in the living room, which he rarely left. The girl laid her task aside, washed her hands in the pail of tepid water, and dried them on her apron. The kitchen door opened onto the yard and the field behind the house. The living and dining rooms were above the kitchen on the main floor, occupying it entirely except for the room that Don Leopoldo had transformed into a bedroom after his mishap. Two balconies looked out onto the village street. The windows on the other side looked out over fields that sloped down to the river. María Antonia climbed up the flight of stairs, holding her apron with both hands. She'd thought that climbing any flight of stairs to where a man was waiting for her was a sure sign that she was going to be raped, in spite of the state she was in, but she was mistaken, and the King of the Belgians, rich man though he was, had never imagined doing that, nor was he in any condition to try, and he had taken her into his home only out of pity and compassion. According to the cook, the King of the Belgians had given himself over to vice. He would send for one of the serving girls and make her urinate in front of him. He would require her to lift her skirt and squat down and urinate in a chamber pot in front of him. The cook said that the King of the Belgians, impotent in his wheelchair, had developed vices. Don Leopoldo was rich, and he could do whatever he wanted to. You could never know what strange vices men would develop, said the cook, and María Antonia had listened to her with incredulous ears. But the reason for her summons was nothing like that. María Antonia went up to where Don Leopoldo was, in fear that he would order her to urinate. At first glance, she saw that there was no chamber pot standing ready, and her distress disappeared. The dining room occupied approximately the same amount of space as the kitchen. It was almost bare of furniture, so that Don Leopoldo could move about freely in his wheelchair. Before entering the room, María Antonia could hear the clicking of the wheels on the parquet. Don Leopoldo wasn't alone. He was attended by one of the servant girls, who was in charge of housecleaning. Another person, a relative, had been pushing the wheelchair and now stood beside it. María Antonia stopped in the doorway, and Don Leopoldo asked her to come in. He'd called her to tell her something, not to amuse himself.

'Your stepfather has returned to the inn, or to what's left of the inn. Do you want to go back there to be with him, or would you rather stay here?'

'I'd rather stay here.'

'It can't be long before your mother joins him.'

'I'd rather stay here,' the girl repeated.

'Very well,' said the King of the Belgians, and then, turning to his companion: 'What did I tell you?'

Don Leopoldo's relative shrugged his shoulders.

'Very well,' the King of the Belgians repeated.

The servant girl who did the cleaning turned to María Antonia and smiled. Don Leopoldo asked to be moved nearer the window, and his relative pushed the wheelchair.

'Come closer,' said Don Leopoldo, making a gesture with his hand.

María Antonia stepped closer to him. The long, gleaming boards of the parquet floor were outlined with great precision.

The vinaceous stain on Don Leopoldo's forehead seemed to have grown, and its colour had a satiny sheen. The King of the Belgians wished to place his hand on María Antonia's stomach, and the girl consented, not that she would have thought of objecting to his gesture, because there was no violence or wicked intention in it; on the contrary, it was a demonstration of compassion and affection. The King of the Belgians remained silent for a moment, palpating her bulging stomach, and then he withdrew his hand.

'It seems to me that you've got a fine baby boy in there,' prophesied the King of the Belgians, with the broad, twisted smile that the hemiplegia of his face allowed. 'How about you, what do you think?'

'Whatever you say, Don Leopoldo,' the girl said.

'Did you hear that?' said Don Leopoldo, amused by her reply and turning his stiff face to his attendant. 'Whatever I say!'

The relative, who was standing beside the wheelchair, grew impatient. 'Come on, leave the girl alone. She'll learn what her baby is soon enough.'

'I have nothing to do with it,' said the King of the Belgians. 'But it will be a boy.'

Then he lifted the blanket that covered his legs and thrust his hand into his pocket. His other hand appeared to be made of wood, like the two small wheels of his chair. He drew out a coin and handed it to the girl. 'Take it. It's your Christmas bonus. It will bring good fortune to the baby boy you're carrying inside.'

'Thank you, Don Leopoldo,' María Antonia said, bringing her hands out from under her apron to receive the peseta. There was a mirror over the sideboard, and she saw herself reflected in it, with the bulge in her stomach and the peseta in her hand, and with a humble glow around her silhouette from the light entering through the window, and she wasn't ashamed of having hastened to accept the coin. There was no shame in that. The door of the converted room that was now Don Leopoldo's bedroom stood open, and the radio could be heard. The war seemed very far, but it wasn't far. María Antonia didn't know if that peseta would prove useful to her during the war or after the war, but in any case, there was no shame in taking the coin and clutching it in her fist and murmuring thanks and feeling her swollen belly with a certain satisfaction.

'Now you can go back to the kitchen,' said the King of the Belgians. 'When your baby comes, someone here will take care of you.'

María Antonia left the dining room. She closed the door behind her and returned to the kitchen with her Christmas bonus. She was satisfied, and she said nothing to the cook. It was possible that the cook got a Christmas bonus double or triple the girl's – that is, a bonus of two or three pesetas – and old María Antonia Etxarri couldn't help smiling at the thought of what the peseta in her fist had meant back then to young María Antonia, the child she had been, above all considering that at the end of her years and her life, when many a calendar leaf had been torn off and cast away, the old Etxarri

woman could pride herself on having inherited a villa and on
having eighteen million pesetas in the bank. But now she was
crying. Now tears welled up in her eyes at the thought of what
that had been like, all of it, the terrible years, the terrible days,
the nights of fright and frost, and tears also welled up when
she remembered the Christmas bonus. A peseta was a lot of
money, and a coin so valuable was rarely seen in a young girl's
hand. The King of the Belgians, half paraplegic, or consider-
ably handicapped by his stroke, continued to be the rich man
of Vera. It was said that he gave out fifty pesetas in Christmas
bonuses. The war had not changed his generosity in any way,
and it's possible that the course of events even prompted him
to make a show of his largesse. With that peseta in hand, the
girl could go on carrying the bulge in her abdomen with complete confidence. She plucked chickens. It would have been
another thing entirely to be obliged to earn the peseta or to do
dirty work for it in some brothel.

Then four more months passed, and she gave birth to her
child. It was so easy that she could have done it standing up.
The young mother's labour was attended by the cook, who
had expertise in this area as well. In those days, the radio
never stopped broadcasting news. Bilbao fell around the
middle or end of April, or later that spring. After palpating
María Antonia's belly, Don Leopoldo had assured her that
the baby inside her would be a boy, but although he was
the rich man of Vera, the fact didn't make him a prophet,
and the baby turned out to be a girl. Around that time, the
nationalist troops that entered Bilbao celebrated a Te Deum
in the basilica of Begoña. Don Leopoldo heard the service

on the radio and wanted the little girl who had been born in his house to be named Begoña. But María Antonia Etxarri thought differently, and she called her baby Verónica. That was the name of the woman who wiped Christ's face. María Antonia thought Verónica a fine name for a girl.

A thick fog came down from the mountains on those spring mornings. It seemed as though the clouds that settled on the mountain crests were torn to shreds by the beech forests. All day long, the village was a raft afloat in fog, although up above the mountains, the sky was blue. In the clearings of the woods, where once snow had lain, patches of rock appeared, cleansed and gleaming like quartz. It was a gloomy, rainy spring. And the wood pigeons, who knew no borders, were arriving from the north. María Antonia had always heard that babies born in springtime were lucky, because mothers' breasts gave more milk in the spring, and it appeared that the saying was true. Her breasts seemed to contain several litres of milk. The cook compared María Antonia's breasts with her own. The cook's breasts had suckled two sons. She therefore knew what it was to have milk, and she acknowledged that María Antonia had at least as much milk as she'd had. On this account, there was no danger. Both women felt the rural pride in bountiful breasts and the ancient fear of flaccid breasts and babies dead of malnutrition.

María Antonia's stepfather had returned to the Etxarri inn and begun to repair the extensive damage. María Antonia's mother hadn't returned; but after wandering in the mountains for several months, the cows, with the exception of a female calf requisitioned by the soldiers, had come back. For her part, María Antonia had no intention of returning to the inn. It would become a prosperous business again when the war ended, or rather, when the war was only a memory, but María Antonia did not envision that future and so had no wish to go back to Etxarri's. One day, the King of the Belgians summoned her again. Had the King of the Belgians summoned her to commit some dissolute act, such as those that were rumoured among the staff and recounted by the cook, that would have been terrible, but it wasn't the case this time, either. The baby was now three months old. The cook regularly felt María Antonia's breasts to be sure that she had abundant milk. Don Leopoldo wanted to speak to her about her future and that of her child. He was the rich man of Vera, and in the midst of war, he knew what the future would hold. Once again, he summoned her to the dining room. Don Leopoldo was alone. María Antonia stood still for a moment in the doorway. Then she stepped into the room with the baby in her arms and walked over the long pinewood boards of the parquet floor as if she were gliding, and the parquet didn't creak. She passed the sideboard without looking towards the mirror that hung above it. Then she stopped and waited for Don Leopoldo to speak. The King of the Belgians made a sign with his hand and said, 'Come closer. Are you afraid?'

'No, I'm not afraid,' said the girl, cradling her infant in her arms.

'You don't want to go back to the inn, right?'

'No, sir, I don't.'

'In that case, there's something I can do for you.'

María Antonia remained silent. And little did she imagine that something more important than her own life, something that would affect both her life and her baby's life, was at stake in that long, sombre room, with windows that looked out on fog, nor could she have conceived the debt her life owed that man's compassion, or what that man was gaining in exchange for his compassion, if indeed compassion was involved, because the child she held in her arms was a capital asset, the interest on which María Antonia hadn't understood, and which this man's decision would make her understand. María Antonia gently rocked her sleeping child in her arms. Don Leopoldo wanted to see the baby. The King of the Belgians rolled his chair near them. He leaned forward and pushed aside the mantilla that covered the infant's face. She was already three months old, a robust little girl with very white skin, perhaps because of María Antonia's good milk, the best the child could have had, according to the cook. Her eyes were brownish under a thin grey glaze, and there was a certain golden sparkle in her eyelashes. Her tiny finger- and toenails were bright and hard, a sign of good health and firmness of character, according to the cook. Her nascent eyebrows were like two tiny strips of down above her sleeping eyes. Her first growth of hair had been cut so that it would grow out in greater abundance. María Antonia thought the child looked like her, but the cook found unfamiliar features in the little face. The King of the Belgians grunted. She looks like a hungry little piglet, he declared. Then he said, 'You're going to go to Hondarribia. You'll be a servant in Isabel Cruces's house. Do you understand what I'm telling you?'

María Antonia moved her head. She'd thought that someday she would have to leave the house in Vera, maybe when
the war was over, maybe if other circumstances required her
to leave, and though the war hadn't ended yet, nor was it
known whether in fact it would ever end, that made no difference, because the circumstances that had arisen, whatever
they were, could be a good opportunity for her. She still had
childish imaginings, and she remembered a song that had
often given her food for thought. *She wanted to live in a house
where you could reach the stars and sleep with the sound of the
sea.* Something of her fantasy was visible in her face. The King
of the Belgians, sitting in his wheelchair, looked at her with
surprise, as if he'd read her thoughts.

'Do you understand what I said?'

'Yes, sir.'

'It doesn't matter whether you understand me or not,' said
the King of the Belgians a little sceptically. He looked with
curiosity at the girl, as if some strange ambition he couldn't
discover might give itself away. 'In any case, you'll be going
into service at Las Cruces,' he concluded.

María Antonia had to visit the Etxarri inn so that her stepfather could see the baby. From the inn she would go to the
villa of Las Cruces, where she was expected. After what had
happened, her stepfather naturally didn't call her a tramp
and a slut, but she wasn't needed in the inn, especially with
a baby, and everyone was glad to see her go into service.
Much had to be done so that years later, after the war was over,
the Etxarri inn might become a prosperous business. María
Antonia never missed the place. When nights were foggy and

stormy, it wasn't possible to touch the stars from the villa of Las Cruces. But one always fell asleep in that house to the dull, heavy sound of high tide.

One of the King of the Belgians' relatives took María Antonia and the child to Hondarribia, where Isabel, who had been advised of her arrival days before, was waiting for her. María Antonia had gathered together all her clothes. She'd acquired some things in Vera, the cook had given her others, and there were a few items she'd picked up from the inn. She put them all into an expandable leather suitcase that was in the attic and had belonged to some traveller of days gone by. Everything fitted into that suitcase. The man who was related to the King of the Belgians didn't utter a word for the entire length of the trip. When they reached the villa of Las Cruces, the relative drove the car through the gate and into the garden, stopped in front of the porch, and told María Antonia to walk to the back of the house and go in by the kitchen door. María Antonia obeyed. She went round the house, entered by the kitchen door, and waited, standing in the kitchen with the child in her arms. It was a fine kitchen. It had a good, modern sink and good larders, but no servants had ever worked there. It was a white, cold place, with glints of aluminium and brass. There was a coal stove and an electric stove with two burners. María Antonia's eye was the eye of an expert. Something made her think that this kitchen could bring bad luck, but maybe she was mistaken, and the contrary could be the case as well, that is, the kitchen could contain both bad luck and its antidote,

as can happen in a health centre or a clinic. After some time
passed, she was called into the drawing room and found herself face-to-face with the mistress of the house. And it's possible that, at that moment, an unknown element was added
to the girl's impression that there hadn't been any domestic
help in the villa, an additional, precise factor that wasn't abandonment or slovenliness or the strange feeling of violation or
punishment that seemed to pervade every corner like a thin,
cold sigh. Isabel looked the way flowers look when they've
been exposed to a winter frost. Not that María Antonia could
perceive this, except through the intuition of what abandonment and violation had signified in her own experience. But
standing in the drawing room, barely past the threshold and
the leaded glass doors, in front of the woman who was waiting for her wearing a blue housecoat and blue slippers, with
her hair caught up in a blue ribbon and her hands folded as if
she were praying, in front of that woman waiting for her with
the person related to the King of the Belgians, María Antonia
understood that something graver than an abandonment had
taken place in that house. Once again, in the first moments
of silence, she felt incapable of understanding what it had
been. Then a sob came from the baby. The mantilla covered
her face, but her tiny hands emerged from the folds like two
extremities with independent lives. Isabel insisted that María
Antonia come closer. When she greeted the girl, the timbre of
her voice was strangely pure and emotional.

'So you are María Antonia?'

'Yes, Señora.'

'I pictured you older. How old are you?'

'Seventeen.'

'Seventeen,' Isabel repeated softly and absently, as if she remembered some happy event associated with that time of life. Then she returned to the present and smiled. Isabel was more than eight years older than the girl who was entering her service, but their difference in age was cancelled out by the hard, laborious young years that had marked María Antonia's features and reddened her cheeks, while Isabel's young years had modelled her face, despite her anguish, in the pale porcelain befitting a young lady. 'Have you brought anything else?' Isabel added, looking at the bundle that María Antonia was rocking in her arms and trying to soothe.

'I have a suitcase.'

'Very good. You can go and fetch it.'

The leather suitcase was still in the King of the Belgians' relative's car. There was a moment of hesitation. The girl stood with the bundled infant in her arms and didn't know where she could put it. She peered around, searching for a suitable spot, feeling stupid and uncomfortable. She didn't know if she should leave the baby in the drawing room the way one would leave a fragile little package, or if she should look for a place in the kitchen. At that moment, Isabel stepped forward, held out her arms, and said, 'I'll keep the child.'

María Antonia handed her the baby, and the Señora received it with infinite tenderness, with inexpert hands, with extreme caution. She stepped away to a window, cradling the bundle in her arms and moving aside the mantilla that covered the infant's face. 'I'll keep Verónica while you go and collect your bag,' she said, turning to face the window, and before María

Antonia went out, she felt flattered that the Señora knew her daughter's name. The drawing room was in semi-darkness. When Isabel moved aside the mantilla and uncovered the baby's face, she gazed at it as if she were examining some precious merchandise that she had just received and that she was prepared to take charge of, always provided that it was undamaged, but her gaze was not without tenderness and not without expectation, as if the precious merchandise had occupied her thoughts for many an hour. When María Antonia returned with the suitcase, Isabel had not moved from her place at the window. In the soft light, her blue housecoat took on a satiny sheen. The baby had stopped crying, like Moses in the arms of Pharaoh's daughter. Don Leopoldo's relative had lit a cigarette and was sitting in an armchair with his legs crossed. For a few minutes, nobody noticed María Antonia's return. Finally, Isabel turned her head and saw that the girl was standing there.

'Come with me. I'll show you your room.'

The two women left the drawing room. Isabel, with the baby still in her arms, went ahead, followed by María Antonia, carrying the suitcase that contained all her belongings. The servant's room, located next to the kitchen, featured a white lacquer wardrobe and an iron bed, bigger and clearly more comfortable than the attic bed in Vera. This one had a thick mattress covered with a red bedspread. At the head of the bed, framed under glass, hung a coloured print of the Virgin of Guadeloupe, the patron saint of the village. A blood-red pinstripe ran through the green-and-salmon-coloured braids of the wallpaper. It was a cosy room, and María Antonia immediately felt that it was, beyond a doubt, the place where her good luck would begin, in spite of the cold and the damp air. The window opened onto the mountain, not the sea, but that didn't bother her. The toilet facilities were modern, that is, as modern as toilet facilities could be in those days, and certainly more modern than anything María Antonia had ever seen, as comfortable-looking, in their way, as the bed, as well provided with handy little white lacquer shelves as the wardrobe, and completely covered with tiles, with a mirror and a light above the mirror; it was a bathroom better than those she'd used in the inn and in the big house in Vera de Bidasoa, and in any case better than any bathroom she would have ever imagined having at her disposal. That was important, and the toilet augured a better future than the white china chamber pots in the attic of the big house in Vera and the washbasin where the water would sometimes freeze, not to mention the possibility that Don Leopoldo would someday choose to indulge his dissolute proclivities at her expense. María Antonia put her suitcase down on the floor.

'Do you like it?'

'Yes, Señora.'

'I'm sure you'll be comfortable here,' said Isabel. 'You'll find it very tranquil.' Then, with a strange, mad look on her face, she added, 'There are no men here.'

Still carrying the baby, Isabel walked out of the room, leaving María Antonia to unpack the few things she'd brought, which included her own clothes and some clothing for the baby. While she was putting them away in the wardrobe, she heard an automobile horn and the sound of an engine. The

man related to the King of the Belgians was leaving. Isabel
stayed in the drawing room with the child. Then she went
back to the servant's room, because the baby had started crying again.

'She must be hungry,' María Antonia said.

Both women went into the kitchen. María Antonia sat in
a wooden chair, unbuttoned her cardigan and the top two
buttons of her shirt, revealing her white bosom with its map
of blue veins, and took out her teat, as frankly and simply as
if she were opening a pantry. The baby changed hands. María
Antonia gave her a dark nipple to suckle. Isabel stood nearby
expectantly, as if she'd turned over the infant to its wet nurse.
Maybe it was in this ordinary, banal, almost wordless way that
everything happened. Maybe there was no distrust, on either
side, right from the start. One could imagine no simpler, more
natural movement, one woman handing the bundled infant
to the other, and the other receiving the bundle in her arms,
as if the women had established a pact between them, and
the functions corresponding to each had been agreed upon.
Or maybe from the moment María Antonia stepped inside,
the two women, without considering any other possibility,
had mutually acknowledged that the bundle belonged to both
of them, as if by a previously negotiated arrangement, since
in that house a maid was needed and a baby coveted, with
equal urgency. Because on one side, there was covetousness
and yearning for motherhood and frustrated motherhood,
and on the other, naïveté and a hint of suspicion, enough
to prevent her from understanding what was paralysing the
young Señora and making her stand by expectantly while

she, María Antonia, suckled her baby. And while the baby fed, gripping the girl's dark nipple, Isabel could neither step away nor even move; her arms were suddenly empty, and she could only contemplate that most profound and essential act of maternity without being able to resign herself to it, gazing not with curiosity or tenderness, but with barely dissimulated covetousness and yearning, maybe because, contrary to what her simple gestures might imply, she was most deeply and bitterly moved, and her perturbation, however she managed to control it, could betray itself only through her eyes. María Antonia held the child away for a moment before giving her the breast again.

'Is she cutting teeth?'

'It's too early for her to be cutting teeth,' said María Antonia, without dwelling on the Señora's ignorance. 'But she has hard gums, and she bites my nipples.'

While the baby kneaded her breast again with tiny but already well-formed hands, the girl sat up straight in the chair. The rounded, pearly white flesh of her bosom seemed to illuminate her face. At her side, Isabel remained silent. There was a special dignity in that situation, whatever the end of the brand-new relationship might be. Isabel had known the baby's name, Verónica, for weeks, because she'd been informed of it at the time when she'd learned that María Antonia would be coming to serve in her house, and as she registered that long, beautiful name, rich in its deployment of vowels, lovely as a sheet of copper, a process of appropriation had begun deep in her heart. It would have been intelligent to think that the spider's stratagem had been put in place, or that Isabel was

moving towards the satisfaction of her desires by following
the dog's curve, that line which apparently goes straight to
its goal but which nevertheless describes, through imperceptible lateral movements towards immediate emanations and
scents, a trajectory that doesn't confirm its objective. And the
scent came from the milk that hadn't flowed from her breasts.
She had bound her breasts so that the milk wouldn't rise in
them, and now she felt her body suffocated by the same op-
pression. It seemed that all the anguish of her solitude and
her frustrated maternity had converged in that spot. For a
few minutes, in the almost mystical silence that enveloped the
scene, Isabel began to feel that an irretrievable part of her life
was being left behind. Fate had branded her existence with
fire and sowed salt in her bowels, and that same fate, which
had toyed with her love and her instincts as with a palette of
garish colours, now placed before her eyes a gentle and tem-
perate scene of ordinary motherhood, as if taking pity on her,
or perhaps so that she might see what she could still reach by
another road, or perhaps to suggest to a tortured, sceptical
heart, anticipating a barren life, the possibility of salvation.
When María Antonia finished suckling Verónica, she lifted
the infant from her breast and moved her to the other side. A
thread of milk ran down from the corner of the baby's mouth,
and the girl wiped it away with a handkerchief. She wanted
to cover her breast, but she couldn't pull her shirt together
while holding the baby. There followed another moment
of hesitation, an uncertain instant in which Isabel held out
her arms and María Antonia, as if she found that gesture of
help natural and kind, handed over the child again, perhaps

because of the Señora's almost supplicant attitude, or because
of an immediate impulse to obey. Probably neither of the two
women had a premonition of what those gestures entailed,
what concessions they implied, what mutual pact. Neither
of them had the clear-sightedness necessary to understand it,
but then again, the situation could also be interpreted differently, and we might entertain the possibility that neither
the act of handing over nor the act of acceptance was inno-
cent. Perhaps each of the two women cherished projects that
would have turned out to be complementary, had they been
compared, but neither of them could have confessed to having such projects. It would have been risky to draw conclu-
sions and surmise that the baby girl no longer belonged to
her natural mother. But if that wasn't the case, and presuming
that life lets itself be guided by spontaneous gestures, bland
or unimportant, we could imagine that something had crystallized there, one of those elemental gestures on which the
course of a destiny can depend. Isabel took the baby in her
arms again. María Antonia covered her breast and buttoned
her shirt and her cardigan. Both women remained silent for a
moment in the cold and sterile solitude of the kitchen. María
Antonia seemed to have turned over her daughter to the common patrimony of the house where she had gone into service.
With a hitherto unseen expression between voracious and domestic, Isabel rocked the baby in her arms. Then she moved
away, whispering affectionate words. She looked satisfied, as
if everything had been worked out in advance, and that might
have been the most accurate conjecture, although it would be
impossible to demonstrate.

'Verónica, eh? They couldn't have picked a better name for you.'

María Antonia finished installing herself in her dominions. The domestic service in the house became organized, which meant that pots started boiling in the kitchen again, and María Antonia was able to put into practice what she had learned from the cook in Vera, in the King of the Belgians' house. Over the course of the years, the old Etxarri woman had washed a lot of plates, had witnessed the arrival of electrical appliances, and had seen her room receive new wallpaper twice, prior to being painted cream and then blue, which was its present colour; but back then, everything seemed to have remained immobile for an indefinite period of time, perhaps the suspended time of the country at war. From her months in Vera de Bidasoa, in the house of the King of the Belgians, María Antonia Etxarri had kept certain superstitions and remembered some pieces of advice. She could see the large kitchen in the great, rambling house in Vera, with its stone floor, and the cook sacrificing the Christmas chickens. María Antonia's cheeks were still hot from the glowing embers of that winter's fires. She would have wished to stretch out her hands to the fireplace again and feel the weight of her pregnant stomach again and let the fire warm the blood of her lost innocence again, and the blood she shared with the child inside her, but even if she'd known how to read the future in birds' entrails, and even if the cook, with all her knowledge, had interpreted them for her, she wouldn't have known how to express it. A few weeks after María Antonia Etxarri's arrival at Las Cruces, Isabel called Doctor Castro and asked him to come and examine the baby. In Vera, the cook had said it was bad luck to have a doctor for a neighbour, because that meant you were next door to misfortune. Furthermore, it was equally bad luck to cross paths with a cripple, because cripples are heralds of twisted destinies. Chance, however, had so arranged things that the neighbour of the house where María Antonia Etxarri was going into service was a crippled doctor, and her first sight of the owner of Los Sauces struck fear into her heart. He was like a storm cloud, a menace looming over the entire house. But even though the old Etxarri woman had retained her suspicion of him over the years, she had to concede, for all practical purposes, that Doctor Castro, a physician and a cripple, shared the same ambiguity as the number thirteen, or black cats, and as such could be a harbinger either of bad luck or of good luck; and it had been her lot, fortunately, to find in him an instance of the second possibility.

The spring air, clean and cold, got under the doctor's raincoat, making its tails billow, swelling its shoulders, and giving him an aspect somewhere between ghostly and grotesque. The raincoat had deep openings under the arms. That had been a popular fashion many years previously, for reasons of hygiene or for greater ease of movement. It was a raincoat from the old days, one of those articles of clothing that survive a man, with big square pockets, a felt lining, and a narrow, round collar fastened with a leather button practically under the Adam's apple. But the wind was coming in through the underarm openings, the raincoat was inflating like a balloon, and the doctor struggled to keep his balance, bracing himself on his cane. It was the early morning bluster, which precedes the strong north-west winds. The view spread out before him, displaying all the shades of green in the thin morning mist and exhibiting the grey-blue or steel-grey watercolour of the sea. Currents rippled the surface, tracing roads on the water, and one could imagine them as roads to nowhere, uncertain, capricious roads that no man could travel, much less a crippled man, the doctor thought resignedly, unequipped for walking on water, not to mention the leg he dragged around like the dead weight of age. Sometimes he set up his telescope on the terrace so that he could watch the ships entering or leaving the Bay of Txingudi or gaze at the cottages and summerhouses on the French shore. The estuary of the Bidasoa was the river Lethe, the river of forgetfulness. The Txingudi was the lagoon of the Styx, which leads to the country of the dead, and that country was the ocean, delicate and most beautiful in its immensity, as placid and powerful as a giant demonstrating his tenderness, its hue barely separated from the hue of the sky by an imperceptible line of light. The rising and falling of the tides, like an astronomical clock, marked the passage of Time. Through the telescope, the view with its miniature details evoked a landscape enclosed in a bottle. If songs had nourished María Antonia Etxarri's imagination in the Las Cruces villa, the imagination of the doctor in Los Sauces turned to more elaborate representations. A man had to open up his imagination in order to feel trapped in Time as in the belly of a whale, whose guts, phosphorescent in the night, were all he could contemplate. Memory acted like a telescope, too, in its way. The doctor had scrutinized distant scenes, figures as old as his raincoat, singular miniatures trapped behind the clear, hard glass of memory, sometimes fragmented, as though seen through the mosaic of a frosted pane, and at other times cut and polished with precision. If set up on the Las Cruces side, the telescope could, with its monstrous avidity, enter a garden scene, or focus on hands putting balls of yarn into a basket, or on the surprising face of a baby no one, least of all the doctor, would have expected to see there; and that was the avidity of memory, always eager to satisfy its need for reliving what has been lived through and for raising to its insatiable mouth a tea-soaked madeleine.

Events had been too sordid and too cruel. Life itself had taken on a purple cast, like the tunics worn by the mad. A great silence and a great calm reigned over the memory of that time, as if Isabel's stillbirth had ushered in a period yet more horrifying because of how deep it was, and how silent. One had to lean over the well of silence and ponder the effect of those two absences, the lost love and the stillborn fruit, in order to be able to imagine the sorrowful nostalgia of having been, so briefly, a wife and a mother. Bilbao fell that spring. Isabel's parents could join her at last. Many bridges had been destroyed. Rubble blocked the streets of Durango. Highways passed through devastated towns and villages, and on those roads, columns of prisoners and troops were moving, either towards the new front or towards the rear. Such was the gigantic whirlpool of events, whose axis of rotation kept shifting. And despite everything, in that corner of the landscape, facing the estuary, the river, and the sea, the spring of that year could have been described as tranquil, suspended as it was between heaven and earth, suspended between the diaphanous light of the sky and the incessantly changing sea. There was the tranquillity of days gradually growing longer, disturbed only by the nightly crackling of radio broadcasts, as if the radio were the dirge, the Dies Irae for men's actions in those days. The doctor's imagination had not been shaped by songs, certainly not, but by the news on the radio. That succession of military reports, briefly declaimed by monotonous or familiar voices, voices cracked or submerged in boiling oil, rose from his Bakelite radio set with the regularity of certain domestic sounds, as if someone were frying something in a frying pan. Hondarribia was very far behind the lines in its unusual corner, above the Stygian lagoon and the river of forgetfulness. Towns and villages fell, and the front moved westwards, out of the province of Vizcaya. The doctor would have liked to live, smell, and feel those times the way he felt the spring, peaceful and inevitable, on the nights of the war reports, but the threshold of those feelings lay on the near side of the very circumstances he was evoking, and only the radio, with its remote nightly litany of songs and orders, allowed him to get close. And the doctor thought that the fall of Bilbao had been the requiem for many things he hadn't tried to recall, not even in his later years.

But if he turned his eyes towards the villa of Las Cruces, he could see that the higher the sap mounted, the stranger the splendour of that spring became. Isabel's parents finally arrived at Las Cruces. Doors in the house were opened and shut, shutters that had been barred for the winter were flung

wide, windows let air into rooms that had not been venti-
lated for many months. Isabel was seen emerging from the
places where she had remained shut up, not only from the
physical places, but also, in a certain fashion, from the reclu-
sion imposed on her by grief. She still appeared enveloped
in mystery. Her gloomy consciousness of the night in which
the doctor had assisted her had marked the nature of their
relations and impregnated his imagination. He saw her go
out into the garden, accompanied by her parents. He saw her
giving the gardener some instructions, as if she were ready to
take charge of the vital fury of spring and impose some sem-
blance of order on the untidy vegetal explosion in the flower
beds. Rose shrubs threw up stalks a metre high with tender
purple shoots, displaying all the vigour of the brambles from
which they had sprung. An obscene juice oozed from the leaf
buds on the trees. The vulvas of the irises were bursting into
wine-coloured or striped flowers. The power of the black,
awakening earth showed itself in a monstrous way. There was
a catastrophic essence in that inexorable and tranquil explosion of spring and in the doctor's perception of it, as if, when
he saw Isabel strolling around the garden on her father's or
mother's arm, amid the vigorous irises and roses, he imagined
a scene from a fairy tale set in a land ruled by a dragon.

Several weeks passed, and then one night Isabel's father
paid the doctor a visit. He knew that the doctor had attended
his daughter, and he wished to convey his thanks. Since he
didn't know the doctor, he had to introduce himself. He was
a little silhouette on the threshold of the door, cut out against
the dark garden. He wore a summer cap, the kind used in

golf or tennis or canoeing or whatever elegant sport had been
played before the war. He'd no doubt recovered the cap from
one of the closets in Las Cruces. The doctor turned on the
porch light. Its forty-watt bulb lent a certain volume to the
sad, pale man who stood before the doctor, haggard and bony
after the months of scarcity that had afflicted Bilbao, and also
a little ridiculous, in spite of the circumstances, because of
that cap, as though the doctor's visitor were a sporting type
who had lost his racket or his golf clubs, or whose canoe had
gone missing, in the war. Publio Cruces was a mature man,
too old to cope with new situations. Everything the doctor
knew about him had been gleaned from the society pages of
the local newspapers before the military rebellion, and now
circumstances had changed so much that remembering those
days was like remembering a geological period in which certain races or certain animals had become extinct. The doctor
invited him inside. Cruces entered the living room as if he'd
been expecting to find there the replica of his own house and
seemed rather surprised to observe that the doctor's house was
unlike his in appearance and layout. The doctor had managed
to acquire a bottle of cognac, whose contents he had been
sampling most parsimoniously, and he offered his visitor a
glass. Cruces courteously refused and sat down in an armchair. The doctor went over to the drinks cabinet and poured
himself a drink, not at all discontented at having been spared
from pouring a second one. Then he dragged his leg over to
the other chair.

Cruces remained silent for a few minutes, perhaps regret-
ting his visit already, although the doctor suspected that the

opposite was the case. He assumed that it represented a relief for the older man to leave Las Cruces and come calling on him. And indeed, Publio Cruces heaved a heavy sigh. The doctor had left a window open. They were breathing the fresh air from the garden and the salt air of the sea. From there, one could see, plunged in darkness, the garden of Las Cruces, from which the visitor had come. Perhaps the sight made him remember the wedding banquet in that same garden, brilliantly illuminated. Perhaps he hadn't ever suspected that there was such a good view of his garden from the villa of Los Sauces.

'I want to thank you for all you did for my daughter. That's why I'm here,' he said, moving his gaze from the window and turning his sad eyes on the doctor. 'Isabel should never have married that Captain Herráiz,' he added, as if his daughter's misfortunes had been a consequence of her marriage.

'I don't think I can express an opinion on that subject,' the doctor said.

'Of course you can't express an opinion on that subject. I understand perfectly. Besides, at this point, opinions are useless. Did you know that her husband was in command of a column of Reds?'

'I did.'

'The man was crazy. Who do you think will win the war?'

The doctor didn't reply. In any case, the crazies would win.

'In Bilbao, we found out that he'd been shot in Alsasua. We couldn't communicate with Isabel. We've learned that you're the only person who was able to help her.'

'I did what had to be done in her case. I can assure you that
she had a very difficult time. I believe it's going to be hard for
her to recover from it.'

'You think so?'

'What happens to a woman when, first of all, her husband's
murdered, and then she loses the baby she's carrying?'

'Oh, "murdered" . . .'

'Call it what you want. A doctor knows how to maintain
his composure, even in the midst of a war, but I'm also aware
of the value of words.'

'That woman is my daughter, and I can't be indifferent to
what has happened to her.'

'I grant you that.'

'I could have been shot if they had found this golf cap in
my house. They're shooting people for less in Madrid. Are you
a bachelor?'

'Yes, I'm a bachelor,' said the doctor, giving his bad leg a
clap, as if to say it was enough for him and he needed no other
companion.

'You're young. Maybe someday you'll understand that an
unequal marriage can turn out bad in every possible way.
Incidentally, I don't remember seeing you at the wedding.'

'I wasn't invited.'

'A mistake. There was surely some mistake.'

'I don't think it was a mistake. I had moved in only a short
time before. And then I had an accident. This leg—'

'I understand,' Cruces said with indifference. Then he added,
'Each of us has suffered a misfortune.'

The doctor raised the glass of cognac to his lips. He was listening to the voice of egoism, a deliberate, sad, weak voice, but spoken out of a dry heart and without tears, perhaps without any feeling other than self-interest, and perhaps expressing the speaker's relief at having survived uncertain circumstances, circumstances in which he might have lost his life for belonging to a fancy golf club. Publio Cruces turned the ridiculous cap in his hands. There was something pathetic in his gesture. Perhaps misfortunes and fear had led him to reclaim his social class with a slightly hysterical and victorious nostalgia, the acutely egoistical feeling that follows fear, even though the fear had proceeded from no real threat, but rather from his imagination of what he could have feared. The months that he'd spent in the city while it was under siege and subject to bombardments had affected him in a peculiar fashion, given that on the one hand he feared Bilbao's destruction and the destruction of his interests, while on the other he wished with all his heart for the arrival of the rebels. His passage through the places where the troops had advanced gave him an idea of the widespread devastation. And his fear, once he was over it, acted like a spring to his egoism, as sometimes happens with weak persons, incapable of conceiving private acts of vengeance, but deeply satisfied when other powers take on that function. After some moments of silence, he put the golf cap aside, crossed his legs, and turned towards the doctor. 'May I smoke?'

'But of course.'

He thrust his hand into his jacket pocket and extracted a cigarette case that contained two pitiful cigarettes bound

together by a rubber band. Tobacco was hard to come by, and
the cigarettes contained a few strands mixed with the shred-
ded stuff used in bad cigars. Publio Cruces offered the doctor
a cigarette. The doctor declined. The visitor took one, tapped
it against the case a few times, and lit it as elegantly as if it
were made of fine Egyptian tobacco. He was inwardly satisfied
that the doctor hadn't accepted the other cigarette, which was
the way the doctor felt about the glass of cognac his guest had
refused. A draft of air carried the smoke towards the window.
The two men knew that they were in conflicting but not irreconcilable positions, at least not directly irreconcilable, even
if one of them expressed his satisfaction at the course of events
and the other showed his bitterness, or his scepticism, or simply the much greater sense of unease he felt at having to be a
mere spectator of those events, a spectator with a ruined leg.
The doctor knew that he was helpless. And yet that helplessness
was what had saved his life, preventing him from joining either
of the two sides, simultaneously sparing him both humiliation
and victory, and thereby allowing him to judge more freely and
generously, or at least that was what he liked to believe.

The visitor sat up slightly and moved an ashtray closer to
his chair.

'Now I must tell you that my wife and I are returning to
Bilbao in a few days,' said Publio Cruces, relishing every puff
of his cigarette with great delight. 'Isabel is going to stay in
the villa.'

'She can't stay there.'

'We've tried to dissuade her, but she's made her decision.
It's where she would have liked to live with her . . . captain.'

'Will she be alone?'

'She won't be alone. A friend from Vera de Bidasoa is going to send a servant girl to move in with her.'

'And she's going to accept that?'

'She's already accepted it,' said Publio Cruces, gazing with disappointment at his burning cigarette, which was swiftly vanishing. 'Besides, we'll come and spend time with her. The real reason for my visit is this: You helped her in her worst moments. We know that if she wants to stay here, at least she'll be able to count on you.'

'It goes without saying.'

'We can't stay here, and she doesn't really want us to,' the visitor said, excusing himself. 'Why not? Can you explain it?'

The doctor made no reply.

'Why doesn't she want us to stay with her?' Cruces insisted, genuinely perplexed.

'It may be that she has her own ideas in her own head,' said the doctor. 'Many people want to remain in the place where they've suffered the most. It's her way of overcoming her grief. Forcing her to check into some kind of sanatorium would serve no purpose.'

'Out of the question.'

'Besides, that sort of thing isn't even possible at the moment. All the sanatoriums have been turned into prisons or barracks.'

Publio Cruces lowered his sad eyes and moved his head. In his most private thoughts, he found it difficult to understand all the things that were going on. There were frustrated passions, and lack of filial affection, and blood – blood, too – and

the refined antebellum golfer sensed all that, but he wasn't
able to specify what was happening. It was as if the situation
had shifted slightly; the deranged person was him, and his suffering was to have been a witness as an entire world collapsed.
Then he looked towards the window again. The moon was
shining. Part of the villa seemed to be illuminated by great
sheets of livid light, between the leafy masses of the trees. He
remained pensive for a moment, as if, upon seeing from that
perspective the villa where his daughter was, he understood
that it could be a house of healing for her, or a place of repose,
or without going so far, perhaps it was actually a good idea
for her to remain there, it would solve a problem for him,
and that last consideration did as much to improve his state
of mind as the reflection that when all was said and done, the
best course of action Captain Herráiz could have hit upon was
to get himself killed. His cigarette was burning out. Cruces
hastily raised its remains to his lips, inhaled, and expelled a
long cloud of smoke, which a subtle enchantment dragged towards the tall rectangle of the window. The expression on his
face was more tranquil. The fresh air cleared off other ghosts
and contributed to renewing his optimism. He stubbed out
what remained of his cigarette and carefully placed the butt
in his case. The shortage of tobacco was a torment. However,
it was said that things were beginning to get better. Provisions
for the civilian population had reached Bilbao, and people
were consuming appetizers of shrimp and beer on the terraces
of San Sebastián. That frivolousness seemed to animate his
thoughts with possibilities he hadn't dared contemplate for
many months. He barely hesitated before silencing his bad

conscience. He also believed it would be inadvisable to expose himself. The relief he dissembled was comparable only to the concern he pretended to feel.

'Naturally, my daughter will want for nothing,' he said, putting the cigarette case back in his jacket pocket. 'We'll visit her from time to time. And maybe later, she'll decide to come home and live with us in Bilbao.'

He rose from the armchair and picked up his golf cap. He looked around, thinking he'd forgotten something, but then he remembered that the cigarette case was in his jacket pocket, and that was all he needed. The doctor likewise stood up. Publio Cruces stepped over to the window. He gazed at his house and garden for a few moments, surprised again to find himself in his neighbour's house and to see the villa of Las Cruces from that previously unknown perspective. Then the doctor accompanied him to the door. The sea was at high tide. They could hear, close by, the sucking sound of the undertow. There were great, torn clouds in the sky, and the salt-impregnated air seemed to bring the visitor an inexplicable sense of euphoria, adding it to the dense, nocturnal euphoria of late spring, as if the year's first season, in drawing to a close, released primitive forces, and the sound of the war stayed very far in the background. The doctor returned to his chair. He turned off the lamp, stretched out his leg towards the dark landscape on the other side of the window, and drank the rest of his glass of cognac.

It had been said that the war would be won or lost in the northern campaign. That had been said, or it was said afterwards, when the course of events could be established. But in the doctor's memory, things followed a more immediate rhythm and a tighter schedule. It wasn't long before María Antonia arrived in the villa of Las Cruces. Her baby arrived with her, but the doctor didn't notice the child right away.

Some days later, he saw the two women in the garden, and one of them had the baby in her arms. Then he watched the other woman receive the baby from the hands of the first. That was all. The scene could not have been simpler, and for that very reason it struck him as unusual. Probably everyone knew. Everyone had known in advance that the girl being sent by Don Leopoldo, the rich man of Vera, was nursing a baby, and probably everyone knew her story, Isabel knew it, her parents knew it, whatever their original intentions may have been, and it was precisely because the girl had a baby that the King of the Belgians had sent her. At Isabel's direction, María Antonia came to see the doctor about her chilblains. The doctor asked if the baby was hers, and the girl didn't reply, she didn't say, 'It's mine,' nor did she say it wasn't hers, perhaps because she took it as understood that the baby could only be hers, included among the services she rendered in the neighbouring house, or more probably because she'd already been instructed not to say anything. The doctor didn't know that María Antonia was suspicious of physicians and cripples, as the cook in Vera had taught her to be. He treated her chilblains as best he could. The girl said that Isabel would pay him for the consultation, and the doctor told her to come back in a few days for a final treatment.

Chilblains. Back then, they were a common ailment. They were little purple flowers, stinging, sensitive, painful filigrees

of veins and capillaries that formed on fingers and toes – and
sometimes on earlobes – and drew, just under the surface of the
skin, tiny, tight, ulcerated nets that would occasionally burst.
Chilblains could bleed and fester. They bloomed in the winter, when it was excessively cold. María Antonia's chilblains
had lingered since the previous winter on two fingers of her
right hand and one finger of her left, and those fingers burned
whenever they touched anything. The doctor ordered her to
take off her shoes and socks so that he could see if she also
had chilblains on her toes. He knelt before her in a humili-
ated posture, a kind of homage, as though Christ were paying
homage to Mary Magdalene. He anointed her feet with tinc-
ture of iodine and with belladonna unguent, a yellow cream
like soft wax, and put iodine and belladonna on her fingertips
as well. He warned her that the unguent was toxic, repeating
himself so that the girl would understand that she must not
put her fingers in her mouth for several days, and that she
must take precautions when handling the baby. María Antonia did as he said. She was extremely careful when suckling,
and in the garden, only Isabel held the baby in her arms. The
burning sensation caused by the chilblains diminished and
eventually disappeared. In María Antonia's eyes, the doctor,
although a cripple, gained a certain reputation.

'If the chilblains come back, I'll put some more belladonna
on your fingers,' he said.

María Antonia didn't blink. 'Yes, sir.'

In a certain way, the circle was closing, as the seasons follow one another and the cycle of the year closes. The fatal
celebration of summer had already begun. A powerful inertia

was moving things and establishing an equilibrium of sen-
timent, adding plenitude where before an abyss of suffering
had yawned, filling with tenderness the endless, disagreeable,
and antisocial hours that seemed to have formed the single,
unrelenting sustenance of life. It could not have been otherwise. Destiny rages among mortals, obeying pacts and con-
flicts apparently well above their heads, in the upper spheres
of chance or providence, as in the days of the mythologies.
And that seemed to have been Isabel's fate until pity was taken
on her, either down in hell or up in heaven – it hardly mat-
tered which – and it's possible that the gods or fate had chosen
the man from Vera de Bidasoa as an instrument of their designs, because the Jovian idea of sending the girl and the baby
came from the King of the Belgians, who knew that Isabel was
looking for a servant, and surely also knew that she had lost
her baby. And in the end, the crippled man played a role, too,
for the doctor saw himself forming part of the fabric that had
been woven around her, the woman with the murdered love
and the accursed womb, not only because he'd been a witness
to her misfortune, but also because his hands had entered her
very entrails, and because he was still nagged by the unjust
but insidious suspicion of his incompetence as a doctor. Chilblains. That had been his big success, a second opportunity
after having been called once before, to attend a stillborn, premature birth. One day during that time, the doctor saw Isabel
playing with the baby in the garden. María Antonia stood a
few metres off, a little uncomfortable, a little intimidated by
the extensive grounds of her new home. Isabel was laughing
and holding the baby, who wasn't many months old. At that

moment, she looked as though all her hopes had been realized. The scene had a special fullness, like scenes that follow a rigorous fast or a long penitence. Then Isabel handed the baby to María Antonia, who received the child after first wiping her fingers on her dress, because she was afraid they might still carry some traces of unguent. The girl was something to see, worrying about her poisoned fingers and taking great precautions as she suckled her baby. It was Isabel who held the infant to María Antonia's breast, while María Antonia, sitting in a chair, kept her hands behind her back. It was a unique, hitherto unseen posture for suckling, one woman raising her bust and pulling her breast out of her shirt with a certain arrogance, and the second woman, as if performing an amorous service, holding the infant's mouth to the nipple. A cradle had been placed under a tree in the garden and covered with a veil of gauze to protect the little creature from the dance of the mosquitoes. Isabel took the child and placed her in the cradle. She bent over the baby; her gesture was maternal, but not kindly. It contained a strange avidity, which the doctor related to the posture of certain all-consuming insects. There was a similarity. Isabel leaned to the cradle in the prayerful attitude of the *Mantis religiosa*, the insect that devours for love, contemplating its prey. With her hands joined and her head tilted to one side, Isabel smiled at the infant. It was a show of affection, a performance compromised by what the woman would have wished to offer her own baby, that is, a gauze-covered cradle in the garden on a summer afternoon, amid the tumult of insects, under the magnificent foliage of a chestnut tree; and so she also offered maternal affection, as if the baby were truly her own. Therefore, to the doctor's eyes, that show hid what was really transpiring and needed only to be interpreted. He couldn't be so naïve as not to think that everything had been decided beforehand. With the rather childish arrogance that the doctor had already observed, María Antonia put away her sturdy peasant's breast and buttoned her shirt. Her primitive intuition concerning the value of affection enabled her to know just how far her power was extending. Not for nothing had she brought the child to that house so that her Señora could have a child. She could admit, with muffled greed, that there had been an interplay of interests. There was credit and debit, with one party giving up her own blood and the other party receiving the blood of a lineage not her own. For the most precious things that María Antonia brought to that house were not her presence and the services that her chilblained hands could perform, but the milk of her breasts and, above all, her baby.

One afternoon, Isabel sent for the doctor to come and see about the child. The doctor, carrying his little medical bag, went down the garden path, circled the garden wall, and limped up the path that led through the garden of Las Cruces to the house. Isabel, who had seen him coming, was waiting for him in the shade of the porch. She wore a white dress printed with little yellow flowers. Because it was starting to get cool in the late afternoons, she'd thrown a small shawl over her shoulders. When she greeted the doctor, she removed her dark glasses and revealed her large, bright eyes. The doctor stopped on the porch for a moment, and she invited him inside.

'Thank you for coming. I think the baby has a little fever.'

'Where is the baby?'

'She's upstairs,' Isabel replied.

The doctor had an intuition, but there had been other foreshadowing signs. The smell of the house had changed. It had been entered by the ample air currents of spring, which had swept away, or carried down to redoubts in the cellar, the squalid odours of winter. He recognized the entrance of the house and recovered as he did so the memory of that tragic night, which seemed to be lodged far away in the back of his mind. María Antonia was in the kitchen. She looked out for a moment through the half-open door, drying her definitively chilblain-free hands on her apron. Under the apron, she wore a dark blue dress, long, cut with a certain elegance, with bulky shoulders like a flower, sleeves gathered at the wrist, and mother-of-pearl buttons. She'd arrived at the house with two changes of clothes, a cotton skirt, and a grey cardigan, a gift from the cook in Vera. The Señora had given María Antonia her old clothes, and the girl had made them her own. After greeting the doctor, she closed the door and disappeared into what was already her territory. Isabel led the doctor into the drawing room and asked him to wait a few minutes. Then she joined the servant in the kitchen.

The drawing room had changed, too. The window was open. The tulle curtains billowed gently. The slipcovers had disappeared from the furniture. The walls had been cheered up with some sparkling silver trays. Painted plates adorned the shelves of a long sideboard. A vase of flowers stood in the centre of the table. A medium-sized insect, gleaming and jet-black, entered the house through the window. It took two tours of the drawing room, felt attracted by the flowers in the vase, and went out again, buzzing like a little artefact. On the other side of the drawing room was the closed door to a smaller room, and opposite it was the sewing room, a kind of diminutive, glassed-in parlour, equipped with a piece of furniture made from wicker and bamboo and filled with little drawers, and a round table covered with an embroidered cloth. The doctor stepped into the sewing room and examined the garden outside. Then he returned to the drawing room. Life in that house could be luminous with the light that inundated the sewing room through its big windows. A life as well-ordered as the dishes on the sideboard, and a practical life, such as the one he had no doubt was being lived in the kitchen. The doctor pricked up his ears. The murmurs he heard came from the kitchen conversation. After a short while, Isabel returned. Suddenly, the doctor felt dizzy. Maybe something was badly wrong with the baby. He said, 'Is there some problem?'

'There's no problem,' Isabel replied. 'María Antonia wants me to convey her thanks to you for having cured her chilblains. She's going to make some maize cakes for you. If she can get maize. The baby's upstairs. She's been sleeping with me for several weeks now.'

Isabel led the doctor to the stairs. 'This way.'

Gripping the handrail, the doctor watched her light legs as they preceded him up the stairs. On the upper floor, the landing opened in two different directions. The doors were shut. One of the corridors led to the bedroom where the doctor had attended Isabel on the night of her stillbirth. Isabel went down the other corridor, which was half dark. At the end there was a small living room, situated like a tower over the sewing room on the lower floor and lit by tall windows. He followed Isabel, whose white dress was luminous in the semi-darkness. When she reached the door to one of the bedrooms, Isabel stopped and raised a finger to her lips. Then, delicately turning the handle, she opened the door.

And there was the baby, lying in a big cradle next to a double bed with a walnut headboard. The shutters were half closed. The afternoon light cut the wooden floor with two vertical lines. The child was asleep. Isabel approached the cradle, bent over the sleeping form, and with infinite care took the infant in her arms. She didn't wake up at first. Then she started gently waving her little hands. She shifted about uneasily for a few moments, and finally she burst out crying.

'She ran a fever last night,' said Isabel, softly rocking the child, soothing her with little pats. 'Maybe we should have waited until she woke up.'

The doctor asked Isabel to lay the child on the bed and open the window to let the light in. Isabel obeyed. The doctor opened his medical bag, took out a thermometer, and, after removing the mantilla that was covering the infant, examined her. The baby smelled like sour milk, a healthy baby smell. Everything seemed to be in order. The room smelled of nappies and talcum powder. The baby had stopped crying, and the light from the window made her close her eyes. Her tiny mouth opened in a yawn, showing her pink gums. She'd probably had one of those inexplicable bouts of fever that sometimes afflict babies. She was a well-formed infant, with cheerful, as yet undefined features that permitted a glimpse into what the lineaments of her face and her expression would be. She wasn't afraid. Although her little pink face was somewhat flushed by a few tenths of a degree of temperature, she showed no sign of illness. As the examination went on, the doctor began to feel a strange vigilance behind his back. He raised his head and glanced round. At one spot on the wall, there was an unmoving eye: the glittering brass pendulum of a stopped clock. It was the captain's cold eye. The doctor was doubtless the first man to enter that room. A big wardrobe with mirrored double doors stood against one wall. A uniform was probably still hanging in there. That was probably where the groom's dress uniform and the bride's white wedding dress were kept. Isabel remained unmoving, her arms folded, in the square of light coming in through the window.

'What's the baby's name?' the doctor asked.

'Verónica.'

The doctor turned back to the infant, who was gently waving her arms with her eyes closed, as if she wanted to levitate off the bed. 'Well, Verónica,' the doctor said affectionately, 'you have a bit of fever. It looks like you're in a hurry to grow.'

Then he turned to Isabel. 'It's nothing serious. Only a few tenths of a degree of fever. It will disappear overnight. Has her mother run a fever, too?'

'Her mother?'

'The servant girl.'

Isabel glared at him furiously. It took only a few seconds for the doctor to understand that he'd committed an error.

The transfer of the baby to that room, her cradle next to the immense, deserted, rather tragic matrimonial bed, signified much more than he'd imagined at first. He should have caught on sooner, while he was climbing the stairs, while he was following her down the hall and passing the closed doors before reaching the room. It was Isabel's real room, the one where she should have given birth, in the bed that should have been her matrimonial bed after her honeymoon. She didn't reply immediately to the doctor's blunder, perhaps because she didn't consider it a blunder. In her imagination, she believed herself the victim of a deliberate provocation. Anger prevented her from uttering a word. Although he didn't think he should apologize, the doctor murmured an apology.

Finally, she said, 'You can consider Verónica my daughter.'

'Your daughter?'

'From now on, you can consider her so.'

Her voice sounded strangely melodious and false, as if she were making an effort to pacify her rancour. The doctor put the thermometer back into his bag. Isabel took the child in her arms. She briefly rocked the little package, its face barely peeking out of the mantilla, before replacing the baby in her cradle. Then, standing bolt upright, her eyes brighter than ever, almost on the point of weeping, Isabel faced the doctor. 'Her name is Verónica Herráiz,' she said, stressing the last name. 'This is her first cradle,' she added, pointing to the cradle, where the baby was once again asleep in her feverish dream world.

The doctor made no reply.

'Do you have an objection?'

'I believe I'm entitled to my own opinion on the subject. I'm aware of certain facts,' the doctor said in an insinuating drawl.

'Are you?'

'Let's leave it at that,' said the doctor, collecting his bag and heading for the door. 'There's nothing wrong with the baby. She'll probably sleep until it's time for her to be fed again.'

'You didn't understand what I said,' Isabel insisted.

'I believe I understood perfectly.'

'Everything's settled,' she said in a firm voice. 'What you know or don't know makes no difference.'

The doctor opened the door and stepped out into the corridor. Isabel remained beside the cradle for a few moments. After ascertaining that the baby was asleep, she half-closed the shutters again and left the room behind the doctor.

'Doctor.'

The doctor turned to her. There was something both heroic and pathetic in the woman's attitude. It wasn't merely a ploy to salve her wounded pride, or an act of vengeance against her enforced sterility. Isabel raised her voice insistently. She had tied together the ends of the shawl round her shoulders and was wringing the fringes in her hands. Her white dress, sprinkled with yellow flowers, made her look like an apparition in the semi-darkness. The closed door to the room where the baby lay sleeping was behind her, and she looked as though she were defending that closed door, or as though she were defending some secret that the intruder might carry off and expose. But nobody in his right mind would have thought that was a secret, at least nobody in the circle of her acquaintance, and it would have seemed even less likely that there was any need to expose it or conceal it or create an unmentionable atmosphere around it. What internal violence had made the woman want to block any suspicion of her frustrated motherhood? Isabel came forward a few steps, her hands clenched in her shawl. There was a deranged glitter in her bright eyes.

'Doctor,' she said imploringly, raising her voice. 'You saw me bear a child in this bed.'

The doctor stopped with one hand on the stair railing. She was hanging on his lips, waiting for him to speak. It was the crucial scene. The woman may have been betting her mental health on a few comforting syllables, on some small hint that would forever signify that her grief and her joy had been simultaneously understood. Within a second, the doctor grasped what his role must be.

'Of course I did,' he said in a kindly tone.

'You delivered my baby.'

'I was here,' the doctor agreed, slowly moving his head. 'I helped you give birth with these hands.' Then he added, 'You mustn't worry.'

She breathed a relieved sigh, as if all the tension accumulated in that minute – a decisive minute for her – had found comfort in the doctor's simple words. She said, 'Thank you.'

And at that moment, it was as though her body were taking on another shape. Her convulsed fragility was being transformed. She released the shawl she'd been wringing in her clenched fingers and joined her hands under her chin to hide her emotion. Then her whole face lit up in a smile. It was impossible to know if she herself believed what she had asked for, that is, the confirmation of something that hadn't happened and to which the doctor had made himself an accomplice, but it made no difference whether she believed it or not, or whether other feelings qualified the doctor's compassion for her madness, or her misfortune. In all probability, everything was settled, as she herself had said. In all probability, the rich man of Vera, her parents, and whoever else considered himself concerned in the affair, probably all of them had settled in advance on providing her with a child, as if the matter lay solely in their power, and they had counted from the beginning on María Antonia's consent, and all that was lacking was the useless concurrence of a physician. In Irún, the archives had been burned. Many parochial registers had been destroyed. There had been sufficient charity and administrative influence, that is, sufficient levels of both charity and administrative influence so that the baby could be inscribed in some register as Verónica Herráiz, and surely, that act of charity and that administrative influence were to be splendidly recompensed by a new Isabel, sensible and filled with determination, or by her father, or by whomever else. The chaotic times, the same disastrous times that were causing so much misfortune, had brought her some succour, and in the room with the outsized double bed, a baby with a second mother was sound asleep. There were always going to be people who would believe that the child was the daughter of the captain whose comrades in arms had put him in front of a firing squad, and as for those who didn't believe it, or who knew or guessed the truth, they would keep silent out of respect for the two mothers, obeying the strange and ancient modesty that envelops the supplanting of one blood by another. The doctor was taken aback for a few minutes. He didn't know if his testimony, delivered from the top of the stairs and directed to the semi-darkness of the corridor where she was waiting, was unnecessary testimony or not, a statement that no registry would ever solicit, but which the woman was eager to hear. Compassion pushed him so far that he didn't think he had lied. He would have wanted his complicity to be accepted by others besides her; he went so far as to wish that he had truly helped her to deliver a child on the disastrous night that now seemed so far away. The circumstances had been appropriate. The meeting in her room, which the mirrored wardrobe doors reflected in a strange concavity, under the unmoving eye of the brass pendulum, had been enough for her, had enabled her to demand his benign testimony as a tribute to her suffering. What was being sorted out wasn't an adoption or an appropriation, but the degree of craftiness and the number of lies that would be necessary to ensure that the grievances life had inflicted on those two women would be in some way compensated. One of them turned over her child and received in return a certain amount of gratitude and, above all, peace. The other received the baby and drained the chalice of her suffering. The doctor was immediately conscious of all this. The situation, suspended and crystallized in a few words, needed no further explanation.

The doctor took his leave. 'I believe I should go. Don't hesitate to call me if you need me again.'

'I'll do that,' said Isabel, relieved. Then she stepped back into the bedroom where the baby was and closed the door behind her. Holding on to the rail, the doctor went down the stairs. He'd left his cane in the umbrella stand, and he headed towards it. On the way, he passed the kitchen door, which was half open again. He saw María Antonia stick out her head, which was expectant, round, and healthy. There was something about it reminiscent of a summer watermelon. Her look expressed a mute interrogation, a desire to know what had been revealed on the upper floor. Maybe she was really interested only in Verónica's fever. When he saw her, the doctor sensed that she wouldn't be capable of going into explanations. Her occupation as a wet nurse was worth as much as or more than her occupation as a mother. Or perhaps she had understood that Verónica's future and her own future in that house, from which no one would ever dare to expel her, were at play in the exchange of functions. One sure thing is that the child had not been given the last name of her first mother's family – if one may so put it – much less her unknown father's family name, but this was the least significant aspect of the whole business. The doctor picked up his cane and turned to the girl, who was thrusting out her full-moon face from the other side of the half-open door. After hesitating a moment, he took a few steps towards her. The girl started to close the door, as if she were afraid of something. Then she stood firm and waited for the doctor.

'Listen, the Señora tells me you're doing just fine here in this house, and I'm sure you are. Is everything all right?'

María Antonia didn't answer him. She pressed herself against the door jamb.

'Is it true that you've handed over your daughter . . .' The doctor stopped before finishing his sentence. It was obvious that the girl wasn't going to reply to that or any other question, because she'd already begun to form part of the house, part of its heart, and her Señora's secret was her secret, too. The doctor looked at her strong hand, which was defending the kitchen door. 'How are your chilblains?' he asked.

The girl, still intimidated by the young, crippled doctor, looked at him in amazement. 'I don't have chilblains any more,' she stammered.

'Glad to hear it. If you're lucky, they won't come back this winter.'

The doctor opened the door to the garden. The afternoon was drawing to a close, and the grass was taking on an orange-tinged gleam. 'You must take care of the little girl,' the doctor said before leaving the house. 'And please, that woman needs taking care of, too.'

He crossed the garden and found himself on the road that went along the garden wall. He'd planned to go back to his house, drop off his medical bag, and go out again. He needed to take a longer walk and exercise his bad leg, which had conducted itself so well, going up and down the stairs in Las Cruces. But the north was still a war zone, and the curfew that had been decreed began at nightfall. By a curious mirror effect, the doctor's memory projected an impression of peace onto those circumstances. It was the astronomical peace of twilight, the interior peace of having resumed the simplest functions of his profession, the strange, recently acquired peace of the house he was walking away from. That summer came the news that Santander had fallen. At the time, the war was being fought throughout the broad territory of Spain, and no one knew how long it would last. Setting up his telescope on the terrace and contemplating the descent of dusk and the face of the heavens, admiring the slow rising of the tide in the molten-gold waters of the Txingudi, and lingering to watch the lights come on, gradually more and more of them, on the other side of the frontier – all that was out of the question. Equally out of the question was going out of the back door and pointing the telescope at the crests of the Jaizkibel and looking for pro-pitious signs in the summer constellations, disregarding the ominous news contained in the war reports. There remained only one refuge where he could find a secret peace, so fragile, so resigned, so newly lodged in his heart that he himself had no way of explaining it. It was the peace of the weak and the just, and it granted him the tranquillity of opening the gate and limping back to his house to pour himself a glass of cognac. There was no sadder peace than that.

The day when young Goitia was to leave Las Cruces dawned foggy. The sun seemed to have camped on the clouds and stopped moving, leaving the world bathed in an uncertain light. As the morning progressed, the smooth surface of the sea and the bulky shapes of the mountains started emerging from the landscape, as on the first day of the creation.

Doctor Castro went out into the garden in his slippers, with a jumper over his pyjama coat, a bathrobe over his shoulders, some old flannel trousers instead of the matching pyjama bottoms, and his cane. He grasped the cane in one hand and with the other held the front of his bathrobe closed. Releasing the robe for a moment, he ran a hand through his dishevelled hair. His head hurt. He'd spent the night dreaming of death. The dream had left a bitter taste in his mouth and an ominous shadow in his heart. But as the fog, like a lavish symphony, gradually lifted before his eyes, he began to recover his spirits. He realized that once again, as had happened on many nights over the course of many years, he'd crossed the barrier that sleep throws up between waking and dying.

The old Etxarri woman at Las Cruces passed through the kitchen and out of the garden door to hang out the laundry with her white, gnarled hands. She had a red scarf wrapped round her nose. She'd done some washing, the clothes were in a tub she carried on her hip, and she was going to hang them out, because she knew, with the knowledge shepherds and sheep share, that the fog would lift before noon. She pinned them to the line, those spectral articles, shirts, kitchen cloths, age-old panties, raising her arms in the thin light, signalling her presence in the mist with the red blotch of her scarf. Then she went back inside with the empty tub. She remembered the days when she was a girl, before she came to that house, the days of Etxarri's inn, the days of the big, rambling house in Vera de Bidasoa. Those were days shrouded in fog, out of which emerged a cow's ghostly forehead, or a soldier's face, or the weather-beaten, sibylline countenance of the cook in Vera. And should she wish to bring all those faces together – the cow's, the cook's, and the soldier's – maybe she'd be holding a good hand of cards, some high trumps that could explain what those nebulous times had been like better than any swindling memory, as heraldic shields explain a family's blood with a bull's head, a helmet, or a siren's face, for she knew about escutcheons, carved in stone and held up by two dwarves, or two lions, or a lion and a cat, and she had concluded that her own history deserved something equivalent to the shields that powerful families ordered stonemasons to carve. She could add Verónica's face, too. That was a happy and never forgotten trump, whose memory accompanied her best hours. And as she remembered all this in the lush morning fog while busying herself with the humble task of hanging out clothes to dry, the old Etxarri woman's heart was moved. Because Verónica Herráiz had been her blood without actually becoming her family, and consequently, in the desolation of her secret, couldn't figure in the heraldic shield that María Antonia, had she been powerful, would have ordered to be carved. The doctor saw her go back into the house with the empty tub, leaving behind her the clothesline, peopled with ghosts. The profile of the façade dissolved into geometrical planes. The roof eaves were a blurry line the colour of slate. The dark green foliage of a laurel tree was outlined against snippets of light without shadow. The doctor watched as the red blotch of the scarf disappeared. The dampness penetrated to his bones, and he pulled his bathrobe tighter as he stood in the doorway. It might have been ten in the morning, and there was great pleasure in believing that time had stood still. Then he heard someone uttering his name, most pitifully, inside the house, with a melodious and sad voice that only the doctor understood. It was Satan, the cat, calling him and demanding a saucer of milk. The doctor went inside to tend to the cat. As the old Etxarri woman had foreseen, in the mid-morning the veil of fog confounding heaven and earth began to lift in a delightful symphonic progression. The doctor's reflections on death and sleep gradually faded. He ate his breakfast while sitting in a wicker chair near the window, still in his bathrobe, with the black cat at his side. His fear of the sleep of death was not resolved, but as the spectacle emerged from the lifting fog, he indulged in the fantasy of dying while seated in a chair and watching the creation of the world.

An hour and a half later, he went to shave and change his clothes. After the long breakfast, the cat was ready for him to open the door. The doctor was fond of late habits, and by the time he finished shaving, it was after eleven-thirty. More or less at that same hour, lawyer Goitia began to get his things together, that is, the suitcases, the shoulder bag, and the heavy trunk of books he'd arrived with several weeks before. This latter item, which felt as if it contained the bust of Cicero, would have to be dragged to the taxi when it came for him later that afternoon. In the meanwhile, genealogical thoughts were assaulting the doctor, too, just as they were exercising the old Etxarri woman. Thus do the generations succeed one another, he thought, like the ages of the heavens and the ages of the heart. This was the third generation. The doctor, musing in the silence of his spirit, was a little saddened to see the boy lean out of the window and shake a jumper, and then to watch the cheerful way he dumped a wastebasket full of papers into the incinerator, where dead leaves from the garden were burned. This was the third generation, which former misfortunes could not reach, and in which were dissolved the vicissitudes of the past and the mysteries of bad luck. Old and crippled, the doctor was aware of his own solitude, as if some curse had fallen on him long ago and not yet run its course, but among his desires that morning, none was so urgent as the wish to see the boy conclude his sojourn in Las Cruces with the same unburdened heart as when he arrived. And of course, with a much better chance of passing his notarial examinations, depending on how well he'd used his time there. He was the son of Verónica Herráiz. And just as his mother had had two mothers without knowing it, the boy was the grandson of both Isabel and the old Etxarri woman, although to all intents and purposes, he possessed evidence only of the first, and neither the old woman nor the doctor was going to offer the boy any revelations about the second. There had been a time when the Goitia family used to come to Las Cruces in the summer, and there had also been a time when their summer visits stopped. One could imagine that Verónica knew who her real mother was and didn't want to spend a summer vacation under the eyes of that mother, who was also the servant. Someone, perhaps Isabel herself, could have revealed the truth to her. Perhaps it had happened that way, and the doctor suspected that it had, but in any case, he hadn't wasted any time trying to unravel *that* mystery. It wasn't important to investigate the most trivial details, or to be more rigorous, or to assume that all this represented an obscure grief for the old Etxarri woman and some kind of frustration for the doctor himself. In any case, nobody had told the boy yet, no one had said to him, Son, this is your grandmother. But the boy was there, and for a few weeks the powerful flood of memories had overflowed the sluice gates.

Young Goitia came out of the house a second time to empty the waste-paper basket. The doctor activated his leg and cane and crossed the garden to meet him. As his neighbour approached the low wall between the two gardens, the lawyer stopped, waste-basket in hand. The tips of his shirt collar peeked out from his high-necked jumper like two triangular birds. He'd put on a pair of old trousers, as if he were moving house. He clumsily shifted the wastebasket to his other hand before greeting the doctor.

'Good morning.'

'Good morning, counsellor. Did you get up early so you could pack?'

'Early? It's eleven-thirty.'

'Let's say the sun has just risen,' said the doctor, waving his cane at the broad, clear sky. 'The hours of fog don't count.'

The boy nodded without conviction. Then he turned his gaze to the landscape and received the warm sun on his face. A faint yellow gleam floated on the air. Fog was still hanging on the mountains above the tender blue of the coastline. Out above the horizon, where the open sea began, clouds were forming a thick disc, as if they were hiding some other piece of land.

'What time's your plane?' the doctor asked.

'Seven o'clock this evening.'

'Won't it be hard for you to go back to Madrid?'

'Oh, no,' the lawyer said vivaciously. Then, by way of excusing himself, he changed the conversation. 'I was carrying
some papers and notes to the incinerator.'

'Notarial secrets?'

Young Goitia, a little confused, lowered his head. 'Not
quite yet. A candidate's study papers.'

'Come, come. I'm sure we're going to have a civil-law
notary,' he prophesied.

Young Goitia smiled again. There was something delicate
in his smile. The doctor loved that face with the same unexpected emotion he felt at seeing the sad cemeteries of autumn
receive the sun's caress. It was, in any case, a symbolic feeling.
The doctor examined young Goitia with interest. Ever since
the lad had come to Las Cruces, the doctor had tried in vain
to satisfy a certain irresistible curiosity. He wanted to discern,
in the boy's face, some remote resemblance to the girl who'd
arrived to serve at Las Cruces with a baby in her arms in the
spring or summer of 1937, and whether because his memory
was failing him or because the caprices of biological inheritance hadn't transmitted any of María Antonia's features to
the young lawyer, the doctor was inclined to think that Goitia
could have received his physical traits, on the maternal side,
from the unknown sergeant who'd raped his grandmother.
And it's possible that old María Antonia Etxarri proceeded in
the same way. For an instant, the doctor wondered whether
old Antonia drew the same conclusion when she saw the boy's
face up close, or whether that was a refinement on his part,
or a tribute he paid to his personal curiosity, or to the melancholy necessities of his failing recollection, which was obliged

to illustrate its own memories with the forced corroboration of some evidence. On the other hand, it required no effort for him to transform young María Antonia Etxarri into the old Etxarri woman, and much more suddenly in words than in reality, for as is often the case with the more well-to-do classes, the doctor felt no obligation whatsoever to discard the habit of considering old a servant who was at least ten years younger than himself. The doctor concealed his brief emotion and offered to accompany Goitia to the incinerator. They walked down to the bottom of the garden, each on his side of the little stone wall. The lawyer carried the full waste-paper basket under his arm like an absurd bundle. The two men stopped when they reached the corner where the low garden wall joined the big wall, crowned with bottle shards, that separated the two properties from the road. In that corner stood the incinerator. It was a metal cylinder where the gardener would burn leaves on some afternoons, spreading abroad a bitter reek. The lawyer opened the incinerator, releasing an odour of wet ash and decomposing vegetable matter. He emptied the basket of papers into the cylinder and replaced its lid. The doctor waited a few moments for the operation to be completed. Then the two of them turned to go back. From where they were, both houses were visible, each on the gentle slope of its own garden. The trees had strewn a circle of yellow leaves in front of Los Sauces, and the geraniums near the porch were decomposing. The virgin ivy covering the façade of Las Cruces had begun to turn scarlet. And that panorama, which the two men discovered at the same time and which seemed to have been veiled to them until that moment, made them stop unexpectedly in their tracks, as if they were both receiving the same discreet message, leaping over the span of the years, not a message concerning origins or the illustration of a common history or a vivid image of happiness or of the tragedy latent in the sumptuous representation of autumn spread out before their eyes, but a message that somehow, for both of them, implied a strange, shared complicity. That couldn't be the case. No fate could permit the abyss of the years to close up between them, and no confidence could endow the vista with the same significance for them both. Where the doctor could see the scene of the saddest and hardest winter of his life, the youth admired two enchanting summer villas dating from before the war. Behind them, on the mountainside, other villas had sprouted. Just up the road, a building was under construction. Time also included those references. Farther away rose the Jaizkibel, omnipresent and rugged, its brow still furrowed in the remaining shreds of fog. The boy remained pensive for a few seconds. The superfluity of colours among the bare trees, like a wrinkled tapestry heavily stained with gold and wine, was shocking.

'I think I'll miss this place. These weeks have been very profitable,' the lawyer said. 'I'll miss you, too, and the old Etxarri woman.'

'Maybe we'll see each other again. Won't your mother come and spend a summer at Las Cruces?' the doctor asked, with the same inquisitive curiosity that had assailed him before.

'No. She prefers to rent a villa in Linces since my grandmother died.'

'Since before your grandmother died,' the doctor corrected him.

'Yes, you're right, since before my grandmother died.'

'Didn't your mother say anything about your coming here to study?'

'It was her idea.'

'Your mother's?'

'Yes. I needed a quiet spot. But I wasn't going to rent a villa just for that.' Goitia raised his hand to his chin, as if something inexplicable had crossed his mind. 'Sometimes I wonder why my grandmother would leave the house to her servant.'

'Notarial secrets,' the doctor said, barely joking.

Young Goitia laughed out loud. 'Who knows, maybe that's it.'

The doctor kept silent. Once again, he appreciated the sincerity, the involuntary innocence of the comment, the brief, insensible oscillation of destiny that allowed the boy to be kept in the limbo of ignorance, on the last day of his stay at Las Cruces and forever. His ignorance was the guarantee of his happiness, after the allusion that had grazed the black, hard matter from which his own existence proceeded. Not even documents could be sufficiently eloquent. No document recorded what the doctor and the old Etxarri woman knew, or what the boy's mother might have found out. And as the doctor saw it, there was no room for doubt that it was better so, that is, that the memory should remain enclosed in itself, without being transmitted to this boy, without even alluding to the obligatory parenthesis between what his mother could tell him someday and what the doctor might have been able to reveal to him. And when all was said and done, the secret could remain enclosed, as in a miniature, in the gorgeous autumnal mystery of the two villas.

The doctor attacked the little upward slope, retracing his steps and poking the wet grass suspiciously with his cane. The lawyer followed him on the other side of the stone wall with the empty waste-paper basket in his arms. When they reached the level of the villas, they separated. Their paths were different. The doctor crossed the circle of yellow leaves, heading for the rotting geraniums in front of the porch at Los Sauces. The lawyer, with the wastebasket in his arms, disappeared under the tresses of scarlet ivy that covered the façade of Las Cruces. As the plane for Madrid wasn't scheduled to depart until seven o'clock, the doctor invited the lawyer, before they parted, to have coffee in the doctor's house after lunch. The lawyer accepted with a thin smile worthy of a schoolboy. He was still embracing the wastebasket, like a young man in a snapshot of some academic prank, as if it were the last day of classes, and in a certain way it was, and also as if he found in the prospect of leaving Las Cruces a nostalgia at least equivalent to the pleasure of having a farewell cup of coffee with the doctor.

In the late afternoon, while young Goitia was at coffee with the doctor, the old Etxarri woman went up to the second floor in Las Cruces and looked into several rooms. Sometimes she carried out this mission with no other intention than to inspect the house and to calculate whether or not she could make a bit of money one day by renting rooms. Two bedrooms and a shared living room looked out onto the garden.

Two other bedrooms with bathrooms had a view of the mountainside. Red ivy covered one of the balconies. The old Etxarri woman hadn't ever thought about moving to the upper floor herself. As far back as her memory of her life in that house could reach, her territory had always been confined to the kitchen and the servants' quarters. The upper floor contained remembered anguish and mysteries that weren't hers, or were only partly hers. In any case, they were account balances that produced no interest. María Antonia Etxarri's pact with life did not include those accounts. She had a firm and grounded sense of things. But she was also a curious old woman, and she liked to listen to the murmur of the empty spaces and to feel, with a shiver, ghosts brushing up against her. She liked to imagine the games of a little girl who no longer existed. She could peer into the shadows and make out the greenish glow of a curled-up, gelatinous shape in the form of a fetus, and she dreaded the sudden apparition of the captain's bloody ghost.

In young Goitia's room, the bags were already packed. The window was open. From there, she could look through the big windows into the living room at Los Sauces and discern the silhouettes of the doctor and the lawyer as they sat drinking coffee. What they might be saying to each other in that conversation intrigued the old Etxarri woman, but it didn't disturb her. She closed the window and went out into the hall. One by one, she inspected the rest of the bedrooms. In one of them, she opened a wardrobe and felt a dirty uniform. She opened a big closet in another room and ran her hand over the clothes as if she were counting lamb carcasses, dressed and hung up. All that could be sold to the rag man one day,

while the scrap merchant would take care of the dining-room
cutlery, once she'd found out whether it was silver or pewter.
Another of the bedrooms on that floor had been Verónica's
until Verónica went to Bilbao and got married and until
the married Verónica went to live in Madrid and until she
stopped spending summers at Las Cruces. There was a leak
in that room. The aureole on the ceiling looked like the map
of an island and was situated directly above a chamber pot.
With the indifference of a cat, the old Etxarri woman passed
in front of a mirror. This was now an undesignated room. But
just as Saint Verónica was left with an image of Christ's countenance stamped on a cloth, the old Etxarri woman still had a
photograph of Verónica, with an inscription that read *To my
nanny María Antonia*. The old woman kept that picture in a
drawer in her room.

After a long while, María Antonia Etxarri returned to the
lower floor. She crossed the drawing room and headed for the
sewing room, whose old, honey-coloured wicker-and-bamboo
furniture was gilded by the late afternoon sun. That room had
been the Señora's sewing room, so María Antonia had never
done her sewing there. She sewed in another room, close to
the kitchen, which lacked the sewing room's big windows but
was well-lighted all the same. She had, however, appropriated
the Señora's sewing box, more to satisfy the unconfessable
envy it had aroused in her for years than out of any real need.
The box contained several thimbles, some of them silver, and
a set of three scissors in three different sizes, all with worked
handles. María Antonia had sufficient time ahead of her to
turn all the objects in the house that she didn't like into cash

and add the sum to the eighteen million in her bank account, but she had no intention of selling that sewing box. Another, smaller sewing kit that had belonged to Verónica contained boxes of pins with coloured heads and child-sized thimbles. María Antonia had kept the little kit, too, even though she remembered that the child had never liked to sew.

She stepped into the former gun room, where young Goitia had spent all those weeks studying. On the desk was an office lamp with a green, glass-paste shade. In María Antonia's opinion, this was not the most appropriate lamp for a young man, because the green light, like the flame of a green candle, was the light that summoned the dead. The window, set at an angle and smaller than the sewing-room window, was an extension of it, just as it was extended in a symmetrical angle on the drawing-room side. The trunk of books, which Goitia had already packed, was ready on the floor. María Antonia had a premonition. The trunk made her think of a coffin. All that was missing was the crucifix. And it was a heavy trunk, too, like a coffin with a corpse in it. Señora Isabel had died like that, small and shrunken, just the right size to fit into that trunk. The old woman figured she would die like that, too. She could already see herself shrinking as the years passed, even though she was still active and robust, and still capable of great exertions. She didn't like that kind of luggage, hollow inside, long and low, with lids and iron fittings and handles, with everything that evoked a coffin. María Antonia opened a window to ventilate the gun room and dissipate her morbid premonitions in the late afternoon air. Then she heard the doctor and the lawyer bidding each other farewell on the porch at Los Sauces.

'You can come back whenever you want, whether you're a notary or a lawyer,' the doctor said. 'You've got two houses in this town.'

'I'm sure I'll be back,' said the lawyer.

'You've got everything ready for your departure?'

'A taxi's coming to pick me up. My bags are all packed.'

'In that case, I wish you good luck.'

'Thank you.'

The lawyer stopped for an instant at the foot of the porch. Then he turned round and said his final goodbye to the doctor. María Antonia Etxarri saw him walk down through the garden at Los Sauces. She watched as he disappeared behind the tall garden wall, bristling with broken glass, that bordered the road. Then she saw him emerge from behind the wall, enter the gate of Las Cruces, and walk up towards the house. The old Etxarri woman would have taken some pleasure in telling him a few tales, ancient tales, about when she was barely more than a child and had had two men like two horses, about the months she'd spent in the big, rambling house in Vera, about the time when a sergeant had possessed her, about her arrival at Las Cruces with a bundle in her arms, and about who knew how many other things. She would have joined her hands, but she wouldn't have found the words. For barely an instant, her mind was crossed by the thought that the person coming towards the house was her grandson, and that now the house was his house, and that she could cook dinner for him, and that the boy could move in with her and stay a long time. But she couldn't demand recognition from him, nor could she claim dividends on the blood that she'd turned over to her

Señora, and she couldn't even imagine doing such a thing. It was simply a warm sensation that she felt in her stomach. It was a deeper respiration, as when the mind feels itself on the verge of receiving a revelation. But none came. She knew she could count on the doctor's discretion. She was confirmed in this almost at once, because Goitia entered the house with the broad smile of a schoolboy on an excursion day.

'I think the taxi I ordered will be here soon,' the lawyer said, consulting his watch.

The old Etxarri woman withdrew for a moment to the kitchen. She was falling back on simple, solid things, because it couldn't be otherwise, nor did she wish that it could be. She had prepared a surprise for the boy. A short time later, she returned with half a *bacalao*, wrapped in grey paper and enclosed in a cloth sack tied with a cord. She said, 'This is half a *bacalao* for you to take back to Madrid.'

'Oh, María Antonia, that wasn't necessary. . . .' said the boy, thanking her.

The old Etxarri woman smiled. Half a *bacalao* was necessary in any circumstances. Goitia went upstairs and came down again with his shoulder bag and the two suitcases. Ten minutes later, the taxi arrived. It entered the gate and went up the gravel road to the villa. Goitia waited for the cab in the foyer. He and the driver hauled the trunk, filled with books or whatever else it was filled with, to the car. Then the cab driver carried out the suitcases and the shoulder bag. He took out a handkerchief, wiped his forehead, and muttered something about luggage loaded with bricks. Meanwhile the boy, with half a *bacalao* wrapped up like a mummy under his arm, took his leave.

'Goodbye, María Antonia.'

In her excited state, the old woman dared to say, 'Greetings to Verónica.'

'I'll give her greetings from you, and from the doctor, too,' said Goitia.

The old woman put her hands in the pockets of her apron and fell silent. The sensation of warmth had disappeared from her stomach. In her pockets, there was a rosary, a much-used handkerchief, two wrinkled thousand-peseta notes, and the key to the pantry. She wondered if she should give the boy a tip, the way grandmothers do with their grandsons, but then she decided that half a *bacalao* was enough. Three quarters of an hour later, she watched the plane take off. From the porch at Los Sauces, the doctor also watched the take-off. The plane rose thunderously over the black waters of the estuary, flying towards the horizon and the open sea. An orangey glow illuminated the fuselage as it described a great half circle in the sky. Then it headed inland, high and silent in the twilit heavens.

The next morning, the day dawned foggy again, as was usual in late autumn. Before breakfast, the doctor, wearing pyjamas, slippers, and bathrobe, stepped out onto his porch. The old Etxarri woman stepped out onto the porch at Las Cruces, with her hands under her jumper and her red scarf wrapped round her nose. When the doctor discovered her, her face was raised to the sky, as if she might be expecting the announcement of a new existence after the passing of the clouds. The doctor, too, would have wished for that, and the thought filled him with melancholy. But the Lord does not grant the exhausted veins of life the privilege of a second youth.

www.vintage-books.co.uk